THE FOOL OF NEW YORK CITY

Michael D. O'Brien

THE FOOL OF NEW YORK CITY

A novel

IGNATIUS PRESS   SAN FRANCISCO

The music and lyrics of *The Sidewalks of New York* were composed by Charles Lawlor and James Blake in 1894.

Needless to say, the giants and extremely old people who play crucial roles in this story should not be identified with the giants and extremely old people who are living among us at the time of this writing. All characters and incidents are entirely fictitious, with the exception of certain public events known to us all.

Cover art:
Hope of the Drowning by Michael D. O'Brien

Cover design by Roxanne Mei Lum

ISBN 978-1-62164-073-8
Library of Congress Control Number 2016931675
Printed in the United States of America ∞

CONTENTS

I

You awake from a dream

You awake from a dream. The dream dissolves in the frosted breath of your mouth. From where you lie on the bed's metal springs, you can see a window permitting light to enter the room. You see rooftops of a neighborhood, old and weary, with chimney pots and bobbing Santa Clauses and television aerials, no longer used. A band of cerulean blue sky has been slashed across the glass, and above it is boiling charcoal. Snowflakes drift down, only a few. It is winter here, which is somewhere you do not recognize.

You swing your legs over the edge and drop your feet to the icy floor. Recoiling, you slip your damp sock feet into plastic beach sandals. You do not recognize your clothes. They are old men's things—rumpled khaki trousers, an undershirt, a wool sweater with holes and unraveled strings of wool. The garments are not clean. You pull a stinking gray blanket around your shoulders.

Your belly, your thighs: you are not fat. You are not too thin. Your face is rasping with days of stubble. You touch the dome of your skull. There is hair, thick, curling, the color uncertain. You can see nothing of your face, though you are in it and there is full sensation. You blink—darkness. You open your eyes—light.

There are layers in existence. Many of these are visible, though flattened into a single plane. The invisible layers are present but incomprehensible. They may be seen in brief flashes, as if hints were scattered as errant snowflakes. The layers are beyond counting. They are in relationship, yet how it works, and why it does, remains indecipherable. You exist as an element of the whole phenomenon and may observe parts of it—yourself a part, of course. To see and understand the invisible, you must wait quietly. You must not frighten it away.

Oh! Is this correct? Can you frighten phenomena? Yes. You can. A deer bolts for the deep sanctuary of evergreens. The fish flashes into deep reeds. The mind hides in deep sleep. Fear may be a necessary part of the whole, preserving the integrity of things. Yet when a man awakes in a cold room and does not know where he is or why he is, he may stand and wave his arms about and make sounds with his mouth, and in this way affect the infinite movements all around him. As you sit shivering on the edge of the bed, you know you should not do this. If you are waiting for the invisible phenomena to appear, it is best not to create confusion. Best not to disturb the layers. But now you are very cold, and your body cannot wait. It makes you stand up and shuffle through the dust toward the window, making small clouds—which is disturbance.

You are a stone dropped into a forest pond, when snow has covered the earth and the stripped birches are sleeping sentinels ringing the pond. The water is not yet frozen. There are a few yellow leaves clinging to branches, exposed nests cupping little mounds of snow, and an elderly tree with wizened apples hanging upon its leafless limbs. Rust red against white, touched by brushstrokes of gold. At some time while you were asleep, there had passed through this region a tentative painter of visual haiku.

So you drop the perfectly smooth, unflawed oval of stone into the pond, and it makes concentric waves, silver foil blossoming from black water. Cold water is always black. Though sometimes, if you are able to walk upon it or bend over it, you may see a carpet of orange and yellow and crimson and Tyrian purple spears on the bottom. Bottles too. Broken eyeglasses. The green circuit boards of abandoned computers. A toy racing car. Lost wedding rings.

Do you remember the autumn thrill of the first ice-walk on shallow water? Beneath is the carpet of leaves. Between it and your rubber boots there is the frozen layer as clear as glass. When you step onto it, it splinters but does not collapse. Then another step, and another. You are looking down into the real world. You laugh when you hear the splintering sound, once a year. It is recognition, the reliability of the seasons, the dependability of the world.

But that is not the point. You mean to say to yourself that if you affect the world of phenomena, it is only in your immediate environs, like a wave dissipating as it is absorbed. Or the weight of a single child in the epicenter of an outward-expanding web of fractured glass. Are you now—at this moment, in this room, this winter— are you now frozen or fluid? Are you the mass of your being, like water? Or are you the wave of your being, like speech and the gestures of your muscles?

You know there is something uneven in this question. Do you need to ask it? The answer must be wrong too. You have taken a wrong turn somewhere; you have fallen asleep and lost yourself. And now you are awake again but have not refound yourself. Though you know the names for things, you do not know how you know. You do not know the way things have come to be, or why they continue to exist and to move. Like yourself.

The sky is divided into strata, or else appears so. Now a flock of small brown birds cuts diagonally across the glass, moving from churning gray into serene blue, circling and darting in unison, whirling, dancing in air, rising again. It is beautiful. This word flows through your mind. Yes, it is a word for something. It attracts and consoles, but you cannot say any more about it.

There is a street below the window. A human being walks past, an old woman in a heavy brown coat, moving slowly, pulled by a little leashed dog wearing a red coat and leggings and hat. Then two other human beings pass by, slender and swift, their legs scissoring. They wear black clothes; their hair is green; their faces are hardly human. They do not look up at you, but they are frightening. The world has become peopled with creatures you have never seen before.

The blanket around your shoulders no longer preserves your heat. You are shivering hard now, your teeth chattering. The room is growing darker. The bird dance has finished; the air dancers depart. Are there other hints out there? Will they tell you your name and your purpose? Will they explain why you are here?

You are pressing your face to the glass, waiting for the answers to these questions.

It is nearly night when the giant comes. You remember giants from the books someone read to you. Someone carried you then, kept you always warm and without fear. They laughed when you laughed, smiled when you smiled. And the rocking horse in the room—that was another room, not this one. And the glowing bunny lamp. The giants were all in books. There are bad giants. There are many of these. There are good giants, though fewer.

You are staring down at the street, watching the giant approach in long easy strides, his enormous body inside a heavy coat of curry-colored canvas, under a knitted cap and with a long scarf flying out behind him, the pennant of a masted schooner, and with his hands in his pockets, his shoulders hunched. You wonder if his head will be able to peer into your window when he passes by it, though your room is high up, for you are gazing over rooftops and the dead Santas and it is many feet down to the concrete below. Nearer and nearer he comes, and his face is raised to the sky. He is whistling. You can see now that he is not as tall as a house, not as high as the layer of building in which you are standing by the window, waiting and observing. Yet there is no doubt he is a giant. His face is not frightening, though you cannot know for certain if he will become dangerous, because giants are willful and some of them would deceive you. It is a beautiful thing to see a real giant, as long as he does not see you.

But that is not always the pattern of things, for the world is, at times, inconstant.

The giant slows his pace and comes to a halt beneath your window. He sees you! His face changes, his eyes narrowing, his brow folding, his mouth opening in an *Oh*. Is he angry? Or is he hungry? Is he the colossus you have always dreaded, always knew would come? Or is he Saturn, who devours his children?

You quickly step back from the window. You hear heavy footsteps, the clumping of large boots on the staircase. There is only one door in the room. The floor is littered with broken glass, mouse droppings, a frozen bat, the bed, the rusty springs. You try to open the window, to climb out and drop to the sidewalk, which is swift and better than being slowly eaten. The window will not open. You sit down on the floor and cover your face with your hands. You sob and sob, for now the ramparts will splinter and shatter. You will dissolve. You will evaporate. You will become something else in the belly of the giant.

Will you become a whistling in his mouth?

You cannot bear to look. You hear his boots splintering the shards of glass.

"Hello," says the giant, his voice like distant thunder. He has whispered so as not to break your eardrums. This is generous. He may eat you, but he does not want to frighten you. He does not want you to bolt into the forest.

"Are you all right?" he asks.

You press your hands tighter over your face.

"You're going to freeze to death here."

You cannot speak. If you are silent, you will become smaller and smaller, not worth the effort of a bite.

"I won't hurt you," says the giant.

Now your sobs become wails, a child in the room of the rocking horse, with the coffin in which you laid a dead golden hamster. The coffin was an empty matchbox, for large wooden matches, with a blue sailing ship on the cover. You made a memorial label for her and pasted it on the box. In crayon: *Beloved daughter. Gone but not forgotten.* And someone helped you bury it in the backyard. Someone helped you make a little cross to put into the soil.

"Don't be afraid," says the thunder, with his hand cupping the back of your head, a hand so large it holds your entire skull in its palm. The hand is warm and holds things lightly. You can feel the contours of its shape, the complex planes you have drawn again and again with charcoal, and perspective, at times with chiaroscuro. Though this hand's strength is self-restrained, it could crush you.

"What is your name?" asks the thunder.

I cannot remember, you think, opening your cracked lips to speak, but fearing that words would vibrate the air, disturb the layers, provoke the giant, and invite a painful conclusion.

"Why are you here? This is an abandoned building and not very safe."

You open your fingers a little, to see if he is toying with you before his meal. The giant obscures the sky, the room. He is kneeling before you. His face is enormous and too close. The eyes are gray and clear, the face is a Bronzino, a lord of that time, though lacking arrogance. It is a kind face. It is worried. It is sad.

The giant gently pulls your hands from your face. You are no longer wailing. You are not sobbing. But you will not look up. This is what people do when they are shot by killers—they look away. To look at a human being, face to face, eyes to eyes, is to say that between us there is recognition. And sometimes trust.

"My name is Billy," the giant rumbles. "I want to help you. I won't hurt you. Are you hungry?"

You nod, instinctively, impulsively, and you regret it. But still you cannot look at him.

The giant adjusts the blanket covering your shoulders, tucking it under your chin.

"All right then. We should find you some food and shelter. You can't stay here. You'll die if you do. Can you stand up?"

It is not wise to converse with giants. Not until their true nature is revealed.

The giant is so strong that when he lifts you to your feet you are standing before you know it.

"Come on. Let's go find a place for you to stay."

Out on the street a bitter wind is blowing. The giant removes his own coat and drapes it over you. Its hem brushes your ankles. He puts your blanket over his back and a hand on your shoulder, and guides you along.

"Am I a child again?" you ask, and are shaken by the words that have come from your mouth. The words are rasping, broken words.

"No," says the giant.

Five blocks, ten blocks. People and cats. Winter birds. Automobiles with smoking tails. Ice in concrete runnels, fumes rising from drains. The enormous hand cradling you—to crush, to guard, it is not certain.

Now you are through a glass door and in a room full of people, seated along a wall, waiting. The people all look up and stare at the giant, saying nothing. A child hides his face in his mother's arm. Others whisper and stare. They do not look at you. They look at him.

The giant helps you to sit on a chair, and he takes an empty one beside you. The metal creaks and bends. He is too large. But even giants need to sit at times. And still his arm is around you.

Now you and he go into a room where a lady at a desk asks for your names. You sit down. The giant stands, his bristling brown hair brushing the ceiling.

The giant explains. The woman looks worried, or irritated. You cannot understand what is being said.

Later the giant brings you to a bright and shining place full of people waiting with their broken legs, bleeding hands, coughing lungs. Everyone stares at the giant. No one sees you.

A doctor inspects your body. Nakedness. Shame. Needles extracting tubes of violet-red fluid. Thermometer. Pressure band. Stethoscope.

"Stethoscope," you say aloud, to no one.

The doctor speaks to you, but you can say no more.

You are laid down onto a sliding tray by two burly black men with friendly smiles. As they strap your body tightly with bands, one of them says, "Don't you worry, pal, this ain't gonna hurt. Try to hold still. Please don't move or we'll have to do it all over again."

They feed you into the open mouth of a machine that hums and buzzes. You hold yourself perfectly still, hoping you will go through the tunnel into another universe. But the bed slides out again and you have not escaped. They unstrap you, help you to stand, take you out to see the giant, who has been waiting in another room.

"He's not ill," says the doctor to the giant. "No trace of drugs or alcohol. No wounds, no head trauma. A touch of hypothermia, but body temperature is rising well. Malnourished too. The psychiatric unit would be best, though without identification and health insurance, we can't admit him. You could take him to the free ward for itinerants at Bellevue. Have you tried the police? Missing Persons bureau?"

"I am not missing," you say. "I am here."

"Yes, you are here," the giant rumbles with a pat that shakes your bones. "Thank you, Doctor, we'll check with them."

The police are busy. You sit on a bench and wait and grow warmer. The giant stands beside you, his hand nearby, ready to reassure you, or to guard the ramparts of your integrity.

A policeman discusses many things with the giant.

"He doesn't look like a street person," says the giant.

"They usually don't in the beginning. This guy's falling through the cracks, buddy. He a friend of yours?"

"We just met."

The giant goes through album after album of photographs, names, places. All the while, the policeman stares at the giant, observing his face, his limbs, the way his hands flip pages. The policeman is not suspicious. He is curious, amazed. You see now that other people observe unexplainable things, are startled and expanded by phenomena.

"You from a circus?" the policeman asks.

The giant glances at him and shakes his head, then returns to the albums.

You are photographed, a burst of light, glow-spots in your eyes.

Later, faces flash across a computer screen. Face after face after face.

"I am not in there," you say, though they cannot hear you. "I am here."

Your fingers are inked and pressed onto paper. You wash them off in a bathroom, the giant standing watch over you.

You return to the desk out there in the office.

"What's your name?" asks the policeman. "You sure you can't remember who you are?"

You do not answer. Who are you, really?

The policeman says to the giant:

"All we know is he's a Caucasian male, early twenties, no distinguishing marks or features. No fingerprint match. No cyber track anywhere. Facial recognition software narrowed it down to about ten thousand guys in this state who look like him, more or less, but can't seem to pinpoint him. And he could be from anywhere. If we had some ID, there'd be a way to start looking. Until then ..."

"Surely there's a place he could go."

"Good Shepherd shelter, not far from here. Want me to call them?"

He telephones. The voice on the other end says that the shelter is full. All the city shelters are full tonight. But there's one on the south side of Jersey that has a bed.

"Long way to go," says the policeman. "Cost you a fortune by taxi. About two hours by bus. Want me to call them?"

"No, I'll find something else," says the giant.

The policeman spreads his arms wide, shrugs. "It's your life."

The giant looks down at you, his face without expression. There is a lot in his eyes, liquid, not cold, not frozen.

"Hungry?" he asks. You nod.

You are in a noisy café. You are sitting on a stool looking across a counter at a street full of cars, neon lights, people moving past the window, laughing, talking, fracturing layers, and building defense walls around the self. You are lifting a bowl of soup to your lips and gulping it down. There are sandwiches beside you, a basket of fried potatoes, a salad. The giant is too big for one of the tipsy stools. He stands beside you as you eat. He sips from a large paper cup, watching you relieve your thirst and hunger.

"Triple espresso," he says. "Keeps me awake for a couple of hours. Would you like one?"

No, you shake your head. You are grateful for his kindness, but—

"Water?"

Yes.

After more water, more soup, more everything else, you want to go to sleep again. Not to hide. Your eyes are closing. You almost topple, but the hand grabs you and steadies you.

"Okay, let's go," he says.

You are walking with the giant on poorly lit streets. It is one of the city's hard places, old places. You pass huddles of unhappy people shouting insults, the new strange creatures in the world. The giant is not afraid. People can shoot you, but when you are as big as he is they do not try to beat you up.

You come to a four-story, red brick building on a side street. Up the stairs to the top floor, and a hallway full of silent numbered doors.

Across three of the doors and parts of the walls, the words "Bedbugs. Don't rent. Don't squat. This building condemned" are spray-painted in fluorescent orange.

"Home sweet home," says the giant, unlocking the one clean door at the end of the corridor. "I debugged my place, and I've been working on the others. The landlord says I can give it a try."

He stoops to get his head under the lintel, goes in, and switches on a light. You follow him inside. You feel it may not be safe to do this; you may regret it. Who, really, is this giant? Is he a good one?

"You can stay here for the night," he says. "It's cramped and it isn't pretty, but you won't freeze, and I can try to help you tomorrow. Sound like a good idea?"

You hang your head and stare at the floor. You are trembling with apprehension. Goodness has no explanation. You cannot trust it. But you have nowhere else to go.

The giant closes the door behind you and helps you take off the coat, which he hangs on a hook by the door. You dare not move. The giant kneels, a mountainous back in a tan wool sweater, a strip of white T-shirt at the neck. Blue jeans. He is unlacing his hiking boots. That done, he points to your feet.

"Sandals in winter," he says with raised eyebrows. "Your feet are soaked. I suggest you take 'em off. I'll get you something warmer to put on. Have a seat."

The apartment is a single room with a kitchenette and a bathroom. The ceiling is very high. The walls are pale yellow, a sunrise in early summer. There are no pictures or posters on them, nothing at all. There is a chrome dining table and a scarred wooden desk with stacks of books on it, along with a desk lamp, paper, pens, and notebooks. A packing crate is its seat. Two large stuffed armchairs fill most of the remaining space. Their arms are missing, the wounds of their dismemberment gaping.

You sit down on the edge of one. The giant again kneels and removes your wet sandals and socks. Your feet are blue. He dries your feet with a towel. He brings socks that he pulls over your feet. Like gunny sacks, though made of coarse wool.

The giant puts a kettle of water on a gas burner.

Two thick foam mattresses stretch along the entire length of one wall. The giant separates them and slides one across the room to an adjacent wall. He dresses it with sheets, a blanket, and a pillow, and on top of these he pulls a green sleeping bag. He dresses the other mattress in the same manner.

"I sleep here," he says, pointing to one. "Even an Abe Lincoln bed is too short for me, but we'll make do for one night. You sleep there. You can lie down and shut your eyes now, if you want."

You remain seated, uncertain, clamping your hands between your knees. The kettle whistles. The giant pours steaming water into a white teapot. He is rummaging in the kitchen to find cups, spoons, a jar of honey. He lifts the window and brings in a carton of milk from the outside sill. From the corner of your eye, you see him gathering a handful of kitchen knives, very dangerous knives, and standing on tiptoe to put them on top of a cupboard, high above human reach.

He turns and notices you watching him. He lifts his shoulders as if in explanation or apology. Now you see that he is not only a titanic human being, a continent of bone and muscle, but is excellent in all ways. If you were to see him at a distance, not knowing his height, you would say, this is what a man should be. Yes, this. For here is immense strength, and it is mastered. Here is perfect form and balance, yet it is without vanity. This man does no harm.

Now the giant brings you a cup of tea. It looks like a thimble in the palm of his hand. You take it in both of yours. You sip its sweetness. He sits down on the other chair, which, despite its missing arms, is too small for him. It creaks and groans beneath his weight. When everything has settled, he swallows his tea in a single gulp. He looks up with bright eyes, and laughs gently.

"I went out to buy a loaf of bread," he says. "Little did I know what I would bring home."

You lower your eyes. You understand, suddenly, that you are a burden. You are an unsolicited weight upon the world. You have misread the world somehow; something in it was wrong. And now you are not where you should be. Though the giant is sturdy enough, it is not good to add burdens onto others.

Some people become rescuers, you think. Some become this in order to strengthen what they are. Some become rescuers in order to become what they hope to be. And yet there would be no rescuers without those in need of rescue.

Silently you begin to weep, because you understand now that you are in need of rescue.

The giant looks at you without speaking, his eyes sorrowing with you, his face sympathetic, listening, waiting. Rescuers, too, contemplate phenomena.

"It is hard for you," he says. "I was once like you. A long time ago, I too forgot my own name. The name love gave to me, and breathed into my ears, and called me to supper, and scolded me, and taught me my path in life. And when I lost that name I thought I had lost everything. But it was only a beginning. A losing can be a better kind of finding."

"What is your name?" you ask the giant, though you remember that he told you before. There is reassurance in names. There is identity and integrity.

"My name is Billy Revere," the giant replies. "Before and after, though I lost it for a while. Are you sure you can't remember yours?"

"I don't know," you say, staring into the distance, a horizon obscured by smoke and dust. "I sense it, but I cannot hear it. I remember I was afraid and I was running from something. I fell through ice, and I fell through frozen leaves below the ice, and then through the ring of fire underneath all layers of phenomena."

"There is a kind of poetry in what you say," replies the giant. "Maybe you are a poet."

"I do not know for certain."

"You do not know what you are or where you should be. I understand. But you are here. And you are you."

You are warm now. The tea has helped, and the giant's words. You hear something faintly in the distance, beyond the sound of police sirens, the clinking of the radiator, the soft bellows of the giant's breathing. It is coming closer and closer.

You look up at him and say:

"My name is Francisco de Goya."

2

The Metropolitan Museum of Misplaced Memories

"Bacon and eggs, Francisco?" asks the giant.

I open my eyes. Where am I? Oh yes, I am lying on a mattress on a floor in the lair of a giant.

I have a memory of saying my name and then toppling sideways, unable to keep my eyes open. I felt myself scooped up and carried, laid gently down onto a mattress, blankets pulled over my shoulders, a light going out, and I was gone.

Now I am here again. There is natural light in the apartment's single window. The giant is standing by the kitchen stove with a spatula in hand and a big smile on his face. The frying pan is spitting.

I sit up, kicking off the sleeping bag, preparing to run if I have to.

"You really slept. Fourteen hours," he says. "If you want to shower and shave, breakfast should be ready when you're finished. I'm making waffles too. Maple syrup. Coffee. Do you drink coffee?"

"Yes," I say, though I don't know how I know this.

"I went out this morning and bought you some clothes, also a coat and boots. I think I got your sizes right. The clothes are on a hook in the bathroom. Put your old ones in the hamper. Make yourself at home."

I am desperate for the bathroom. I close its door and take care to slide its bolt into locked position. Are there dimensions to the personalities of giants that are better left unknown? He could have overpowered me but has chosen not to do so. This tells me something. Though I do not feel safe, neither do I feel unsafe. His name is Billy, like a little boy strolling through a wheat field. My name is Francisco, like a little boy on a donkey revolving around a grape press. Or a darker Francisco wrestling with the witches embedded in oil paint. Beyond that, nothing is certain.

My face in the mirror is disturbing. Who are you? The eyes tell me nothing, large and brown with black lashes and brows. A head full of heavy dark curls. Olive skinned. Am I Italian? Or Middle Eastern?

There is a fresh safety razor and soap on the sink. I shave myself carefully. A new toothbrush in its cellophane package, a tube of minty white. I brush my teeth. I rinse and brush again.

The bathroom is floored with a chessboard of black and white ceramic tiles, many of them cracked. The walls are peeling plaster. The bathtub is ancient and deep, an oval quadruped on four lion paws poised as if to leap. An iron ring suspended from the ceiling surrounds it, with a curtain to keep the water from spilling all over the floor and out into the apartment, and then into the corridor and down the public staircase, making rapids and waterfalls and hazards for those who live in the building, and when the water freezes as it reaches its estuary on the sidewalk, an extremely dangerous zone for unsuspecting people passing by. How full of treacheries, follies, mistakes, is existence. Is it safe to take a shower?

After disrobing, I stand under a jet of steaming hot water and remember, before it is too late, how to master the curtain engineering in order to keep the water within the chamber (slide the rusty rings on which the curtain hangs and completely surround yourself; do not forget this). I am also learning that life is fluid; I am liquid, not frozen. I move. I can speak. I possess my small morsel of identity, and on the other side of the door is a giant who, for reasons known only to himself, wishes to help me.

There is no shampoo, only a bar of orange carbolic soap. When I am clean and have dried myself with a towel, I put on the new clothes: white boxer shorts and T-shirt, jeans, a thin dark-blue pullover, a bulky maroon cardigan. There are new socks too, which are slightly too large but smaller than the giant's. Everything is stapled with price tags: Hospital Auxiliary Thrift Shop—New to U.

New to me. Everything is new to me. The world. My name. My face. The face is certain. The name may be something pulled down from the swift-flowing currents in the sky. It is close to my true name, I think. It must be. It is meaningful to me though not quite right.

We eat quietly, facing each other on opposite sides of the kitchen table.

"I found a two-dollar chair at the flea market," he says. "It's yours for the duration."

"There is little space in this room," I reply. "I take up too much of your space."

"*I* take up too much of my space," he says with a grin, chewing on bacon, his face looming over me, though he is feet away.

"I will leave after breakfast. I am sorry to have been a burden to you."

"You aren't a burden, Francisco."

"You have spent money on me. And you are too tall for one mattress."

"I'll get another. You can stay as long as you need to."

"I will go after breakfast."

"Of course. If you wish. However, I have a suggestion."

I look at him curiously.

"We need to find out who you are. We could have an interesting time of it. Like a game or a mystery story."

I shake my head. "You must go to your work or to school," I say. "You have spent your money to feed and clothe me. You own nothing. I do not wish to offend you, but I think you are poor."

"Oh no, Francisco. I am very rich. I have a small pension that pays for everything I need, and then some. I'm studying too, but there's no time pressure on that."

"You are a student?"

"In a way. I wanted to be a paramedic, but my size was a deterrent and they wouldn't let me into the course. And no one would have hired me even if I had graduated. I don't fit easily into ambulances, you see. And sometimes people in crisis are frightened of me. So I study paramedicine on my own, and I volunteer at shelters on weekends, but most of the time I walk around the city looking for people in trouble."

"You help them?"

"Uh-huh, I try to."

"As you helped me."

"It makes me happy when I can do any small thing. So you see, you're doing me a favor. And if you're worried about me, uh, hurting you, you don't need to be. I'm not unbalanced. I'm not a crazy person. I used to be, but I'm not now."

"But *I* am now."

"I don't think you are. I think you've suffered some kind of trauma."

"Which is why you were right to hide the knives on top of the cupboard. I do not know if I am good or evil."

The giant blushes mightily.

"I'm sorry," he says. "You were a stranger."

"I am still a stranger."

"But not as much as you were last night. We're sharing a meal and having a good conversation."

The giant stands up and in one step crosses the room to the cupboard. He retrieves the knives and puts them back into a drawer. He sits down and smiles.

"Another waffle, Francisco?"

"Yes, please."

We are walking north out of the regions of fear.

"You are very big," I say to the giant. "That is why people do not try to hurt you."

"You're wrong there," he says. "I'm a challenge for some guys, you see. They jump at the chance to bring me down. Good story to tell after the fight. David and Goliath, except the bad guys are David." He walks another half block before he adds, "They aren't really bad. Just angry. They feel trapped, without choices.

28

They know me now and there's no more trouble. I've got nothing to steal, and I'm the last person in town who's likely to be an undercover cop."

Now we are walking along Fifth Avenue, the most expensive street in the world, the giant tells me. We are going to a museum.

"The Metropolitan Museum of Misplaced Memories," he says. "The lost and found of the human soul."

It's a cold day, but the boots he bought me are fleece lined, and the coat is warm enough. It's corduroy fabric, striped vertically in a variety of colors. It is not a pattern I would have chosen—I realize now that my tastes are sober and conservative, despite my vagrancy.

"What city is this?" I ask.

"It's New York. One of the biggest cities in the world."

"Oh, now I remember. Yes, I know the name. There was a giant ape here—on top of a building. I can see it in my mind. Did I see this with my eyes?"

"You might have seen it in a movie."

We meet other pedestrians. Those who are not distracted by their own affairs, or the sidewalk at their feet, always blink rapidly and stare at Billy as we pass. Most of them stop and watch him from behind. They do not see me. At traffic lights, every head in every car turns and stares at him.

"Am I a child?" I ask the giant. "Truly, you can tell me."

"Children do not shave, Francisco," he says, lumbering along without a pause.

"Then am I a dwarf?"

"No, I'd put you at just over six feet tall."

"How tall are you?"

"Ah, the question I'm asked by every human being I have conversed with since I turned fourteen. I haven't measured lately, but last I checked I was seven feet eleven and a half inches high."

"You," I declare emphatically, "are a giant!"

"Technically, medically, no. I don't suffer from gigantism or acromegaly. Mythically, imaginatively, I suppose I'm a giant in most people's eyes. In reality I've inherited a genetic code that made me grow normally in every way, just somewhat more in terms of quantity."

"Were you a very large baby?"

"Quite ordinary, nine pounds something, I think."

"Are your parents exceptionally tall people too?"

"They were. Both under seven feet, though. They had me when they were older, in their forties. They passed away some years ago."

A cloud washes over his face and is quickly gone.

"I am sorry. Are you alone in the world?"

"Brothers and sisters, aunts and uncles, you mean? None. I'm without any family now. But I never feel alone in the world. Do you?"

"I feel as if I have always been alone. But not today."

"Good!" he says, thumping me on the back, making me stumble forward. A hand flashes out and steadies me.

"Here's the museum."

This is a very big building, ceilings a hundred feet high, just the right size for the giant. In a place like this he can be comfortable. Straighten. Stretch. Advance without a stooping neck and a nagging fear of banging his head on lintels, drawing blood, creating dizziness, falling down, hurting people he would bury beneath his body. In order to keep up with him I am forced to trot. He knows where he wants to go. Through gallery after gallery, annex and alcove and more Minotaurian galleries, people stare at him. He never seems to notice.

"It is rude to stare," I gasp, nearly out of breath.

"They can't help it," he murmurs, slowing his pace, allowing me to catch up.

I come to a halt, distracted by a painting of a man standing on the earth holding the hand of a woman who is floating sideways in the air. It is very beautiful and strange. Is she rising, or is she descending from the heavens? Is he tethering her to the earth with his love?

"Look at this, Francisco," says the giant, pointing to a detail in the painting. "Tell me what it is."

"It's the Eiffel Tower."

He nods up and down, smiling. "Excellent!"

"I like it too."

"I mean it's excellent that you recognize it, have a name for it." He pats me on the top of my head. "It means everything is still there inside your mind, stored away in attics and broom closets and cupboards and cellars. We just need keys to open the locked doors."

On we go at a trot.

When we next come to a stop, I am in a gallery of old dark paintings full of movement and mysterious colors. The colors in the portraits are unique: a tangerine vest above jade-green leggings, a queen in a black dress riding a swollen horse with a too-small head, a flaming red peony on her black bonnet. I know these paintings. These portraits are old friends. I think one of them is a self-portrait of me as a child. I was very gifted, you see, even at an early age.

The portrait captures me standing with my arms open wide before me. I'm wearing a red pantsuit adorned with a silver-white sash and satin slippers. I am feeling somewhat uncomfortable because of the ruffled lace neckpiece, but I have learned to live with it. On the floor beside me is a green birdcage, full of little birds that seem content enough to remain where they are—well-fed prisoners. The cage's door is open. At my feet is an Asian jackdaw, pecking at a piece of paper. One of its legs is tied by a string that I hold lightly but firmly in my hands. Yes, this is what the painting is about: the illusion of freedom. Sitting beside my feet are three cats peering intensely at the jackdaw—a detail that tells me it was painted on one of my low days.

"This is what I looked like as a child," I inform the giant.

"I can see the likeness," he says, pondering the image thoughtfully.

Suddenly I am feeling very uneasy. I don't know why.

"What is written on the paper the jackdaw is pecking?" I ask. "Do you see what I see?"

The giant peers close.

"It looks like garbled Spanish, or maybe a nobleman's crest?" he says.

"Look closer."

"Sorry, that's all I can see. It's not very clear."

"It's the skyline of New York City, in the future, the boy's future, actually *my* future back then, if you see what I mean."

The giant frowns, squinting his eyes. Shakes his head.

"And the numbers. They don't make any sense to me. Do they make sense to you?"

"Are they numbers, Francisco? They look like random strokes of a pen."

I bend closer to inspect. My eyes are inches from the canvas surface. No, these are certainly numbers:

09—11—20—01

I shake off the inexplicable mood. We move on to other paintings, some with overtly frightening themes: firing squads; battles; monsters; a colossus; a crazed demigod; blood; gore; witches floating in the air, tumbling a disoriented man who is their plaything. He doesn't know who he is or where he is, and he has forgotten his name.

"I know all of these paintings," I inform the giant. "I am fairly sure I painted them."

The giant leans over and reads a label beneath a painting of a colossus, a bad giant.

"The name is yours, all right," he says in a musing tone. "This is a clue. We are making progress. Do you know how old you are, Francisco?"

I shake my head.

"The year you were born?"

I stare at my empty hands.

"It says here you were born in 1746. This makes you around two hundred sixty-five years old. Would that be about right?"

"Yes, it must be. What year were you born?"

"Nineteen eighty-one."

"Are you sure? Is it possible we have all been deceived?"

"Maybe. But then there are memories to go by. Public records, news events, things you can check against your

33

personal recollections. For example, do you remember wearing fancy clothes in a palace, painting a picture of a princess surrounded by old ladies and a dwarf?"

Straining as hard as I might, I can't recall any such experience. I shake my head.

"Okay," says the giant. "But that doesn't prove it didn't happen. The memory may be locked away temporarily."

"Yes, that could very well be the case."

"Genetically and theoretically, it is possible that many of our presumptions about human life are broad generalities, which ignore astonishing exceptions. For example, I myself am something of a genetic and theoretical anomaly. Yet here I am before you, standing in my size eighteen Nike jogging shoes—breathing, emanating heat, desiring a cup of espresso. By the same token, Francisco, the aging factor in our genetic makeup is a tag on our double helix. If something in your helixes was amiss, or in *advance* of most of mankind, it would explain it."

"It does not explain why I look so young *now*."

"But it does, Francisco. It's simply that you age more slowly than the rest of us. Let's do some math here. You appear to be twenty-four or twenty-five. Yet if you made these paintings all those years ago, you are about two hundred sixty-seven years old. Thus, it looks to me like you age ninety percent slower than most people."

"I don't believe the figure is accurate, Billy."

"Probably," he sighs. "I failed math in high school, which is why I never graduated. Thank heavens for basketball."

"What do you mean?"

"A university gave me a full basketball scholarship and let me in without a high school diploma. But that's beside the point. The important thing here is we now have an indicator that science doesn't get everything right. For all we know, there are countless extremely old people living among us."

"And you think I am one of them?"

"What's your earliest memory? Does anything come into your mind? It might turn a key in a lock."

In a flash I see a scene.

"A boy in winter. It's me. I'm surrounded by snow. I'm wearing ice skates, holding a hockey stick. I'm wearing a blue hockey team sweater with a white maple leaf on it. My cheeks are flaming red. I look about eight years old."

"Hmm, if it's a memory, how would you be able to see yourself?"

"Maybe I saw a photograph of myself."

"Or maybe it's some other boy you saw with your eyes. That could explain it. Anything else?"

"A television set, black-and-white pictures. Outside on the street there are old cars. Television antennas on the houses."

"No satellite dishes?"

"No."

"Okay, this is progress. It's not Madrid in the seventeen hundreds. It's probably the 1950s. And maybe you're a Canadian. The sweater is the Toronto Maple Leafs." The giant regards me with a look of penetrating deduction. "*And* your accent is definitely not one of New York City's dialects, nor anywhere near it."

"Bedford-Stuyvesant?" I ask. "Rude Babylon?"

Where did these names come from?

"Doubtful," he says. "Besides, you speak with a whiff of English accent. Not New England and definitely not Brit. Close your eyes again. What comes into your mind?"

"I'm walking on thin ice. It's splintering under my feet. I can see my boots, which are black rubber with red rims. I'm carrying a tiny yellow racing car in my mittens. The ice breaks, and I fall straight down into the water. Fortunately it's not over my head, only up to my chest. I push away the floating chunks of ice and struggle toward shore, breaking more and more ice with each step. I am crying. It is not a man's crying, it's a child's. Somehow in all of this I have lost the car."

"The tiny yellow car, you mean?"

"Yes, a yellow Matchbox car."

"Good. Now we have another clue. We've narrowed down your origins to an Anglo-Saxon country north of the warm zones of our continent."

"I don't think it helps identify me. A lot of people live there. Millions."

"You mean in Canada?"

"I don't know whether or not I come from Canada. But it's a fact that thirty million people live in that country."

"That can't be true!"

"I do not tell lies, Billy."

"Then you fabricate in order to evoke a deeper truth."

"That is lying."

"Okay, you embellish."

"Truly, there are that many people in the north."

He grins like a detective who has discovered a trail of blood.

"How, may I ask, do you come by this information?"

"I don't know."

He chuckles, a rumble of distant thunder.

We make a stop at the New York Public Library, farther south on Fifth.

"Excuse me," the giant says, addressing the crown of an information clerk's head. He is trying to keep his voice down. Even so, it booms. She looks up from an index she has been perusing and stares at him through her thick glasses. She jumps a little when she beholds the questioner. She is a sweet girl in a calf-length dusky-rose dress and a pink angora button-up sweater touching her collarbone.

"You remind me of a portrait by John Singer Sargent," I tell her, hoping to normalize the atmosphere. "You're standing by a lake with cobalt-blue waves, melon hues on your rose dress, your bare feet in the white sand, and the closest wave is kissing your toes."

But this doesn't really help. She looks at me for a second and then back to the giant, swallowing hard, her eyes blinking rapidly. The other clerks along the information counter have dropped what they are doing and are staring at us. They are cynical or indifferent young maidens with exposed bodies. Our maiden is not, and in the silence of our hearts we treasure her. Nevertheless, despite her graces, she is frightened of the giant.

"Can you please tell us where we can find information about Canada?" he asks.

She looks way up into his face and chokes out the necessary catalogue numbers.

We go off to find a book about the country we have been discussing. In one of them we learn that Canada has thirty-five million people. I thought it was thirty. Which could indicate that I have been out of contact for a while, or, alternatively, did not have my statistics correct in the first place.

We are heading home now, going deeper into the regions of darkness southwest of Central Park. The giant tells me it is called Hell's Kitchen. He insists that we stop at a café, because he needs a cup of espresso badly. On the roof of a structure that looks like a railway car, a green neon light flashes a name, on and off and on: *Dina's*.

"I love this place," he says as we go in. "It's so retro. Nineteen thirties."

After we have squeezed into a leatherette booth, a saucy woman in a polka-dot minidress and red high heels, with a bow in her hair, purple lipstick, purple fingernail polish, heavy purple eyeliner, and an elephant tattoo on one of her bare forearms, the name *Alexander in India* beneath it in Greek letters, takes our orders.

"Do you know what year you were born?" I ask her timorously.

She cocks her head and grimaces, as if now she has seen and heard everything.

"Never ask a girl her age, honey," she says wryly.

With a sinking feeling, I realize I have been insensitive. If she is an extremely old person, born in the golden age of the Macedonian empire, she might not wish to discuss her past with strangers.

"Your orders, boys?"

I ask for water. She frowns.

The giant asks for coffee. She smiles.

"Ultra-mega-espresso for me," the giant elucidates. "Five cream, no sugar."

"Comin' right up, Billy," says the woman, and off she goes to fetch it.

"You know her," I comment, somewhat in awe.

"Most everyone knows me in these parts. At least by sight. I stop in here nearly every day, usually after my jog around the park."

"It is a very large park."

"It is. I run around it three times per day. Not three separate times, you understand, but three in one go. One of the problems with an ultrasize body is that sometimes hearts don't quite fit the job they have to do. Don't grow as fast as other parts, and in some cases stop growing before they should. That's what a doctor told me once."

"Do you have a heart like that?"

"Mine is on the more hopeful end of the spectrum. But I take no chances. Ever since high school I've been training it and forcing it to expand." He pauses, inspecting me with a riveting look. "By the way, are you as hungry as I am?"

Are you as hungry as I am? I consider this carefully. What, really, does it imply? Will my growing trust of him be shattered in an instant? Is the truth of the matter that *he* is hungry? If there are no other food sources than me, will he . . . ?

"Yes," I say, swallowing a lump of fear.

"Me too. I'll have you for lunch."

My heart jumps and begins pounding. Is he telling me he is going to eat me? How could he be so blatant about it! No, no, he's only saying he wishes to have me as a guest. I cannot get used to his voice, kept at low volume but pitched so deep. Such a voice, such a tone, might or might not indicate sinister intentions, and yet his face is set in a guileless expression, his eyes twinkling with habitual benevolence.

Back in his apartment he parks me on a chair and tells me he has to go out again for eggs. We're going to have an omelet for lunch, he explains. We had eggs for breakfast, I remember.

"Is that a good idea, considering the state of your heart?" I ask.

"These are free-range eggs. Good for the heart. If I don't get a lot of protein, I start to go downhill."

He goes out and is back within three minutes, carrying eight brown eggs in a wicker basket. He shows them to me in passing. The shells have rusty speckles and a few dark smears that don't look healthy to me. He washes them off at the kitchen sink, slaps a frying pan onto a burner, starts cracking eggs.

"The girls are being generous," he says over his shoulder. "They know I have company."

"Your neighbors gave you the eggs?"

"No, my hens gave 'em to us. I'll introduce you later."

Out in the corridor, he leads me to a door in the wall at right angles to his. He unlocks it and we enter a stairwell. He flicks a switch, and a naked light bulb illuminates wooden steps leading upward to a trap door, which he opens with his head and shoulders. Above this is a plywood cabin containing metal rubbish bins. He opens one of their lids and scoops up a can full of seeds.

"Combination laying mash and scratch," he explains. "They love it. Plus all the household table scraps. I also get throwaways from the restaurant two blocks south of here. The girls go crazy over anything green. But they don't like sushi paste. In summer I collect bags of grass whenever the park is mowed."

We step out onto the flat roof. The outer rim is fenced with high chicken wire. An extravagantly colored rooster is strutting around, crowing, looking sinister. He spots me, arches his neck, spreads his wings, and darts toward me with intent to kill. The giant steps between us, and the rooster and I slowly back away from each other.

The giant scatters seed and makes strange high-pitched calls, incongruous with a throat like his—until now, I have heard only his basso profundo. The girls come running helter-skelter, a crew of disparate breeds, large and small. Also a speckled black-and-white game hen with a long fantail. Their coop is a lean-to affair built onto the side of the shack. It has a row of nesting boxes. On the other side of the shack is a pigeon coop. Twenty or so pigeons of mottled coloring, mostly white and caramel, are huddling there against the cold. A few of them fly out their open door and wheel up into the sky. From other directions, shimmering blue-gray pigeons swoop down, hover, and enter the coop. The giant fills their trough with seed. A frenzy of cooing and pecking ensues. Here too there are nesting boxes.

"They'll be laying again a few weeks from now," says the giant with a paternal smile. "Small eggs, but lots of them."

I walk to the edge of the roof and stare out over the rooftops of nearby buildings just like ours. A few streets away, office towers and apartment blocks shoot upward, steel and glass crystals rising from shadowed canyons. I lean through a hole in the fence to catch a glimpse of the street below. A hand grips the back of my coat and gently tugs me upright.

"Let's get out of the wind," murmurs the giant as he frowns over the hole, weaving it closed with strands of wire.

We go back down to his apartment. Like many colossi, he is accustomed to striding across the face of the earth, forgetting that lower ranks of creatures must move at a different pace. I am exhausted. I drop onto my mattress and fall asleep.

When I awake again, he is coming in the door, jiggling a key in its lock. He closes the door and waves at me. He is wearing jogging pants and a hoodie, sweating, his cheeks enflamed, a frosting of frozen moisture on his forelock. He is carrying a large piece of foam slab. He grins in triumph.

"Huge discount, the price is right. They were tossing these into a dumpster. Clean as a whistle and long enough to complete my bed. What a day this has been. What a truly great day!"

He is deliriously happy over the discovery of a trifle. Tumbling in a vortex of disproportion, I am being cared for by a child. I am lost in a strange land, peopled with creatures I have never seen before. There are giants in the world, but now I know that some of them are good.

3

Homeland security

We are lying on our backs, trying to drift into sleep. The electric lamp and the crystal chandelier in the center of the ceiling are turned off, but enough city light filters through the window that I can dimly make out shapes in the room. The city is noisy, despite the lateness of the hour.

I am feeling warm under the sleeping bag, no longer so afraid. I am not hungry either, since the giant made a five-pound hamburger-and-onion-and-spoonful-of-diced-pickle meatloaf for supper, most of which he ate.

"We are very fortunate people," he murmurs groggily, for now the daytime current of his ideas, goals, and habits is giving way to a slower flow of consciousness. The determined course of a mighty river disseminates into streams, and then into a myriad of trickles.

I cannot think of anything to say.

"I am so fortunate to have a place like this," he goes on. "It's been condemned by the building inspector as unsafe and unhealthy, and the landlord wants to sell it. But he's going to wait a couple of years until the real estate market recovers. I live here rent free, keep the boiler in the basement going, make sure no one busts in and wrecks the place. One by one the other tenants have left, and the landlord won't rent to anyone new. He might keep the building and renovate it into deluxe rental apartments, or he might sell it as is. Until then I have a home."

"Where will you go when you leave?" I mumble.

"I don't know, but I'll find something. New York City must be full of these grand old places that no one wants. I scout around now and then. Did you notice the crystal chandelier?"

"Yes."

"Doesn't that strike you as odd, Francisco?"

"In what way?"

"The ceiling is twelve feet above the floor, which is a tremendous boon to a person like me. Even the chandelier is higher than my head. But why such a marvel for a tiny room hardly bigger than a closet?"

"Maybe the people who constructed this building liked chandeliers."

"It was built in the eighteen hundreds. This entire floor was once a single apartment with many rooms, the home of people with money. It was broken up into little flats after the war."

"Maybe all the rooms in the building have chandeliers."

"No, they don't. I've been inside every one. The other three apartments on this floor are empty now, and only one of them had a chandelier, but the last tenant tore it out and took it away when he left. His apartment was as small as this one."

The giant sighs.

"It's sad," he continues. "The way some people get trapped in a corner and then do foolish things, because they think it's their only way to survive. My neighbor's name was Jimmy de Locke, he told me. After he left with the chandelier, I began to wonder if it was a pseudonym."

"You mean alias," I correct him. "If he was a writer, it might have been a pseudonym. If he was a thief, it would have been an alias."

"He was an old man. He never washed or shaved, and he drank a lot. Sometimes I took him a plate of meatloaf when he'd been drinking too much and wasn't eating. His room was just like mine, except it had stacks of unopened boxes of electronic equipment in it. But I never saw any books or papers or typewriter or computer."

The giant pauses.

"You know, Francisco, it's interesting the way you come up with the perfect word for this or that, but you can't remember where you come from or what happened to you. In my studies, I've read about brain trauma. It seems to me you may be a victim of a ministroke, maybe a series of them, but it would have been some time ago because the MRI showed no trace in your brain. The doctor at the ER said there was no evidence of skull fracture either, no lumps, no abrasions, no scars."

"Do you think I have become mentally ill? It might have happened because I have lived too long, seen too much."

"Like an overload, a blown-fuse kind of thing? Maybe. Or it could be a case of your brain just needing a holiday and taking it without asking your permission. It packed your belongings into boxes and stuffed them into a storage room in the attic of your mind. Then it locked the storage room and the attic door and pocketed the key."

I sit up in bed and lean back against the wall.

"So everything—*everything*—could still be up there," I say, feeling a strange mixture of hope and dread.

"Uh-huh, it probably is. And nobody's forcing you to unlock the door and unpack all that stuff. It's only if you want to. Only when you're ready."

"I want to. I feel lost without it. I do not know where to go, where to direct my life. I know only that I am Francisco de Goya and that I once painted fine works of art. I also know a few important words like *stethoscope* and *alias*, and I can read the Greek alphabet, but I don't know why I know these things."

"You also know you were a boy in a cold land."

"Yes, I wore skates. And I had a toy car, which I lost under the ice. There were lost rings too, underwater, buried by colored leaves, a life frozen in time. Beyond this, I see nothing."

"Do you want to see more?"

I hesitate. "Y-yes, I think so."

"Okay then. The more things we look at and the more places we go, the more you'll remember. We need to find the pocket where your brain put the key and forgot about it. Maybe it's not just one key but many keys—a keychain."

I nod in the dark, though he cannot see me.

"Of course, there's a lot to discover in New York City," the giant continues. "A lifetime's worth. Even I will never plumb the depths of it, because it's always changing, growing mostly. It swallows other cities too. It's as big as the world. But you have to make a start somewhere. So my suggestion is, tomorrow we'll resume our search. If you agree, we'll begin with a clue and follow it to its end."

"Which clue?"

"Hmm, that's a good question. We already know that you are an artist, and quite old. The other main clue is the hockey."

"The hockey?"

"Yes. Skates, snow, hockey sweater. What you described is too distinct to be merely a phantasm."

"What is a phantasm?"

"An ethereal imagining."

"You are a very intelligent person, Billy."

"Some basketball players are *highly* intelligent, Francisco. I am not. I think I'm an average sort of person. But now and then I've met geniuses on the court. You get talking in the locker room, go out for a jumbo espresso, the fraternity of the exceptionally tall. People open up to me, you see, whenever they get over their initial fear."

"They reveal their minds."

"Yup. And I reveal mine too. Or I did, before I grew too tall to play."

"When did you become too tall to play?"

"Well, I reached six foot four when I was fourteen years old, and was six eleven when I turned seventeen and got the scholarship. I was over seven feet when I had my accident and forgot who I was for a while. I think I mentioned that to you. Anyway, when I recovered from the accident, I wasn't much good for professional basketball, and the university let me go. I tried to play

47

pickup games in vacant lots, but at a certain stage I real-ized it was unfair of me to continue, since I just dribbled over to the hoop and dropped the ball in, every time. It really frustrated shorter players. But you see my point."

He has thrown a lot of images into my mind, some of which I do not understand. Confused, I shake my head.

"The point is, it's good for people to open up to oth-ers. Sooner or later, a person has to make a choice to trust. You gotta start trusting someone, even if it takes you places you hadn't expected, even to hard places."

Do I trust this giant? I know he is good. But what if *I* am not good? What if I am hiding a crime, have become my alias, like Jimmy de Locke?

I hear a mammoth yawn, like a low note on a tuba.

"Well, it's been a long day. And tomorrow we're going to Toronto," murmurs the giant.

"Toronto! Really?"

"Yup. Good night, Francisco."

"Good night, Billy."

At eight o'clock in the morning, the giant comes tromp-ing up the staircase and into the apartment, waking me from a dream I can't remember.

"Our ride will be here soon," he declares with a look of boyish enthusiasm. "Get dressed and wash, but don't worry about breakfast—I've packed some food, and we can eat along the way."

Downstairs, a delivery van sits idling by the curb in front of the building's entrance. Its driver is waiting by the double doors in the rear, a corpulent man in his fifties wearing a creaking brown leather jacket and a matching cap. He opens the doors with a subtle amused look, shaking his head as if this beats all, despite the fact that a delivery man in New York City has probably seen plenty. He chuckles as we climb in.

The van's cargo area is empty, save for a rug on the floor and mattresses positioned along the sides like two sofas facing each other. The giant sits down on one, and I take the other. There are no side windows, though a sliding glass in the forward wall gives access to the driver's compartment. It is closed. We can see him. He can see us in his rearview mirror. He makes the engine roar and pulls out into the street.

"Here we go, Francisco," says the giant.

"Is it a long journey to Toronto?" I ask.

"Mmm, pretty long. About eight hours to the border, and then a few more hours to the city. I've hired this man for three days. We'll sleep in a motel overnight, if they have motels in Canada, and we'll do some exploring the next day, look at the sights and major landmarks. Back home the day after that. If you ever lived there, I think you'll recognize things, get the juices flowing, remember more and more. One step might lead to another. If not, at least we tried."

"It must have cost a lot of money to hire the driver and his vehicle."

"Not too much. Besides, it's worth the adventure. I haven't left NYC since my accident."

"When was your accident?"

A flicker of pain passes through his eyes.

"The year 2001."

"Were you badly hurt?"

"Uh-huh. Spent about three months in the hospital, a couple more in rehab."

"Did you fall down a staircase or get hit by a subway?"

"It was a car accident. My parents had driven here from our farm in the Des Moines valley—I'm from Iowa originally. They'd come to visit me at college and watch me play in a big game. There was a scout from the New York Knicks there that night, and I scored high. Me and my folks were pretty excited on the way back to the hotel. Dad wasn't a very good driver to begin with, and he'd never driven in a city as huge as New York, at least not like this one. But it wasn't his fault, the accident."

"What happened?"

"Our car was Dad's invention. He welded it together from an old Dodge station wagon and a John Deere grain hopper. It had a big back door and the small hopper bolted upside down over the rear passenger section, the roof cut out—something I could sit inside without crunching. We rode in it for years. We got broadsided by a car that went through a red light. It was racing to get away from a police car, and it hit us at top speed. The police car crashed into us too. Everyone died but me."

"I am very sorry, Billy."

He nods, eyes moist, firming his lips to keep them from trembling.

"Thanks."

We say nothing for a while. We enter a long tunnel under a river, and on the other side a sign tells us we are now in New Jersey. Through the front window I watch canyons of passing high rises.

"The Statue of Liberty," I say, pointing at a statuette on the vehicle's dashboard.

"Bravo, Francisco, bravo!" says the giant, his shine restored.

"Like the jackdaw," I reply.

"The jackdaw? What's a jackdaw?"

"The bird on a string in the self-portrait I painted. The one we saw in the museum."

"Oh, right. We call them grackles, kind of a blackbird. But the statue doesn't look anything like a bird."

"No, but the idea. Freedom."

"Mmm," he says, turning inward to his own thoughts, musing. He is sitting with his knees up, feet wide apart, forearms on knees, hands clasped between them. His eyes grow drowsy, then they close. His head droops. He sleeps.

I notice for the first time the white striations on the back of his skull, showing through bristling brown hair. Scars from the accident. For a time I watch his head bobbing with the motion of the vehicle.

Who is this giant? Why is he helping me?

The driver pulls off the turnpike we've been traveling on and rolls into a rest stop. The giant gives him money, and the man goes into a fast-food restaurant to order takeout food. Ten hamburgers for Billy, two for me, two for the driver. Large paper cup of coffee for the giant, water for me, cola for the driver.

The three of us sit together in the back of the van consuming our meal. When the giant has finished eating his hamburgers, he opens the paper shopping bag he brought along and extracts a meatloaf sandwich. Plus a quarter pound of cheese. The driver watches him eat it.

"You sure have a big appetite," he comments at one point.

"I am a large person," says Billy. "Large people need a lot of fuel, because we burn up way more energy than shorter people."

"I noticed," says the driver. He slaps his knees and says, "Well, it's another hour to the border. Ready to go?"

So, away we go, ever northward through fields and forests and small towns dozing under blankets of snow. The sky is overcast, but nothing is dropping out of it. Blackbirds rise cawing from old cornfields.

The giant removes a gallon jug of milk from the bag and drinks half of it down, his head tilted back, his larynx rising and falling in his neck.

When he is finished, he says with a smack of satisfaction, "I used to drink three of these a day when I was growing up. I needed a lot of calcium."

"To make strong bones."

"Yes, Francisco. Otherwise you get a brittle skeleton. Doctors always told me I have very strong bones. Also, my teeth don't have a single cavity. Must have been something in our water at the farm. It was a dairy farm, three hundred head, never any shortage of milk. So you see, I've been fortunate from the beginning."

"Was it cause or effect?"

"What do you mean, Francisco?"

"Did you grow so tall because of genetics alone, or did all that milk *make* you grow, plus the mysterious thing in your water?"

"Mum and Dad didn't grow like me. Nobody on neighboring farms did either. We had everything tested—water, milk, feed. Dad didn't like growth hormones in the feed. It was always a hundred percent pure grain and mash. There wasn't anything in it that would've caused my condition. That's the wrong word. It's not a condition like a medical disability. It's a special gift. As I said, I'm one of the luckiest people in the world."

"Except for the accident."

"Yes, you're right," he murmurs, sobering, looking away.

"I am sorry. I should not have brought it up."

"That's okay. It's good you're an honest person."

But I can see I have hurt him. We say no more until the van slows and passes an American flag on a pole, then uniformed guards and a set of single-story buildings. We do not stop. Slowing still more, we glide past a flag with red sidebars and a red maple leaf.

"Canada," shouts the driver through the glass panel. "Got your papers?"

The van stops at a gate, and a uniformed lady steps up to the driver's window.

"Where are you going today?" she asks.

"Toronto," says the driver, handing her his passport.

"Where you coming from?" she asks as she flips through the pages.

"New York City, the Big Apple."

She smiles. "Carrying any cargo?"

"Just two passengers."

She looks in the window, but can't see me and the giant.

"Would you open up the back, please? I need to have a look at your passengers' ID."

"Sure thing, lady." He raps on the glass panel. "Time to get out, guys. Have your passports ready."

The giant pulls a lever and opens the back doors. He steps out first, just as the lady comes around to meet us. By the time I am out, she is not seeing me at all. She is open mouthed and staring up into his face. She doesn't say a thing.

Two other Canadian border guards come out of their building and walk over, young people in uniform, all of them mute and wide-eyed.

The lady clears her throat.

"Um, could I see some identification, please?"

The giant fishes in his trouser pocket and brings forth a crumpled piece of paper.

"All I have is my birth certificate," he says. "I was born in Iowa. I live in New York now."

She takes the document and examines it closely.

"William C"—she squinted to get a better look—"Revere, Des Moines, Iowa, August 15, 1981," she reads aloud. "How come the C name is scratched out?"

"The C is for Cicero. I never really liked it. I got teased about it a lot in school. It's a middle name, not a family name. My dad was a fan of an author named Cicero."

"We're going to need more than this," she says, looking back and forth between the paper and the giant's face.

"I'm sorry, it's all I have. All I ever needed, really. I kept my university student card for years, but then I lost it."

"Driver's license, or anything else with photo ID?"

"I never learned to drive."

"Social Security number?"

"I don't have one."

"Virtually everyone in the U.S. has one, sir. Are you living in the country illegally?"

"I'm not illegal, ma'am. I really am from Iowa."

"Well, you sure don't look like a terrorist."

The giant shakes his head. "No, I'm not."

"Are you running away from something, son?"

I now realize that she is talking to him as if he is a child. She has concluded that he is some kind of handicapped person, perhaps a gargantuan imbecile.

"I'm not running away from anything, ma'am. I'm just trying to help my friend here. He has amnesia."

The woman turns to me, seeing me for the first time.

"Do you have any identification, sir?"

I shake my head glumly.

"What is your name and your present address?"

"My name is Francisco de Goya, I think. I am certain, however, that I live with this gentleman, Billy Revere, in Hell's Kitchen."

The woman tries to suppress a smile. The other guards chortle. The giant tells her our street address.

"All right, gentlemen," she says. "Come into the station, and we'll do some checking."

The guards herd the three of us travelers into the lobby of a waiting area, and the woman goes behind a counter to a desk. We stand around while she taps away on a computer keyboard. She slips the driver's passport through a machine, then returns to the waiting area and hands it to him. They talk for a few minutes. Then she turns to the giant and me.

"Neither of you has any records in U.S. and Canadian systems, not if you've given me your real names."

"I know mine is real. And we're pretty sure about Francisco's."

"Right. Well, your driver confirms your address. I'm sorry, but it's not enough. We can't let you into the country without more identification than you've provided. You'll have to go back through the U.S. border station."

"Is that necessary?" the giant rumbles—a high-note rumble, which is due, I suspect, to his feeling some tension over what may turn out to be a wasted journey. "We have pretty strong hints that Francisco is a Canadian."

"Such as?"

"He ... he likes the Toronto Maple Leafs. He used to play hockey in the 1950s."

Brimming with merriment, all official eyes fix on me.

"I'm a Montreal fan myself," the woman says.

"Edmonton Oilers," says one of the other guards.

"Vancouver Canucks for me," says another.

"And this 1950s business," says the woman. "Your friend doesn't look anywhere near old enough for that."

"His appearance is misleading," says the giant. "He ages slowly ... very slowly."

"I see."

She hands the giant's birth certificate back to him. Then, with a laugh, she adds, "I really regret it, fellows, but you can't come in. It's been great meeting you."

She offers her hand to the giant. He bends down and takes it in one of his own and gently shakes it with a sorrowful look. She shakes hands with me too. One by one the other guards come over and shake the giant's hands.

"Okay, guys," says the driver. "It's a no go. Back to the good ol' U.S. of A."

We pile into the van. After a U-turn, we putter toward the stars and stripes, with the Canadians all gazing after us, waving good-bye.

A minute later we are braking in front of the American border patrol station.

The officer at the gate barks at the driver, scowls at the passport, scans it into the computer, then comes around behind the vehicle and yanks the doors open.

"Get out!" he yells at us, his right hand on the butt of his pistol.

We get out, raising our hands in surrender.

The conversation that follows is much like the one we had with the Canadians, though in an entirely different style. We give our names. The giant's birth certificate is read closely and with suspicion. His scanty identification and my lack of any identification increase the tension to the breaking point. The driver is told to take his vehicle to a pull-off lane near the gates and to wait there.

"Into the station," the officer snarls, eyeing the giant with particular attention.

Four burly guards conduct us inside, and down a hallway, with the giant hunching over because of low ceilings. We are directed into an empty room without windows.

Presently, two men in dark suits arrive, along with a third in uniform. I read the badges on their breasts: U.S. Department of Homeland Security. The border guards leave, shutting the door behind them. I hear a lock click. The agents of Homeland Security command us to take off our clothing.

At first we do not understand the order. They bark at us. The giant and I slowly, painfully remove our clothes. We stand naked before them, trembling, our faces flushing, bare feet on the cold linoleum, hands crossed over our private parts. A thorough search of our bodies ensues. Then we are told to get dressed.

Questioning begins. They want to know what organization we work for. Are we Islamic or Islamic sympathizers, America-haters, America-lovers, super-patriots, militiamen? The list goes on and on. They are not satisfied by our answers. Where do we live? What is our place of employment? Why are we trying to enter the United States?

The giant tells them a number of things about himself: his address, the university he attended, what he does now—"a freelance paramedic in self-training"— the farm he grew up on. He explains that we were trying to *leave* the United States. It was supposed to be a kind of working holiday, he says; we had never seen Canada before—well, he himself hadn't, though possibly his friend Francisco is a citizen of that country.

"*Are* you a citizen of that country?" one of the suited men asks me in a voice so low it is freighted with threat.

"I don't know," I say.

"You don't know?"

"He lost his memory and we're trying to find it," the giant explains.

Disbelieving and very unhappy, the agents say nothing for a few moments, staring coldly at the giant, trying to intimidate him.

"You're members of an al-Qaida terrorist cell, aren't you? Your jump-off base is in Canada. That's how you normally get into our country. We've had eyes on your cell for months, and we tracked you all the way."

"All the way from New York?" the giant asks, confused.

The agents scowl in unison.

"Don't waste our time with the dumb cover stories. You're terrorists and we have you in custody. Talk now, or you're on your way to an intensive interrogation center."

"A center we maintain in another country," adds one of the others. "A country where the niceties of the law are more flexible."

"What country is it?" the giant asks, genuinely curious.

They do not reply.

Clearly they are interested in him only because they have a set of questions they must ask all inexplicable people. Or possibly because he is an oddity. But any sensible person would know that if he were a terrorist, he would have come prepared with documents aplenty and a cover story. Besides, terrorists prefer to be invisible, and he is too big to hide in a crowd.

"Billy can't even drive a car," I say, hoping to clear up the misunderstanding. "He can't even fly a plane."

Why did I say this? Why a plane?

"A suicide jet, you mean," says the uniformed guard.

"Well, any kind of p-plane, r-r-really," I stammer.

"R-r-really," the agent mimics.

The giant and I nod up and down, trying to convince them of our sincerity.

The agents confer with each other in low voices. The giant and I exchange glances. *Don't worry*, we are saying to each other, *don't worry*.

We are handcuffed, our arms behind our backs.

"Sit down," barks an agent.

We look around the room. There are no chairs.

"On the floor!"

We sit down on the floor. It is very uncomfortable, and promises to become unendurable.

The agents leave the room and lock the door.

We sit there for what feels like three or four hours. The giant nods off, his head on his knees. I stay awake, groaning and trying not to cry.

Eventually the agents return, uncuff us, and help us to our feet.

We stand there rubbing our wrists, wondering what will happen next. The agents stare at us, shaking their heads. One of them jerks his thumb.

"Get outta here," he says.

It is dark outside, snow blowing sideways. We meet with our driver in the parking lot. He is pacing back and forth, fuming, in a state of controlled rage. He glares at the giant and me. His van is raised high on jacks, all the tires off, the doors off, the floor and wall paneling off, the engine hood off. The mattresses are spread around on the ground, torn open with their foam stuffing removed.

Workmen are busy reassembling the vehicle.

"You're going to pay for this," the driver growls at the giant.

"Of course, I will," he says. "I'm so sorry. There's been a misunderstanding."

"Yeah, a misunderstanding, all right. Look, you freaks, I have a life to lead!"

"What happened?" the giant asks. "Why did they treat us this way?"

"You tell me! You're the terrorists."

"We are not terrorists."

"Yeah, yeah, yeah—blah, blah, blah. Well, I got terrorized plenty."

"I am really very sorry."

"You better be. The only reason you're not getting tortured right at this very minute is because of me. I got a legit passport, see. And I verified your address, told them the whole story. Then, after they had their coffee and doughnuts, I guess they checked with Canada Customs, just a hundred yards over there. Then they got on the blower and their computers and they found out who you are, which is to say a certifiable idiot. Turns out you used to play basketball, and one of the goons loves basketball. He'd heard about your college team, saw a game once, not a game with any giant in it, but he knows who you played for. Anyways, it was enough to make him get on the phone and track down the team's manager. And the manager identified you, okayed everything you told them. So now they believe what you said ain't no lie."

"How do you know all this?" asks the giant.

"Because they told me about it after they uncuffed me." He holds up his wrists for us to see the raw red marks on his white skin. "Gave me a soda and apologized for thinking I was an Oklahoma bomber or something like that. They also apologized for dismantling Bessie, which is why they're being so thoughtful about putting her back together. Suddenly they're all nice manners after giving me the third degree for hours, grilling me about you guys."

"This is horrible," says the giant. "You have endured a lot for our sakes."

"Haven't I just!"

"Didn't they mention my farm? I told them about it because it proves I'm an American citizen."

"Yeah, a farm in Idaho somewheres."

"Iowa."

"They thought it might be a secret militia center. Turns out it's not, and you're not. It got sold about twelve years ago, right?"

"Yes, it did."

The driver hurls a disapproving glance at me.

"And *you*! They found out there's nobody with your name, your age, living in Canada. You got no record anywhere, no trail, no nothing. But you did *come* from the States with us, and you weren't trying to get *into* the States all wired up with a bomb, which is what they thought at first."

"That can't be right!" says the giant. "If they thought Francisco was wearing a bomb vest, they would have shielded themselves from the very beginning."

"Okay, then they probably thought he was smuggling bomb parts. Anyways, he's dark skinned and dark eyed, and he looks suspicious. He looked suspicious to me from the get-go this morning." The driver sends a look of disgust in my direction. "Inch Allah," he snorts.

"Well, it has ended quite positively," says the giant with something like wonder. "We're free to go."

"Yeah, soon as they've finished with Bessie."

It is well after midnight by the time we are able to climb into the van and leave. Nobody waves good-bye.

4

Hidden rooms of the mind

I ride in the front passenger seat beside the driver, to make sure he won't fall asleep at the wheel. The giant sleeps in the cargo hold, on scraps of foam we salvaged from the border parking lot. I am supposed to talk to the driver, keep him alert.

"I don't know your name," I begin. "I'm Francisco."

"Yeah, I know you're Francisco," he snarls sideways.

"And you are ..."

"Call me Hal 9000."

"Nice to meet you, Hal."

"Look, we don't gotta talk. I'll just drive and you stay quiet. I've met a lot of fools in my life, but nothing—I mean *nothing*—matches you two. I got busted because of you. I got harassed in a big way. And I almost got put up in a nice cozy hotel in Guantanamo."

"They apologized to you," I say. "Why didn't they apologize to us?"

"Figure it out," he snaps.

"Your last name is unusual, Hal. Nine thousand sounds like a number. What are your ethnic origins?"

"Shut up, Francisco."

For the next eight hours we converse no more. The van gets trapped in morning rush hour into New York City. We arrive at our apartment building around 10 A.M., and there we are dropped on the sidewalk. After Hal is satisfied by the additional money the giant gives him, he roars away in his vehicle without saying good-bye.

We trudge wearily up the staircase to the fourth floor, and the giant unlocks his apartment door. Inside, he stands still and turns his head this way and that, listening, like a hunting dog sniffing the air.

"Someone has been here," he says.

"Is anything stolen or broken?" I ask.

"I don't think so. These were intelligence professionals. Homeland Security, I'll bet. They tried to leave no trace of their investigation, but I can see that my books are stacked in slightly different order. And the blankets on our beds are wrong. The wrinkles have changed."

"You have an excellent memory, Billy."

"For the small details, Francisco. On the big picture, I'm not so good."

I yawn.

"You were awake all night, and I had a great sleep in the back of the van. You should crash."

"I beg your pardon, Billy?"

"You should go to sleep. I'm going out for my jog and an espresso at Dina's."

After he has changed into his jogging suit, he is off for his run. I strip down to my T-shirt and boxers, pull my sleeping bag over myself, and drop away into an abyss of sleep.

When I wake up it is early evening. A blizzard is blowing out there, the window rattling, the radiator pumping heat. Billy is seated on his packing crate, bending over his books, making notes with a pen and pad.

"Supper, Francisco?" he calls when he notices me sitting up. "It's Chinese."

We eat out of numerous little paper cartons crowding the table. I am too groggy to talk yet, but I am very hungry. Billy supplies light commentary, domesticating the atmosphere, which feels both familiar and unfamiliar. It is homey.

"I got a tremendous haul from my friends at the restaurant," he says. "While you were napping I went down to beg some throwaways for the girls. They gave me these, a party order that someone never picked up. You'd really like these people. A family from Hong Kong. The kids and grandkids are the waiters. They speak English with a British accent. But the old mom and dad who own the place don't know our language. They do most of the cooking. I'm closest to them. We communicate without words."

"Without words, Billy?"

"Uh-huh. It's another kind of language, I guess. It's all in their faces, little gestures, emanation of warmth, free food they're always pushing my way. They really love me. I love them too. I hire the mom to make my clothes. A cousin of theirs who has a discount store down in lower Manhattan makes my shoes. He was a master cobbler back in the old country. My Nikes aren't really Nikes. They're convincing facsimiles."

"Size eighteen," I contribute between bites.

"That's right. Hey, it sounds like you have a memory for details too, Francisco."

Billy makes a pot of green tea, and after it has steeped he pours it into cereal bowls. We are sipping from the bowls contentedly when I am struck by a puzzle.

"I don't understand why they talked about a suicide jet," I say. "What is a suicide jet?"

"A suicide jet?"

"When we were being interrogated by Homeland Security at the border, one of the agents asked us about it."

"Ah, yes. They were probably referring to the Twin Towers, Francisco."

"What are the twin towers?"

"You know—nine-eleven."

"I don't know what you mean, Billy."

"September 11, 2001?"

"Did something happen on that day?"

"Yes, something very bad happened. Thousands of people died, right here in New York City."

"I didn't know. I never heard about it."

"You never heard about it?" says the giant, sitting straighter and gazing at me with some concern. But he says no more.

I can't stop yawning.

I return to bed, lying on my back, lazily observing his evening activities. He washes the dishes, takes a bag of garbage out to the corridor, and goes up to the roof to collect eggs and feed the girls. On his return he washes a basket full of eggs, whistling melodies quietly so as not to disturb me. He reads for a while, humming and jotting down notes with a scratching pen.

It is a comforting sound, like family. Like sharing a bedroom with a brother. It is all so normal. I no longer think of him as *the giant*. Whole hours go by without me experiencing amazement over his size. He is who he is. I am who I am. But who am I?

Later he showers and comes out of the bathroom in pajamas and socks, brushing his teeth. Is that a long-handled dish scrubber in his foaming mouth? Or is it a toothbrush for a horse? Yes, I think it is.

Off goes the light, and I hear him rustling down into his covers, sighing, yawning, scratching, chuckling to himself.

"We had quite an adventure, didn't we, Francisco," he mumbles, drifting off.

"You spent a lot of money for my sake, Billy. I don't know how I can repay you."

"You don't have to repay me. Money is only numbers on paper. And I have a few numbers on paper in a bank over on Forty-Second Street. The sale of the farm gave me a fresh start in life, you see, and there's some of it left, not much but enough to get by. Also, there's my little pension from the insurance company."

"But I might never remember who I am. What if you lose all your numbers because of me?"

"Lose a few numbers on paper? Where's the harm in that?"

"It's harmful if you lose the numbers you need to buy milk, and hamburger for your meatloaf."

"Francisco, it's pure pleasure to see your thoughts flowing like this. You're using more and more significant words. And ideas. Talking together seems to be helping."

"But what if I discover who I am, and it's not good? What if it's better I don't remember?"

"I remember what it is to have no memory," he says, looking thoughtful. He pauses. "If you get what I mean."

"Yes. I do."

"Even if what you discover about yourself is sad or humiliating or even tragic, it's still better than losing yourself. We have to be who we are, Francisco. There's no running away from ourselves—not in the long run. And when a person faces himself—truly faces himself for what he is—he can make a new start, deal with the weaknesses and work on strengthening the better parts."

"Is that really possible?"

"I know it is. Besides, I like you staying here. You're excellent company."

"You are a very kind person, Billy."

"Mmm. Hey, I have a question for you: Are we the boy in the red suit in the painting, the boy holding the string? Or are we the blackbird tied to the string?"

"Do you mean you and I, or do you mean human beings in general?"

"Human beings in general, all of us."

It is a serious question. I strain my mind to understand it, and then when I understand it, I do not know the answer.

"Any thoughts?" he asks.

"I can't . . . I would, but . . ."

"It's all right. You don't need to figure it out all at once. But my personal opinion is, when you painted it you were probably trying to say that we're the boy *and* the bird. The bird is part of ourselves. It's about freedom, you said."

Suddenly I am flooded with quiet exultation. More than this—I feel immense gratitude for my new friend. He understands. He sees what I see.

"Yes, the painting is about freedom," I say in a choked voice. "But I don't know why."

"Okay, but it's a good start. You're remembering more and more."

"Maybe. I hope so."

"It's a drawer inside a cupboard of your mind. The cupboard just opened a crack, and you can see that the drawer inside it is open a crack too. We just need to find the light switch so you can see everything in it."

"Billy, yesterday you said it was a locked attic, with more locked chambers inside, all locked, everything locked."

"Uh-huh, I did. But the attic door is opening now."

"Is it? I don't feel it is. I have scraps, a thought now and then, like a leaf floating on a pond. Some thoughts rise up from the bottom, some sink back down to the bottom; some stay afloat, and when winter comes they are locked in ice. But all my thoughts are disconnected, like the bit of paper the jackdaw is pecking. Why did I paint a bird pecking a piece of paper? I can understand the purpose of the string, its meaning. Yet the paper is a useless distraction in such a painting. Why did I put it there?"

"You must have had a reason."

"Maybe it was a message to my future self."

"Hmm, now that sounds a bit complicated. Could it be the bird was just pecking at paper that day, and you painted what you saw? It doesn't have to have a meaning."

"But why does the paper show the skyline of New York City? And why the numbers? It's all so disconnected."

"Everything's connected, Francisco. We just don't see the connections. You have to look deeper and farther for that to happen, and you have to wait for the right moment. You can't make it happen by sheer force of will."

Now everything that my mind is straining to understand collapses into obscurity. I hold my head in my hands and rock back and forth. My tears become audible, splashing like stones dropped into a still pond. The ice has melted, but it is black beneath the surface.

"Are you all right, Francisco?"

"I do not understand anything," I groan. "Nothing." I hit the sides of my skull with my fists. "Nothing."

"In time you will. I feel sure you will."

"No, no, I am a house with all the doors and windows boarded over and nailed shut."

For several minutes after that, nothing more is said. I rock and rock my body, holding my head tightly lest it disintegrate, letting the agony in my chest burst and bleed.

I hear him thumping around in his sock feet. A light goes on, blinding me. As my eyes adjust, I see Billy standing by the desk lamp, regarding me with some worry.

"Francisco, everyone has locked rooms in their minds," he says in his quietest voice. "May I show you mine?"

"If you wish," I say out of duty, though I do not really want him to reveal his innermost thoughts, his memories, his lavish abundance of life, when I have so little of these.

"Okay, stand back. Over here. Sit at the table."

I crawl off the mattress, get myself upright, and pull on my jeans. I lurch to the table and sit down on the two-dollar chair.

A cupboard door opens. A squeak-squeak, a popping cork, and then a dusty bottle is in front of me, with two glass tumblers. Billy fills both with dark red wine.

"This is a very important day for me, Francisco," he says. "What I would like to show you hasn't been seen by anyone else but me."

He sips from his glass. I take a sip from mine.

"I would like you to see it," he continues solemnly. "But only if you want to see it."

I am curious now. Distracted, I feel pain receding into the background.

"Okay," I murmur in agreement—a contract, a covenant—and take another sip.

Billy opens a kitchen drawer and removes a hammer, a screwdriver, and a chisel from it. He goes over to our mattresses and pushes them aside with his foot. Then he kneels down and faces the wall. With hammer and chisel, he taps and pries, little by little lifting off an inch-wide wood strip that covers a joint in the wall panels. When it is off, its nails dangling, he leans it in a corner. Moving three feet to his right, he begins tapping and prying another strip. When he has it off, a central panel is revealed. He removes a bronze pin from a hole in the crack and pushes the panel, and it slowly squeals open on unseen hinges. Beyond is a rectangle of absolute darkness. He steps inside.

I remain seated, staring at the empty space. I do not move. Will he come out again? Does he want me to go in there without light? And if so, what is waiting for me there?

Suddenly he is standing in the doorway, smiling encouragement.

"Come on," he whispers.

Slowly I go to his outstretched hand and take it, a child wrapping his fingers around an adult's. Without haste, without compulsion, he draws me into the lightless void. He closes the door behind me and now I am standing alone, shivering in total black.

"B-billy, are you here?"

"I'm here. Don't be afraid, Francisco."

I hear the bellows of his breathing somewhere close, then a click, and a tiny blue light appears above me, followed by a string of lights flickering into life in sequence: red, orange, yellow, green, blue, violet, white, and then the pattern is repeated in loops and coils, the air above my head filling with expanding constellations of them. As more and more become visible, the room begins to glow.

Billy's shape looms in the corner. He is standing perfectly still, his smile tentative, proud of what he is showing me and yet uncertain about my reaction.

"What is this place?" I ask him.

"My hidden room of the mind," he murmurs shyly.

I turn in a circle, taking it all in.

The room appears to be at least twice as large as Billy's apartment. Against the far wall stands a tree in a pot, twelve feet high, its topmost branches brushing the ceiling. Its limbs and myriad twigs are leafless and painted pure white. It looks like the vault of a medieval cathedral, or a too-tall apple tree rooted in mysterious

Iowa water. Fine wires are strung from branch to branch. Billy strides down the length of the room and stoops beneath the tree. He pushes an electric plug into a socket, and the tree ignites, filling with white stars. Now the room is very bright.

Everywhere I look, I see more and more novelties. There is an antique dressmaker's manikin to my left. To my right is a floor-to-ceiling bookshelf loaded with old dusty volumes and ribboned ledgers. Beside it is an unpainted oak cupboard, its doors missing, its shelves displaying clay gallon pots with obscure blue symbols baked in their glaze, and liquor jugs stained by sun and age to pale hues of blue and amethyst. On one shelf there is a white ceramic vessel in the shape of a whale, its tailfin smashing down on a sailing ship. Other shelves display arrowheads and a thumb-size stone carving of a man riding on the back of a dolphin. Interspersed with these are numerous natural items, such as giant pinecones, a brown lotus pod with its black beads rattling inside like a child's toy made by gods, a tarnished silver bowl containing the seed casings of a eucalyptus tree. There is so much more, I cannot take it all in at once ...

A gilded birdcage with an open door hangs from the ceiling on a wire.

On an ornate dining room table, its varnish like rosewood or tinted ebony, sits a large antique mantle clock. Billy winds a key in its back, and it begins to tick.

"It was broken when I found it in a dumpster," he explains. "I turned it into something else."

When he opens the circular glass door on its clock face, a light goes on within it, revealing the absence of hour and minute hands. In their place are nine planets orbiting a sun. Each of the planets is a colored marble held on a rigid spoke revolving on an axis behind the central sun, which is a semitransparent glass sphere, orange, with a light inside it.

"You made this?" I exhale in wonder.

Billy nods, pleased by my reaction, but diffident.

He reaches over and flicks a switch on the clock's back side.

Music begins to rapidly plink and plunk from somewhere inside. It is a music box. I know the melody, I know it, I know it! Out of the waters of memory a song rises to my lips, and with my untempered voice I hoarsely sing a verse:

> "Boys and girls together,
> me and Mamie O'Rourke,
> trip the Light Fantastic,
> on the sidewalks of New York."

I sing it again and again, because it is the only verse I remember. But it triggers something, and suddenly I know it is not a verse but a refrain. Then an actual verse surfaces:

> "East side, West side,
> all around the town,
> the tots sang 'Ring-a-Rosie,'
> 'London Bridge is falling down.'

> "Boys and girls together,
> me and Mamie O'Rourke,
> trip the Light Fantastic,
> on the sidewalks of New York."

Billy whistles along, his notes perfectly in unison with my voice and the mechanical melody. He begins to dance around the room in slow motion, his arms held out as if he is waltzing with a giant bride. He is smiling beatifically with eyes closed, yet he never misses a step or bumps into things.

When the music clock falls silent, I rewind its spring. Again I sing, and Billy dances. After the third time around, he lowers himself onto a horsehair sofa, eyes still closed.

I sit down on a voluminous horsehair chair facing him.

"A lot of these things are very old," I say.

"They are," he says, nodding in agreement. "I've collected them from garbage bins, flea markets, dumpsters. It hardly cost me a penny. Except I had to carry the tree on foot, because I found it in the Connecticut woods and it wouldn't fit on a bus. A long walk home but worth it."

"It is very beautiful."

"Isn't it! Like a tree in a snowy woods, catching stars in its branches."

Billy gets up and opens a window near the tree. Gusts of blizzard blow in, with sprays of snow crystals, making the branches sway and tinkle. He turns off the colored overhead lights, leaving only the tree's white stars. For a time, we savor an enchanted winter's eve in the forest. However, the room grows swiftly colder, and he is forced to close the window. The radiator is clanking.

"How long have you lived here, Billy?"

"Since I got out of the hospital. That's twelve years ago. Little by little I've added to my collection, whenever

I find something that has a story—or looks like it's hiding a story, like a secret or a cherished memory."

"What kind of story?"

"For example, inside the old clock, under the floorboard of the spring chamber, I found a letter written in 1898, penned by a young lady to her beau. Would you like to see it?"

Presuming that I would, he gets up and turns the colored lights back on, as well as an Atlantic seaman's lantern that has been outfitted with a light bulb and wires. Now the room comes further alive with the emerging reds and purples of the tattered Persian rugs carpeting the floor, and the gold-brown paintings on the walls. I also notice black-and-white framed photographs of indeterminate subject matter. I will look at them closely when I can.

Billy fetches a cigar box from one of the cupboards and puts it on my lap. I open it and find a packet of flattened cigar bands from numerous tobacconist companies, plus an old-fashioned shaving razor, ivory and steel. Beneath this is a mauve envelope, smelling of centuries-old bookbindings. Inside is a slip of rag paper, also mauve. Penned on it in a flowery hand is a message.

I read:

"New Year's Eve, 1898.

"My dearest Roger,

"Mama and Papa will understand one day.

"Will you meet me tonight at eight, the rink in Central Park? Bring your skates, as shall I. There will be music, I hear ~ a band playing Viennese and John Philip Sousa. My brother Pip will drive me in the horse and cutter and has promised to keep our secret.

"Thank you, beloved, for the book of Christmas poems, which I read and reread avidly, with a thought of you on every page.

"Your faithful
"Phoebe."

The envelope also contains a yellowed newspaper clipping, a column of text beneath a photo of a handsome man in military uniform, with medals on his breast. "Roger Bennadine, 1880~1918, R.I.P." is written above the photograph in the same flowery script as the note. The clipping is an obituary. The deceased was a member of the American Expeditionary Force and fell at Cantigny, the Somme, France, on May 28. He is mourned by his beloved wife, Phoebe, and their six children. The newspaper lists their names. Phoebe's home address is given.

"I visited the house once, not long after I found these," Billy says. "It had been turned into apartments, with a bagel shop on the ground floor. No one knew where the family had gone. I spent some time researching in the NYC archives and finally located one of Phoebe and Roger's grandchildren, a retired schoolteacher living in the Bronx. I phoned her and arranged to meet with her, because I wanted to give her the clock and the documents I found inside it."

"Did she not want them?"

"Sad to say, she didn't. I think she felt nervous about my size when I showed up at her apartment door. She wondered what I wanted from her. I reassured her that my only intention was to give her a family heirloom. But she told me the clock wouldn't match her decor, and she already had trunks full of old family papers. Then she politely but firmly closed the door. So I brought it home."

"That is sad."

"People are afraid of many things—sometimes of the past."

"One must *have* a past in order to be afraid of it."

"It's not always so, Francisco."

I sigh, thinking, *Let's not talk about that right now.*

Looking around, I say, "You have many treasures here."

"Yes, many pasts. Most of the messages and stories are embedded silently in these objects, which were so dear to people long since departed from the earth. Some of them must be interpreted, deciphered; others we can simply read. Here, look at this."

At the bottom of the cigar box he finds another piece of paper, and hands it to me. It is brittle, mottled as if long ago stained by moisture, its fold lines badly frayed.

"I found it when I cut through the wall to make the door."

I read:

"My name is Elizabeth Rose Walcott.

"Today, September 11, 1901, the workmen are replastering a wall of my room, after installing the new knob-and-tube wiring for electricity. Papa has purchased for me a lovely porcelain lamp in the shape of a ballerina. Its incandescent bulb is very bright, so I won't need the gaslight anymore.

"Today, also, I am reading Plato. I do not like it. Tomorrow is my fifteenth birthday.

"If you are reading this in the future, please remember a girl who once lived in these rooms and thought about you. And would you also kindly say a prayer for me?

"Sincerely,
"Elizabeth."

I look up.

"Where did you say you found it?"

"In the laths—the strips of wood behind the plaster. The note was tucked between two of them. She must have been an ingenious kid. Imagine trying to sneak a letter into the kind of thing those workmen were doing. I like to think of her getting up in the middle of the night, tiptoeing into the room holding a candle, then scooping out the wet plaster, hiding her letter, then re-plastering the hole with her hands, spreading it softly with her fingertips, giggling. Maybe she finished the job by flattening the surface with the edge of a book or something—maybe her Plato."

"Or she might have charmed a workman into cooperating with her conspiracy."

"It could very well be. She was quite a whimsical gal, or dreamy perhaps. And she thought about *us*, far off in the future. Every year I have a birthday party for Elizabeth, just her and me."

"Did you ever find her?"

"I found a record in the city archives. A Walcott family lived at this address until 1907. It took me a long time to find the rest of the trail. There was a professor Peter

Walcott who in 1907 began teaching at a small college in New Jersey. I finally found Elizabeth's grave in a cemetery near Princeton. She died in a nursing home in 1972, age eighty-six. She was a philosophy professor for most of her life."

"I wonder what she was like. She sounds very nice."

"I think she was. I would have married her in an instant, if we had lived in the same era." He pauses. "Have you had enough? Have I bored you?"

"I'm not bored, Billy. But I am very tired, and we both need to sleep. Can we come here again tomorrow?"

"Of course we can. So you don't think I'm unbalanced?"

I shake my head.

"It *is* rather eccentric," he adds uncertainly.

"I do not know what is unbalanced and eccentric, Billy. How can such things be measured?"

"Usually by how odd one's behavior is compared with the majority of people."

"Does this worry you?"

He thinks about it. Then he laughs. "No."

We step out into the apartment, which now seems barren. Billy closes the door and pins it tight. He turns out the light, and we go back to bed.

The next day he leaves before I wake up. I find a scrawled note on the kitchen table:

Good morning, Francisco.
    I'll see you at suppertime.
                        Billy.

Beneath it is another note:

Dear F,

You seem to be getting better and better. If you feel you want to go out by yourself, please keep this card with you at all times, in case you forget where we live.

Take care,
B.

Under this is a pocket-size piece of cardboard, on which is printed:

MY NAME IS FRANCISCO DE GOYA.

I AM EXPERIENCING HEALTH PROBLEMS.

WOULD YOU KINDLY BRING ME BACK TO MY HOME AT:

This is followed by a street number on West Forty-Fifth Street.

I have no intention of leaving the building on my own. Though it is painful to admit, I know I am totally dependent on Billy's generous hospitality, his guidance, and his patience with me. I wish it were otherwise, but I don't know how to change myself.

During his absence I open the door to the hidden room of his mind by pulling out the lock pin. When I enter the room, I find it is no longer dark inside. Light filters through three windows on the left-hand wall. The glass is opaqued with amber-hued paint. I lift a window sash and poke my head outside. The view is a red brick wall of the neighboring apartment building. I close the window and turn on the ship's lantern and the strings of Christmas lights. The stars have lost their brilliance in daylight, but they diffuse their colors warmly. After the starkness of the apartment, this room exudes a consoling sense of home—a familiarity, a recognition, though I have never lived in it. Perhaps the embedded radiance of its dormant histories is welcoming me.

I sit down on the sofa, feeling reservation about intruding on Billy's privacy. These antiques and mementos are the relics of other people's lives, but, still, he has rescued them and cared for them, and in some cases, such as the musical cosmic clock, he has re-created them as new phenomena. They contain stories and messages that he has deciphered. Cryptic though they may be to me, I respect them as objects he has lovingly interpreted or reshaped with his mind and his hands, without thought of profit or public attention.

After all these years, I am the first to see what he has created, and thus it is clear that these things have been, until now, his private meditation—indeed, his private language. Yet he told me last night that I can return to see more. Did he mean that I may enter this sanctum unaccompanied? Or did he imply that I must be guided through it by Virgil?

"Who is Virgil?" I ask with a skip of a heartbeat. A leaf rising from the sodden darkness at the bottom of the pond.

I have not yet looked at the paintings and photographs. I get up and wander around.

A large moody landscape in a gilded frame hangs beside a primitive painting of a horse. The horse is sorrel brown and approximately equestrian, its body split horizontally by the warped panels of wood on which it was painted. The varnish has been crackled by age, possibly by weather. Written in flowing script at the base of the image:

Benny's Vermont Dark Ale.

I move on.

Next is a painting of men rowing a racing scull on a placid river bordered by autumnal trees. This too is crackled, with some damaged spots repainted amateurishly. I frown my disapproval. I hope the repairs were not done by Billy, whom I have come to admire greatly. I want no pall of criticism to fall upon our relationship. I begin to wonder why I care so much about art.

After that comes a section of wall filled with black-and-white photographs in narrow black frames. One of them stands out dramatically. It is two feet wide and eight inches high: an ocean liner on the high seas, white foam at its bow, smoke from its stacks streaming behind. It is heading west at top speed. A printed caption: *R.M.S. Titanic.*

In another, a well-muscled teenage boy in a sports uniform bends over a basketball in midbounce. He is looking up at the camera with an expression both determined and gleeful, expecting the very best from life.

Beside it is a photo of a middle-aged man and woman with broad open faces, looking proud, the same teenage boy standing between them. He is dressed in a suit and tie, with a suitcase at his feet. A shock of blond hair falls over his forehead. The parents are reaching up, their arms draping around the boy's shoulders—he is more than a head taller than they are. In the background a two-story clapboard house rises from the crest of a hill. Beside its front veranda is a stone well with a hand pump. Scrawled across the bottom of the image are the words:

We'll miss you, William. Love, Dad.

and

Have the best year of your life, son. Love, Mom.

Then a larger shot of William, an eight-by-ten glossy with wide creamy matting, nonglare glass, and a narrow box frame.

He is wearing denim farm overalls, two straps over his bare shoulders and chest. He is straining with an arched back and chin held high, lifting a calf that must weigh two hundred pounds or more. His eyes are squinting with the physical effort, and the delight of his accomplishment. His grin is as wide as a field. He is laughing, either silently or aloud.

The only other photograph is of a teenage girl about sixteen or seventeen years old. She is wearing a formal dress with a pinned corsage. Her hair is piled high and bound by a ribbon. Her face is long-shaped and plain, but there is plenty of character in it. Her expression is feminine, generous, loving. She is smiling into the camera, and presumably at Billy, who, though invisible to me, is absolutely present to her when the shutter opens and closes. It would seem that he is still so.

I move on, pondering.

On the opposite side of the room stands a bank of small wooden drawers, hundreds of them, each of their fronts about six inches square with a round ceramic knob. I pull out a drawer. Its interior is a foot long. Inside is a collection of mushroom-top metal buttons.

Picking through them at random, I learn that they come from various nations and military services. Anchors and wings and crossed rifles.

I close the drawer and open another. This one contains handmade bone buttons.

In the next are coils of fine brass wire, neatly bound by their stems.

In drawer after drawer I find an incongruous array of items, thoughtfully sorted, either worthless or not very valuable, but intriguing nonetheless:

- —A collection of small brass bells, including colored Christmas bells that one might affix to a wreath.
- —Canceled postage stamps of recent vintage.
- —Lapel pins, some quite old, some newer, all of them emblematic of wildly disparate themes, political, commercial, tourist, academic, and religious.
- —More cigar bands, which are miniature artworks, meticulously saved by someone over a long period of time.
- —Five round, Chinese-red Tiger Balm containers, empty.
- —Packages of incense cones, mainly purple.
- —Spools of pink embroidery cotton.
- —Four little balsa wood boxes that once contained cheese, their lids stamped with French and Italian logos and printed medallions for past awards. The boxes no longer smell of their former contents.
- —Knitting needles.
- —Crochet needles.
- —Sewing needles, a spool of white thread, and a spool of black thread.

—Illustrations of World War II aircraft, cut from magazines.
—New York subway tokens.
—Straight pens with packages of nibs as sharp as razors.
—A sealed plastic bag containing a single light-green sock with a red stripe and a hole in the heel, powdered with copious dust or white ashes. It is a young child's.
—A dried flower corsage.
—More black arrowheads.
—Broken pieces of fern fossil.
—A highway map of the central region of the United States, along with a water sample receipt, stamped by an Iowa state agency, certifying that the sample was completely free of biological or chemical contaminants.
—Marbles, solid colors.
—Marbles, glass with inner swirls.
—Marbles, giant size, glass without internal patterns.
—Miniature gears, mainly brass and thin steel, one copper.
—Pinecone-shaped weights for clock pendulums.
—Seven crystal doorknobs.
—Broadway theater tickets from the 1960s and '70s, more than two dozen famous and non-famous productions.
—Nozzles for pumping up leather sports balls.
—Glasses for watching three-dimensional films.
—Paper party hats, toy trumpets, and whistles.
—A false beard and mustache. (Has Billy worn this?)
—Electric panel fuses—20 amp, 15 amp, 10 amp, 5 amp.

—A toy fire truck.
—Golf balls stamped *Eliot's Driving Range*.
—Several snail shells, small and large (one as big as a golf ball), various patterns.
—A library card, New York Public Library, expiration date, January 1952. A man's name, *Giacomo Loncari*.
—Three plastic pharmacy containers, prescription sedatives, *Wm. Revere* typed on the labels. They now hold colored beads—red, white, and blue.

Surfeited, I close the drawer. There are many more I have not opened, but they can wait. I go back to the apartment, lock the door to the hidden room of the mind, lie down on my mattress, and fall asleep.

Billy returns to the apartment for supper, flushed from the cold wind of the still-unabated storm. He is looking impossibly cheery. He has found a stuffed water bird at a flea market. It is dusty and nearly colorless, a damaged white crest, a few wing feathers missing. Triumphant, he intends to clean it up and repair the feathers. He tells me it is a hooded merganser.

5

Voices in empty rooms

We work together on the merganser in the evenings.
Most of the restoration tasks are too delicate for Billy's
fingers, which are twice as long and thick as mine. We
take turns gently brushing off the dust, blowing against
the grain of its feathers. But I am in charge of washing
its crest, a near-circular fan. After several rinses, employ-
ing a warm damp cloth with surgical care, I bring the
crest from dirty gray to white. This painstaking process
is repeated again and again over the rest of the body
until the original colors emerge. I am feeling more con-
fident because now I can contribute something to Billy's
life. It is a terrible thing to be locked into the role of the
constant taker.

He has "borrowed" feathers from the girls, and with
careful experiments—trying them for size, snipping and
remolding—facsimiles are created, indistinguishable
from the bird's true plumage. You would never know
that the poor thing is the survivor of bird catastrophes.

We like to chat as we putter side by side. I am putting
a dab of glue to the base of a rooster feather—a delicate
job, I don't dare blink. He is using large-handled scissors
to snip pigeon feathers into shape.

"Billy," I ask, "why was the hidden room of your mind sealed up?"

"Sealed up?" he murmurs, not really listening.

"When you first showed it to me, you had to take wood strips off the door before you unlocked it. It looked to me like you never go in there."

"Mmm," he replies, still concentrating on what he is doing.

He lays down the scissors, sits up straight, looks thoughtful.

"Before you came, Francisco, I opened it up maybe once or twice a year. I'd spend a day in there and then get back to my usual life."

"But why don't you keep it open all the time? You could have a much bigger apartment, full of wonderful things."

He smiles. "They are wonderful, aren't they."

"But why?"

"I do better keeping my life simple. If you live with amazing things all the time, after a while you stop seeing them."

"Stop seeing them?"

"You stop listening to them."

"Listening to them?"

"They go silent and flat. They don't change, of course. But your mind changes, gets dull, stops wondering. The room reminds me not to forget the past, but I know you can't live in the past. I keep my eyes on the present and looking toward the future. That way you never say to yourself, 'There, I've got all I need.' Like a chipmunk who's stuffed his nest full of acorns and baubles. He just goes to sleep for the winter."

"But how can you understand the present—or the future, for that matter—without understanding your past?"

"I do try to understand the past. But the most important thing is to keep your eyes open for amazing new things in the present and future."

"I don't get it."

Billy's eyes sparkle with what appears to be a secret joke, or possibly a wealth of cryptic information.

"Francisco, I really love it when you argue with me."

"I am *not* arguing!"

He laughs. We return to our feathers.

A week passes, and the merganser is fully restored. We are very proud of it. Its bearing is regal, its crest a crown. "The King of the Water Birds," Billy calls it. It sits on the kitchen windowsill for days after that, and we cannot look at it without feeling a swell of pleasure.

One evening, after dishes and egg washing are done, Billy looks at me and says, "This is your bird, Francisco."

"It's ours, Billy," I retort.

"You did most of the work, things I couldn't have done," he insists. "I want it to be entirely yours."

"Thank you, but we can share it," I reply. "Unless this is a good-bye gift. If you think it's time for me to find another place to live, I'll understand. Truly."

"No, no, Francisco," he says with a furrowing brow and emphatic thrusts of his hands. "You can stay as long as you need to, or want to. Whether it takes a year or ten years for you to find your memories is okay by me."

I am unable to say anything. Why is he so good? Was I this good in my unknown life? I doubt it very much.

"I expressed that poorly, Francisco. What I meant to say is, I hope you find your memories as soon as possible, for *your* sake, not because I want to hurry you on your way—which I don't—if you see what I mean."

I nod uncertainly.

"There are plenty of signs that you're recovering," he says with a bright look. "You sleep about ten hours a night, and another six to eight hours of naps during the day. Sleep's a great healer."

"I feel stronger," I admit. "My mind seems clearer too, but there's still not much in it."

"I notice that whenever you aren't thinking about your amnesia, it seems to take a backseat. When we talk about other things, you come up with words I don't know, but I always find them when I check in the dictionary."

"It helped me when you showed me your special room. There's so much in it, so much to think about. And I love the stories you tell."

"Hey, thanks. I love it that someone wants to hear them."

"Billy, who is Giacomo Loncari?"

Billy raises his eyebrows.

"Giacomo is my landlord. How did you hear about him?"

"I found his old library card. He must have lived here at one time."

"He sure did. For about sixty years. He was still living on the ground floor when I first rented a room. He was quite old then, and he's older now. He lives in an apartment on Lexington Avenue, with a twenty-four-hour nurse looking after him. I visit him sometimes. On nice summer days I take him out for a jog in the park. He has a motorized wheelchair, and he likes to race me with it. Of course, I let him win sometimes."

"And who is the young woman in the photograph?"

Billy's face grows still. He drops his eyes for a moment, then looks up with a noncommittal smile.

"She's someone I cared about back home, before everything changed."

"Changed because of your accident?"

"Actually before the accident."

He is staring at the floor, at nothing much maybe, possibly a vague memory. The smile is gone. He is breathing through his mouth.

"It happened when I came home for summer vacation, after my first year at college," he begins. His tone is neutral, as if he is removing an unneeded implement from a store of forgotten items with little value in themselves but too good to throw out.

"I asked her if we should become engaged. I told her we could wait a few years before the wedding, but as far as I was concerned, she was the only one for me. Forever. I was just eighteen at the time, but even then I knew my own heart. She told me she felt the same."

"Did you marry?"

"No, we never did." He shakes his head. He is still staring at the floor. "Francisco, have you ever been completely in love—a forever love?"

"I don't know if I have or not."

"Oh," he says, looking up, embarrassed. "I'm sorry."

"Why didn't you marry?"

"The last time I saw her, we were saying good-bye at the Des Moines bus station. It was September, and I was heading east for my second year. She looked me deep in the eyes and said, 'I love you very much. I will always love you.'"

"That's beautiful."

"Francisco, when a woman says this to you with a certain kind of look, it can mean one of two things. It can mean exactly what it sounds like. Or it can mean she's preparing you for a broken heart—the heart she knows she is going to break."

Billy tells me this without a hint of bitterness.

"I don't understand," I say. "What happened?"

"She wrote me a letter a few weeks later. She told me that it would be impossible for us to marry. She was only five feet six, she explained, and I had just crested seven feet and was still growing. I probably weighed three hundred pounds, and none of it fat. It wouldn't work, she said. Biologically and psychologically it wouldn't work. I wrote back and pleaded with her, argued that many short women are married to very tall husbands. I asked her what she meant by *biologically* and *psychologically*. She sent me a reply that spelled it out. She said it might not be possible for us to have a child, or maybe even a normal sex life, and even if we did conceive, the baby might be a giant like me. Giving birth could kill her. And she didn't want me to go through life thinking I had killed my wife. She wanted me to be happy. She encouraged me to find someone very tall to love."

"It's plain to see she still cared about you."

"I think she still did at that point. But it made me feel grotesque. Like I was a monster."

"You are certainly not that."

"I argued and argued, letter after letter, but in the end she wouldn't budge. She fell for some other guy and married him."

Billy stands up and rubs his eyes. He sighs, "Well, it was a long time ago."

I say nothing, but I am thinking about the photo enshrined in the other room.

Winter must be drawing to a close. The days are sunnier now, and snowbanks are melting away into the city's storm drains.

Billy tells me I have lived with him for nearly three months. More and more often, he takes me on walks or trots to his favorite places: the view from the Battery. Washington Square Park. Madison Square Garden, a basketball game between the New York Knicks and the Brooklyn Nets, during which I fall asleep.

On one occasion Billy asks me if I would like to see the site of the World Trade Center.

"What is that?" I say, feeling suddenly uneasy.

"You remember. The Twin Towers. The place where so many people died."

"No, I don't remember it," I blurt with too much intensity. "I don't want to go there."

"Okay, Francisco, I understand. It was the worst disaster in the history of New York City. You've had some stressful experiences, and other people's sufferings would be too much for you right now."

I swallow the lump of fear in my throat. I don't always grasp his thinking, but I know he means well.

Life goes on. We visit the zoo in Central Park, the Frick art collection, the Empire State Building (a giant ape once stood on top of it and fell to his death), and the American Museum of Natural History (our merganser is finer than theirs). We have also developed the habit of eating our Saturday night suppers at Dina's.

"Hi, Billy! Hi, Francisco! What'll it be today, boys?"

She still has the elephant tattoo on her forearm, but the Greek letters are missing. It must be painful to have a tattoo removed.

On a warm afternoon we take Giacomo Loncari out for a jog in Central Park. When I first meet him, I discover that the landlord is a wizened little man held in place in his wheelchair by straps.

"How do you do, sir," I say. He grunts in reply. As we go down in the elevator of his apartment building on Lexington, he examines me from the corner of his eyes, suspicious and, I think, hostile. However, I can see he dotes on Billy.

We progress slowly enough along the sidewalk until we arrive at the entrance to the park. As soon as Billy's feet hit the broad walkway he begins to trot, pulling ahead. Giacomo squeals with excitement. His gnarled hands work just fine on the throttle, and the wheelchair rockets forward, gaining on Billy, zigging and zagging to avoid the occasional pedestrian who fails to notice the looming stampede of a giant and a runaway mechanical stagecoach. I am running now too. Before long I'm forced to admit I cannot keep up with either of them. I collapse onto a bench, scattering pigeons. A matron in a suede coat and diamond earrings is sharing the bench with me. She leans over and asks:

"Did I just see what I think I saw?"

"Yes," I say somberly, nodding, "it was a giant."

"You saw it too?"

"I did."

"And there was something chasing it?"

Again, I nod.

"How very singular," she says with a look of pleasure, straightening a silk scarf at her neck. "Well, I suppose it's to be expected. This *is* New York City."

One night, Billy takes me to the Chinese restaurant a few blocks south of our place. When he ducks inside the front doorway, making many little bells chime, employees appear from all directions, smiling broadly, bowing. The grandparents who own the restaurant emerge from the kitchen and hasten over with happy cries to pat Billy on the arm, to beam possessively upon him, to guide us to our seats. There aren't any other customers at this point. Ours is a wide booth covered in red leatherette. Billy fits into it without too much discomfort, his legs stretched out so his knees won't lift the table. I sit across from him but remain unnoticed.

The owners' children are suddenly busy talking Chinese into cell phones. The waiters and waitresses, the grandchildren, are busy talking New York English into their cell phones. The grandparents hover over us, pressing close but held back a degree by a certain oriental reserve. Soon the restaurant is packed with their friends and relatives, all ordering meals, all observing Billy. The tables closest to us fill first. There is even a transfer of money between two parties who exchange tables. Handheld devices and cameras flash, taking photographs and videos.

A man arrives with a cardboard box wrapped in ornamental tissue and tied with a red cord. Inside is a new set of shoes for Billy. Much haggling ensues. Billy tries to push more money on the man than the cobbler wants. The man steps back, will not take the cash. Billy can pay for the materials, he says, but the labor is free. Billy insists on paying for both. The man refuses, his "face" offended. Billy accepts defeat. Smiles erupt all around. Then, we feast.

The hailstorm of eggs on the roof grows steadily heavier. Now Billy spends a good deal of time each day boiling them and then chopping them up to make egg-and-mayonnaise sandwiches. The entrance to the apartment is congested with bales of day-old bread, which he has begged from local bakeries. Our mornings are spent making sandwiches, and throughout afternoons and part of the evenings we distribute them on the streets. More often than not, people refuse our offers—even obviously needy people. I try to imagine what it is like to be suddenly confronted by a total stranger who happens to be an enormously powerful eight-foot-tall man, bending over you with an incongruously childlike face, urging upon you a sandwich wrapped in wax paper. Would you trust him? Would you even engage him at first sight?

Wherever we go in our rambles through the poorer districts of the city, many people swerve to avoid him, or simply stop and stare. If he tries to speak to the gapers, they break into a trot. Mainly they do not see me, unless I split up with Billy and keep a half-block distance between us. Interestingly, the truly hungry are always glad to accept a sandwich from *me*. I gloat over this.

I suppose Billy has experienced enough rejection in his life to be untroubled by people's doubts about his intentions. Cheerily, he presses ever onward. Most of his successes are in neighborhoods where he is known, or on the breadlines where he regularly volunteers.

One afternoon, Billy and I work side by side at a soup kitchen run by a local church. He hands out sandwiches and bottled fruit drinks to street people. I ladle hot soup into styrofoam cups. I wonder what is in their minds. Doubtless, most of them, if not all, possess a full set of memories. They have a lot of dignity in their own way, even though there is plenty of variety in temperament and character—like people everywhere. There are con artists among them, of course, but that is true of every level of society. Then it hits me like a blow: though I'm not a con artist, I *am* a social parasite.

"I'm a social parasite," I mumble despondently during a lull in the serving.

"You're what!" Billy scowls, jerking his head back and staring at me.

I dare not repeat what I said. I try to deflect:

"I was just talking to myself."

"You are not a parasite," he breathes in a low rumble. "You are my friend. And these people are our friends."

Chastened, ashamed of myself, I seal up my negative mood and try to focus on meeting the needs coming down the line. I begin to notice that when you serve soup and sandwiches to needy people, they almost always express their sincere thanks. They usually give a word or a smile, a look in the eye, a joke, a compliment. Now and then they try to tell a little story. I learn to listen, to respond appropriately.

For five days this week, Billy has stayed close to home. I hear him sawing and hammering somewhere in the building. Occasionally I hear the screech of old nails as they are being pried from wood. I smell the sweet-astringent odor of wall paint. He is repairing things for Giacomo, I presume.

I am sleeping less during daylight hours. I am reading things now, short passages from his dusty old book collection. It's a pleasant distraction and it exercises my mind. I cannot focus for long and sometimes feel disconnected from the material, though it is now always intelligible. For both my sake and Billy's, I keep a Webster's Dictionary in the apartment. I seldom go into the hidden room, other than to look for a book. There are hundreds upon hundreds of *National Geographic* magazines in there too, shelf after shelf of yellow spines. The older ones are more interesting—the 1920s to 1950s. There are fewer copies toward the end of the century, none after the turn of the millennium.

How do I know the meaning of things like years, decades, millennia? And the vocabulary, which seems to be well stocked and functions instantaneously? Is neutral data stored in one cupboard of the brain, and personal items in another? It is totally perplexing. Was I hit on one side of the head? Was I assaulted or did I fall? Or did I strike against myself from the inside out, so to speak?

I am washing the supper dishes when Billy comes down from the roof with a basket full of eggs—the fourth of the day. The pigeons are laying again, further increasing the daily harvest.

When we have finished our chores, I sit down at the table and Billy surprises me by bringing out his single bottle of wine. He squeaks the cork off, pours me a tumblerful, and another for himself. I have lived here for three or four months, and this is our second drink together.

"Wine?" I say.

"Tonight we are celebrating!" he declares with a grin.

"What is the special occasion?"

"You'll see."

He takes me down the corridor to one of the other apartment doors. A stepladder leans against the wall. A cloud heap of speckled plastic sheets lies nearby. The spray-painted warnings about bugs have been sanded off.

"This was Jimmy's place," he explains. "Now it's yours, Francisco."

He pushes the door open and we go in. I smell fresh paint. He flicks a switch and the room is illuminated by an overhead light. Is that a chandelier hanging from the ceiling? Yes, it is!

"Didn't cost me much," he says. "Missing a few crystals, and nearly electrocuted me rewiring it, but it was fun, kind of mini shock therapy."

I stand by the doorway, taking it all in: There is no furniture. The hardwood floors have been scraped down to their original surface, pristine, save for a few dents where bedposts or dressers long ago left evidence of their presence. The walls are pale yellow and bare of decoration. The foot-high baseboards are enamel white, as is the single window frame. The glass shines, offering a view of another brick wall.

Sitting in the exact center of the floor is a yellow toy car. In fact, a Matchbox racing car.

I stare at it, paralyzed.

"Was yours plastic or metal?" Billy asks.

"I don't know," I whisper, choking, feeling bats flitting about in the attic of memory. I see my rubber boots, and beneath them a web of cracks radiating slowly outward. I hear splintering ice. My heart is hammering hard for no reason.

Billy drops to his knees with a thump-thump and bends over the car. He picks it up and guides it along the floor, making *vroom-vroom* sounds with his lips. He launches it hard, and it zings across the floor and crashes into a wall. Chuckling, he crawls over to retrieve it. Turning around, he goes *vroom-vroom* again and pushes it. It races on its whizzing wheels across the room toward me.

I kneel and catch it in my hands. It is metal. And now I remember that mine, the one lying at the bottom of a pond somewhere, was also metal.

It's my turn. I skim the tires a few times and shoot it back to Billy. My aim is bad, and he is forced to leap in order to catch it. He misses and rolls onto the floor, guffawing, making the window rattle. Then, up onto his knees and *vroom-vroom*.

Back and forth we send the car. Soon I am smiling, and before long I am laughing. It is a strange sound—or strange to me—and now I realize that I have not laughed in a very long time, not since the thing that happened to me—whatever it was.

Billy pulls a small red car from his pocket, grins with raised eyebrows, and sends it flying across the floorboards in my direction. It crashes against a wall. I fetch it and send it back to him.

The playing gathers momentum. Now we are side by side, thumping around the room on our knees, pushing our cars in a race. We're making *vroom*s with our lips and squealing tires with our throats, and crash sounds, and more *vroom*s as we circle and sideswipe each other, spin out of control into a head-on collision, and then resume the race.

Without warning, the door bangs wide open and we hear a shout: "What the . . .!"

With our tires still spinning, we look up and see a man standing in the open doorway pointing some kind of rifle at us. He quickly leaps inside the room, followed by four other armed men. They are dressed in black clothing and combat boots, their helmets and visors masking their faces. The letters *FBI* are stenciled on their flak jackets.

"Down on the floor, hands behind your backs!" one of them shouts.

We flatten ourselves, hands behind our backs, our cars still in our hands.

Thin beams of red light are trained on our heads.

"One move and you're dead!" barks a soldier, policeman, robber, killer—we don't know what they are, but we're not going to move a muscle.

We lie there for what feels like an hour or two, listening to heavy boots storming on the stairway and up and down the corridor. I hear doors splintering somewhere in the building.

Muffled conversations, sometimes in and out of our hearing range. The invaders speak as if Billy and I are inanimate objects. From the corner of my eye I see two men in suits and ties, with badges on cords about their necks. They confer with the combat men.

"Any sign of a factory, any components?" asks one of the suit-and-tie agents.

"Nothing, sir."

"Packages, metal drums?"

"Nothing. Some dusty stuff in the cellar, just shovels and tools, broken bicycles, a bag of toy cars, old household junk. The only electrical is blown screw fuses for a panel box, but no wiring spools, no timers or remotes. Otherwise the place is empty, except for an antique collection in one of the rooms on this floor. It took some time to go through the drawers and cupboards, but all we found was the weirdest collection of trinkets you ever saw in your life. It's a no-threat situation."

"All right. Collect any cell phones you find, and the computers too."

"There aren't any, sir."

"Are you serious?"

"Not a single electronic device anywhere in the building. Just our own surveillance tech."

This is followed by a long silence.

"Okay. Take out all our wires. It's a false alarm."

"When they said *plastic* and *rewiring*, it sure sounded like the real thing."

"Yeah, well, *plastic* and *rewiring* are common words."

"Yes, sir."

"Let's get back to the office. I need to chew off some ears at DHS."

"I just called them. Seems their border people sent a red alert when they arrested these idiots, then forgot to tell us they were cleared."

"Better safe than sorry."

"Yup."

"Okay, evacuate."

They are gone. Billy and I sit up and rub our stiff limbs. We look at each other. Did this really happen?

We take a stroll through the building. To our great relief we find that the troops and agents entered the hidden room of the mind through the doorway in our apartment, which had been open at the time of the visitation. On every other floor, the apartment doors have been kicked in. The bins of chicken feed on the roof have been toppled, their contents spread about for sifting. With a sigh, Billy sets to scooping it up and refilling the bins. He sweeps up the chaff in a dustpan and throws it outside for the girls.

That done, we go back to my new room and play race cars until bedtime.

Billy informs me at breakfast that the room is not intended to be my separate apartment; he is not kicking me out, not even subtly, he hastens to assure me. He wants me to leave it empty so that I will fill it only with mnemonic prompts, in the hope that accumulated visual triggers will reach a critical mass.

Yes, those are the words he uses: *mnemonic* and *critical mass*.

While Billy is washing our laundry in the bathtub, and hanging it to dry on wooden folding racks he has erected by radiators, I return to my new room. Like my actual mind, it is not entirely empty, because the yellow car is still there in both. I hope to fill the room with objects that match the flotsam and jetsam retrieved from other portions of my brain, which are still shut off from my consciousness. Of course, I have no way of telling whether my memories have been permanently erased, but if a few small items have already made it through, then others might follow.

I close the door and turn off the chandelier. The window provides enough dim light. I sit down cross-legged on the floor in the center of the room, and close my eyes. The car in the palm of my hand weighs next to nothing, as a key weighs next to nothing yet can open castle gates or unlock the launch buttons of nuclear missiles. Why does this little toy mean so much to me? I sense that straining to recall the reason won't help, and could even make it harder. It is important not to push. Simply resting with this single solid prompt may be the answer to it all.

What else do I remember?

Mittens! I am wearing mittens. What color are they? Beige wool, woven in Scandinavian patterns. My boot tops have red rims. My cries are those of a child. Ten years old, eleven?

At the bottom of the pond, only two or three feet below the ice, are countless colored leaves. And broken bottles covered in slime. Green circuit boards from computers.

Into my mind's eye flashes a new scene. It is no longer winter. It is autumn, and an old bearded man in checkered shirt and suspenders is standing beside a woodpile, holding an axe. He lifts the axe in both hands and brings it down on a computer sitting on a chopping block. Again and again he smashes. He is enraged, snarling, gritting his teeth on ugly words. He picks up the pieces and hurls them into the middle of the pond. He grabs a black bottle from his trouser pocket, puts it to his mouth, and clamps his teeth on the cork, which he pulls out and spits onto the ground. He tilts his head back and gulps down the bottle's contents. When it is empty, he shoves the bottle at me.

"Here," he growls, "cash it in for a two-cent refund."

I am frightened by his mood but glad to receive the bottle. On its label is a sorrel horse.

My eyes fly open. Jumping up, I run out into the corridor and down the hall, enter our apartment, and go through the doorway to the hidden room of the mind. There on the wall is the primitive painting of a sorrel horse, and beneath it the words *Benny's Vermont Dark Ale*. Beneath this, in small print that I had not noticed before:

Benjamin Uffington Brewery
Tadd's Ford, Vermont ~ est. 1799

The giant's voice erupts behind me, startling me: "This seems to have caught your attention, Francisco."

"Where did you get it?" I ask him.

"At a church rummage sale in Harlem. Why? Is it a clue?"

"I d–don't know. It might have triggered a real memory. In my mind I just saw an old man drinking from a bottle with this label—a brown-horse label. On the other hand, the painting might have induced a scene in my imagination."

"Which do you think it is?"

"I'm not sure, but the scene in my mind seemed so real."

"Mmm, dreams are like that too."

"And so are real memories. But the trail ends there, Billy."

"Then there's only one thing we can do."

I look at him.

"We visit Vermont," he says, his eyes shining at the prospect of another adventure.

It takes a couple of days for Billy to search for a hired driver with a high-ceilinged minivan. He thinks it's better we don't ask Hal 9000 to do the job. In a secondhand bookstore he finds a map of Vermont. In the public library he does some research on New England breweries.

While he is putting together our plan, I spend long hours sitting in my room of hidden memories. The horse painting is now hanging on the wall. The yellow car is on the windowsill. I sit on the floor, waiting, waiting for voices in empty rooms.

For a time I listen to the subdued echoes of car engines, garbage trucks, police and ambulance sirens, the occasional thumping of Billy's sock feet in the hallway, or his boots on the stairs going down to the street entrance, his boots returning an hour or so later. I nod into a half sleep.

"Here," growls the voice of the old bearded man, "cash it in for a two-cent refund."

With this I am wide-awake, feeling a stroke of fear. I see his face now, thrusting the bottle at me. His mouth twists bitterly, his eyes snapping with hatred.

"You killed them, you little parasite!" he roars.

Now the fear becomes terror and I back away from him. His face dissolves.

I open my eyes. I am sitting alone in the room, my heart racing.

I close my eyes.

"You love your tragedy," says a woman's voice. "You love it more than you love me."

I cannot see her face, only a feminine hand, young, a ring on its wedding finger, thrusting a piece of paper at me. I take it and look closely. On it is a photo of New York City's skyline, and below it are numbers:

09—11—20—01

The paper dissolves, the hand dissolves. I shake my head to clear it of these phantoms. I leap to my feet and pace around the room. I am angry now. This is not a memory! Not a real preamnesia memory. My subconscious has taken the paper the jackdaw pecked in my self-portrait and conflated it with imaginary scenes that are no more than manifestations of subliminal emotions.

"Get out of here! Get out of here!" I yell.

I am pounding the sides of my skull with my fists when Billy comes into the room and finds me.

"Are you all right, Francisco?" he asks in a subdued voice, his face worried.

"I'm all right," I whimper. "Yeah, I'm fine. I'm fine."

"Have you got a new clue?"

"No. Yes. I just realized something. I found out that my mind plays tricks on me."

He chuckles. "Now, that's a fact. Happens to all of us. You just have to spot the tricks."

"It cheats! It lies!"

"Sometimes it embellishes to evoke a deeper truth."

"What!"

"It tells us stories so we understand things better."

"Billy, I don't *have* a story. And I don't think I want one anymore. But one thing for certain, we are not going to waste our time on a trip to Vermont."

6

The mystic mountains of Vermont

Our driver is a lady in her late forties. I can't see her eyes through her sunglasses. Why is she wearing them before sunrise? Her expression is neutral, as if she's content enough to have the job but not overly excited about it. She is chary of words. Her ponytail is gray. The lip of her New York Yankees baseball cap is low over her brow. She is wearing dark-blue janitor's overalls, with the logo of a winged bus and *Icarus Rentals* stitched on the breast. An incongruously large Swiss watch adorns her thin wrist. Her salmon-pink sneakers manipulate the pedals as if they were part of her body, requiring no thought.

The vehicle is a fairly new, white, eighteen-passenger van, which she drives without haste or impulsiveness. I am sitting beside her in the front seat. Billy is in the very rear on a wall-to-wall padded bench that allows him some comfort, his arms stretched out along the back cushions, his legs extended down the center aisle.

On the dashboard sits a small glowing screen with an animated map that is constantly changing. As we maneuver our way northward out of Manhattan, the machine speaks a few times in a tinny Japanese accent, and then the driver turns down the volume. At a red stoplight she removes her sunglasses and flicks her eyes again and again at the rearview mirror, doubtless watching Billy. The light turns green and we glide forward.

"The fast route or the scenic?" the woman asks us.

"The scenic, please," Billy answers.

"I'm Roberta," she says out of nowhere.

We tell her our names.

"Uh-huh," she replies and inserts wired plugs into her ears. I follow the wires to their source in the console, where a vivid orange bar of light silently registers the fluctuations of strong music being played, inaudible to Billy and me.

We are in Connecticut by the time the sun comes up over Long Island. Roberta puts her sunglasses back on. We leave the main highway at New Haven, turning north toward Hartford and Springfield. There are more and more farms along the way, and the land is rising. Soon we are in the Connecticut River valley, following beside the water, hills to the right and the left, gold light on the western slopes, numerous woods with pale-green budding leaves, mares and foals in pastures. There is heavy southbound traffic, commuters heading toward the larger cities, but our lane is relatively open, the cars moving at a good clip.

I do not know what lies ahead of us today—a breakthrough or another disappointment. I am feeling a mixture of expectancy and apprehension. Even so, the greenery and vistas spreading all about us have a soothing effect. I turn around to see how Billy is doing. He is gazing at farms and fields and forests, his chin tilted high, eyes happy. This is the second time he has left New York City since his accident, years ago, the first in a season of warmth. He catches my eye and smiles.

He opens the paper map on his lap, bending over it, squinting.

"The Appalachians, Francisco," he says, pointing ahead. "North of here they get higher. Fewer and fewer people too. Though you might see Iroquois running through the trees. Maybe a few colonists firing muskets at redcoats."

As long as I've known him, Billy has been more or less perpetually cheerful, his frequent laughter ranging from hearty to light. But he has never joked or quipped until now.

I turn around to show him my appreciation, but he is already back to his map. If you didn't know what you were looking at, you would see nothing more than a friendly jock relaxing after a game. You would think: *Nice guy*. And beneath the thought, unstated, possibly even subconscious, would be the summarization: *Dumb*.

How very little I have considered his life. Preoccupied by my own problems, grown accustomed to his endless generosity, have I slipped into an attitude of entitlement? There's another word for it, I think. Yes—*narcissism*.

Maybe that's too harsh. You break your arm, and the arm demands attention. You break your mind, and the mind demands attention. But at what point does the attention become obsession? When does the fixing make the problem worse? I don't know when. I don't know anything, really. I return to watching the trees.

We stop for a break at a town called Brattleboro. We all get out of the minivan to stretch our limbs. The hills have become soaring round-top mountains covered in thick woods. Vermont is to the left of us, New Hampshire to the right. There are a lot of birds winging and singing in the treetops. I inhale deeply, astonished by the air's sweetness, its purity, its organic perfumes. The river rustles in my ears.

Billy offers me a sandwich from his shopping bag. I eat half a meatloaf on rye. He eats two whole ones. Roberta declines the offer. She walks off a ways and talks into her cell phone. Her voice is loud; she is giving instructions about the care of a cat—to her teenage offspring, I presume. Then she is talking to a friend about a bowling date. Then she is reporting to her home office. She lowers her voice for this one, but the word *giant* wafts toward me. Fortunately, Billy has been jogging down the highway and is just now turning around to head back in our direction. Roberta is making another call—the subject matter is "sleeping around" and "morning-after pills".

I have noticed this social norm on the sidewalks of New York. People use cell phones as if these instruments are magical erasers of other living creatures. With the tap of a button, humanity dissolves into nonbeing, or at best is frozen into an abstraction. Conversations of the most intimate sort are publicly broadcast without regard for who may be listening, the willing and the unwilling. On a busy street, there is so much of this happening that you are never quite sure which phrases belong with other free-floating fragments.

Two days ago, I returned to the art gallery on Fifth Avenue. The Metropolitan Museum of Misplaced Memories, Billy calls it. I went alone, because I wanted to inspect, without distraction, the jackdaw's paper in my self-portrait. The painting was unchanged. As before, the skyline of the city and the mysterious number stirred in me profoundly uneasy feelings.

Walking home on Fifth, I noticed that the avenue seemed unusually deserted. Then I realized that it was after seven o'clock in the evening, with most of the businesses closed and office workers gone. Exactly at the moment I passed the entrance of a soaring glass skyscraper, a woman came out through its doors and walked rapidly a few paces behind me. In a single glance I had taken in a lot of details: late twenties or early thirties, incredibly beautiful, blond, slender, long legged, and fit, wearing gold jewelry, a tailored black suit, and high heels tapping the concrete in a determined manner. She carried a leather valise with gold initials on it. A lawyer, I thought, or a rising executive.

Though I could hear her heels swiftly closing the gap between us, I refused to turn around to gape at this vision of splendor. Nearer and nearer she came, a cloud of exotic fragrance enveloping me. As she passed me on the left, her arm brushed mine, and she breathed throatily, "I love you."

I veered slightly to the right and increased my walking speed. But to no avail. She kept pace with me, and again came the passionate "I love you!"

In split seconds I analyzed the situation and discarded a number of options. *Life is not fair*, I began. *She is too beautiful and powerful. You will adore her and become enslaved. She will manipulate you. She will break your heart. You will break hers. Your handsomeness, such as it is, means nothing. You are mentally ill. You are a clock with a broken spring. You are destitute and a beggar.* Et cetera, et cetera.

As vistas of devastation opened before me, I was about to break into a sprint when suddenly she pulled ahead. Then I noticed the cell phone in her left hand, pressed to her ear. And the last thing I heard before she disappeared around a corner was, "Kiss the kids for me, honey, I'll be home at eight. I love you!"

Billy is huffing and puffing beside the van, doing post-jog ligament stretches. Roberta folds up her cell phone, pockets it, and pops the audio plugs back into her ears. We all take our seats. The journey resumes.

At White River Junction we turn off the highway and head northwest on a secondary highway that weaves its way into increasingly rugged country. Now and then we pass old farms and homesteads, a cupola-topped barn with a copper weather vane flashing in the sun, occasionally small villages that must have had greater populations at one time. Our second rest stop is merely for a short bathroom break in the bushes. While the others are thus engaged, I walk on a few hundred yards to a crossroads hamlet of six houses, all in various stages of disrepair. In the village square stands a life-size bronze statue of a Civil War soldier, commemorating the fallen of that place—about sixty young men. Surrounding and encroaching on this community, once so vital with potency, with hope, the forest devours its memories.

Roberta and Billy pick me up where I stand contemplating the names, the forgotten lives. A few miles farther on, we turn right onto a paved route that heads into wilder woodlands, following it for a while until we divert onto a series of narrowing roads that take us more or less in the direction of north-northeast.

Shortly after 1 P.M. we come to another village. As we decelerate, we pass a hand-painted sign, "Welcome to Odium!" We crawl past four houses and a gas station with an archaic red pump, an Out of Order sign tied to it with baling twine. Seconds later we are leaving it behind, and pass another sign, "You are leaving Odium. Come again."

Roberta checks her dashboard computer.

"Some of these places aren't on the GPS," she says, "but it looks like Tadd's Ford is. It's a mile ahead."

The van goes over a rise and dips down into a fold in the mountains, entering a serene green valley with a patchwork of farms and woods, a cow in a meadow, and a creek meandering through the fields. At the bottom of the hill, we come to a sign that informs us we have arrived. To our right is the village proper, perhaps ten or more houses, a mixture of old architectures, some with Dutch roofs, some with high peaks and the spikes of lightning rods rising from blue ceramic orbs. The sidings of sheds and homes are wooden shingles, either white-washed or unpainted. There is a single gas station and corner store, its outer walls decorated with rusty sheets of metal advertising Coca-Cola and cattle feed.

Across the street is a log building with a covered country-style porch. A sign on the roof tells us it's Myrt's Café. We park in front of it. There is also a Post Office sign in its window.

Billy and I get out of the van and tromp up the steps to the front door, leaving Roberta standing by the van, tapping on her cell phone. Billy ducks his head low, and I duck too, since the makers of the café designed it for people shorter than both of us. The door opens to the sound of jingling bells. Inside, we note the post office wicket directly before us. Three freestanding tables with chairs are positioned to our left, beside the front window. At one of these sits an elderly man in a checkered work coat and matching cap, reading a newspaper with a cup of coffee beside him. He looks up, holds us in his gaze for a time, then looks down and resumes reading. It seems that a giant entering his personal environment makes no impression whatsoever.

Stretched diagonally across the wall behind him is a bobcat pelt. Beside it are crossed snowshoes. Colorful quilts in clear plastic wrappers hang from the rafters. Across from the window, a serving counter with spin-top stools runs the length of the room. Leaning over it on the working side of the counter is a lady who appears to be in her late seventies, and might even be a hearty octogenarian. She is reading a paperback book. Her gray hair is finely braided and wrapped around her head, held in place by bobby pins. She wears wire-rim spectacles and a flowered print dress under her apron. She looks up slowly, loath to leave what she is reading. Perusing us, she pauses over Billy, and straightens her back.

"Help you?" she asks in a toneless way, devoid of all welcome. It is not so much unmannerly as it is guarded. Across her round healthy face there is written a history, generations upon generations of careful sifting: insiders and outsiders, locals and aliens, year-round people and summer people, newcomers and the ancestrally rooted. Without doubt, she is a permanent fixture.

I step forward. "Yes, ma'am. We're trying to find the Benjamin Uffington Brewery."

"Uffington's," she replies, looking out the window. "It closed down years ago. Nothing to see there now. Are you looking to buy beer? I have some malt ale and lager in the fridge, but none of the microbreweries."

"Thank you, no," says Billy in his deep rumble. Her eyes dart to him, and stay on him.

"As you wish," she says with a tone of philosophical musing. "Though I always say a slice of homemade pie and a beer, even on a spring day, is mighty nice."

She points to a pie rack under a glass dome on the counter:

"Lemon custard. Raisin. Apple. Pumpkin. Got to admit the pumpkin is last autumn's, but I canned it fresh and I use plenty of sweet spices."

"I would appreciate pie," says Billy. "May I purchase the whole pie?"

"You surely may," she says with a twitch of her thin blue lips that I take to be a smile.

"The pumpkin, then, for me, and another for my friend."

"A small slice of apple, please," I say.

"Do you have espresso?" Billy inquires with bright-eyed optimism.

"Nope, no espresso. I could make you some regular coffee extra strong, just add a spoonful of instant."

"That would be perfect, ma'am."

As the woman busies herself cutting pie, I glance at the book she has been reading. Its title is *Blue Mountains Quilt Patterns*.

"I'll have one of them lemon custards, Myrtle," the old man at the table calls out.

"Coming right up, Cory."

As she unhurriedly goes about her business, I say to her, "So Uffington's Brewery shut down."

"That's right. In 2002, if I recall."

"Do you remember the people who lived there?"

"Oh, I remember them well enough. A bank owns the land now, last I heard. Thinking of buying the place?"

"No, no, not at all," I say too hastily. Her eyes dart at me and linger, assessing.

"A lot of city people come up here trying to buy land cheap," she says, bringing out her words at a ponderous rate. "They want the old farmhouses for summer places. It's not right. For hundreds of years, men and women and children sweated to clear those fields, pulling out stumps, picking up rocks, building stone walls, putting up their barns and homes. Now it's all sliding back into forest. You walk through the woods just anywheres around here and you come across a field wall. Used to be these hills were pastures. Big families lived up and down the back roads, kids running in and out like flies in the slits of a raisin pie. We had a two-room school built in 1840, before the war, and two more rooms added over the years until after the Hitler war. In the fifties, the young men started moving away to Montpelier and Burlington and such places, for the work mostly. It got so you couldn't raise a family by farming anymore. Then in the early seventies, some hippies broke into the school and had a drug party, burned the place down. They were building communes in the hills in those days, not far from here, though they're mostly gone now. At the time of the fire the population was shrinking pretty grim, and the few kids we still had were being bussed up to Saint Johnsbury for school."

"That is a great pity," Billy sympathizes. "I was raised on a farm, and I know what a loss it is when it's gone."

"Lots of good things gone these days," Myrtle says, placing a slice of pie in front of me and a whole one in front of Billy, with forks for us both. "Sure I can't get you some beer?"

"Just the espresso, please."

"Water for me," I add.

She serves the old gentleman his pie and returns to us. Billy is served his coffee in a soup mug, with a pitcher of cream beside it. I am given a glass of water and a paper napkin, with the image of an antlered stag on it.

She places a cloth marker in her book, closes it, and says:

"You sound like nice boys. Where you from?"

"Iowa."

"New York City, I think."

"Uh-huh. So, why're you interested in Uffington's?"

Billy answers. "In my home I have a painted sign for the brewery, very old. It has a brown horse on it."

"Yup, just like the labels. That'd be Benny's Vermont Dark Ale. It was sad to see it go."

"So we thought we would drive up here and learn a little more about where it came from, what its past was. I hope you don't think we're intruding."

"Oh no," she says, warming to him. "It's just we get antique dealers from the city scavenging everything within thirty miles. They'll buy a milk churn for a dollar and sell it in the city for a hundred. Take an old picture off the wall of an abandoned house and sell it for a thousand. It isn't right. It's like selling your love letters."

Billy nods sadly. "All the love and labor people put into things they made. Then to go treating them like numbers on paper."

"Ain't it so. More pie, boys?"

"Yes, please. Lemon, if you don't mind."

"Mind? Heck, you can have it on the house."

"Myrtle, if it would mean anything to you, I'd be happy to return the sign to you as a gift. It might be a good memory for your store. Don't you agree, Francisco?"

"Yes, I do."

Now the lady is smiling wide, her crooked brown teeth displayed in a moment of guileless pleasure.

"That is very nice of you," she says. "Very nice indeed. I can't say how many years it's been since I was more touched. But you just go on keeping it down there wherever you live. And you'll remember us, won't you? A piece of Tadd's Ford right there in ..."

"In New York City."

"Well, that's fine," she says, wiping off the counter with a rag, her eyes wet. "That's just fine."

"Myrtle, can you tell us a bit more about Uffington's?"

"Well, I think I can, some. A Colonel Uffington was in the Revolutionary army and afterward got a land grant in Vermont after we kicked the British out. He wasn't a good farmer, so he built a grist mill on the race higher up the river."

"That river?" I ask, pointing out the window to the wide but not very impressive creek running through the valley.

"The very one," she says. "So he put up the mill, and before long he'd built the brewery off to one side.

He loved his ale, you see. Plenty fine water upstream, fed mostly by springs from the mountain. The buildings are still there, but the roofs are gone. Vandals made off with everything they could carry, and busted up the wooden barrels—hand-carved staves with straps made in the Franklins' own forge. They kept them for years after the breweries were supposed to change over to metal barrels. Things were tough in Prohibition years. The Franklins had troubles with the law in the twenties, but the company recovered under FDR."

"Who are the Franklins?" I ask.

"The Franklin family. They bought the company in 1899, just before the last Uffington died, about a hundred years after the mill and brewery were founded. But they kept the name because the beer was known far and wide as a right good drink. The last of the Franklin line ended a few years ago now. The wife, Dorothy, she passed away shortly after the turn of the century. The husband, Benjamin, he died a year later. I never got to know them real well, because they leaned more to the western side of the range and the people who live that direction. They got their mail at Graniteville, did their shopping there too, I suppose."

"Did you say *Benjamin* Franklin?" I exclaim.

"Oh, lawd," she laughs, "he wasn't the famous Ben Franklin. But you can see why those people kept giving the name to their boys. For generations it ran in the family, and sometimes there was four generations alive at once and living under the same roof. Can you imagine what it was like for the women to call them to supper? And of course the original Uffington was a Benjamin too."

"So this Benjamin Franklin you mentioned was the last owner?"

"He was. They had a daughter but she left home early on, and I've never seen her since her parents died. She married a man from the city—I'm not sure where—and I guess she never wanted to claim the old place after her parents were gone." Myrtle sighs. "Same as all our young people. They all go away. My sons and daughters too. Most of mine live over in Manchester, New Hampshire, and one in Montpelier, but they come home for Christmas some years and a few weeks every summer."

Billy decides to widen the discussion:

"My friend Francisco may have lived here at one time. Did you ever know any people named Goya?"

"Goya? No, I can't say I did." She shakes her head. "No, no one by that name this side of the mountain."

We scrape our plates and finish our drinks. Standing, we make our good-byes, shaking hands. Billy is careful with old people's hands, little bird bones you could crush with a wink.

"Come back, now," says Myrtle, seeing us to the door. "Come back anytime."

The old fellow stands, throws some coins onto his table, and comes outside with us. He straightens his cap and peers judiciously up the road.

"Three miles that way you come to a fork," he says, "just before the highroad dips down over the range. Take the right fork, and it'll bring you to the old Franklin place. Watch out for potholes."

We thank him, and hop into the van. Roberta is still talking into her cell phone. Without ending her conversation, she turns the ignition key and lets out the brake. With one hand she steers us into the enveloping, enduring trees.

It doesn't take long to reach the Franklin place. For the people of this region, perhaps, a few miles means another country, another community. For us, the distance is next to nothing. As we bump and rattle along the fork, with a rampant creek roaring beside us all the way, Roberta slows the vehicle to a crawl. Five minutes farther in, she brakes and turns off the engine. Ahead of us, beyond a few saplings blocking the road, are the faces of three dilapidated buildings, gray and white and rust red. Billy and I get out, leaving Roberta to resume her communications with the world.

As we walk into a clearing through knee-high grass, we see that it was once a wider, more open space. The remnants of a waterwheel lie rotting in the creek, which gushes down cold and fast from the hillside above. Wisps of mist play about the banks. The trees crowd the buildings, the two largest of which are roofless. The mill is a square fort of hand-cut stone blocks greened by moss and spray. The brewery is the larger brick building, which stands farther back, with copper pipes jutting from its side, leading to a catchment basin above the water race. Painted on its front wall is the brewery's name and an image of a life-size sorrel horse, faded and peeling. The front doorway is open, its massive wooden doors hanging at an angle on hinges that are pulling away from their frames. Swallows dart in and out of the open windows, building nests. To the right of the brewery stands a two-story clapboard house with glassless windows, its porch half-collapsed, bricks from its chimney scattered about the roof shakes. There is a clothesline off the end of the porch, a loop of wire sagging between a post and a tree, like loose rigging on a sailing ship. The high-standing grass is speared with last year's dead burdock and mullein. Overgrown lilac trees are blossoming purple and white. The sun shines down on us, but it doesn't dispel the chill in the atmosphere.

Billy and I have not yet entered any of the buildings. We are simply soaking it all in. Rather, he is waiting quietly while I look. I have the oddest feeling that I know this place—yet it is a knowing without memories attached to it. My mood, which had been expectant only moments before, and elevated by the pie and the lady at the café, now plunges.

Billy clears his throat and asks, "Does anything look familiar, Francisco?"

"It *feels* familiar, Billy, but there's nothing attached to the feeling. No pictures in my mind, no scenes, no memories."

We spend an hour going through the mill and the brewery, imagining what they once were. They are empty shells now, echoing with the lost eras of their abundance. The house has been stripped of furniture, save for a white enamel cookstove in the kitchen, missing its top plates. The smoke pipes have also been removed. There's an occupied bird nest in the open chimney, quite busy with comings and goings. In every room, we find evidence of the many lives, the many Benjamins and their families who lived here. The birds-eye maple floors are scored and dented in a hundred different patterns. The embossed wallpaper, once white, now dark ivory, is badly stained by water leaks. There are paler squares and rectangles where pictures once hung. In upstairs closets, we find messages scrawled in crayon or quill and ink: "I love Taddie Archer," and "Benny owes me thirteen pence," and "Papa is mean," the small protests and ardor of simple people. We know that numerous babies have been conceived and born in these rooms, have grown up and grown old and died in these rooms. These empty spaces are not so much hollow as hallowed by vanished stories. But they are not mine.

"Do you feel you know this house?" Billy asks as we pick our way carefully down the ominously creaking staircase.

"I feel something. But there's no name for it."

Outside in the yard, we come upon a trail of broken weeds leading into the maple trees behind the house.

"This looks recent," says Billy. "No farther back than last fall, but it could've been made this spring." He kneels and fingers a few crushed stalks. "There's winter film on it. So it wasn't this spring. I wonder where it leads."

"Just a deer trail," I say.

"I don't see any pellets. We used to have deer on our farm, but they never made this kind of trail. No, Francisco, people made it. And it's going somewhere. Let's take a look."

He leads the way into the trees. We have not gone more than a hundred yards when the trail comes to its end in a clearing. On the far side sits a log cabin rising from high grass. To its right and farther back is the glitter of sunlight on water.

The cabin door is unlocked. Going inside, we see little at first, for there is only a small window. As our eyes adjust, the details emerge: it is a single room furnished with plain wooden chairs, a plank table, and a cot. The smell of mildew and musk is strong, as well as the stench of decaying matter. On the table sits half a loaf of bread furred with blue mold. On a sideboard, unopened cans of beef stew, smoked salmon, liver paste. On the floor there's a littering of empty cans. The most telling of the debris is a heap of empty liquor bottles scattered haphazardly about the floor. More such bottles sit on the windowsill. One is open, half-consumed. It is vodka. For the most part the alcohol was whiskey. I inspect a frying pan sitting on the woodstove in the corner. My gorge rises when I bend over it and the stench of decay hits my nostrils. It looks like hamburger patties, fried to the point of near carbonation, leaving just enough meat to rot.

"Look at this, Francisco," Billy says in a whisper, pointing to the bed. On its rumpled vomit-stained sheets sits a handgun. He picks it up gingerly and turns it over and over in his hands. It's a revolver, full of bullets. He places it carefully back on the bed.

"What happened here?" I gasp.

"I don't know, but it looks like someone fell apart pretty badly."

"Maybe teenagers had a drunken party."

"It could be, but it seems more like one person stayed here awhile. He left and hasn't come back."

Billy bends and inspects a colored photograph, a page torn roughly from a magazine and tacked to the wall above the bed. He straightens abruptly, exhaling.

"What is it?" I ask.

"The Twin Towers," he murmurs.

"The what?"

"Nine-eleven. Remember I told you about it? Thousands of people died?"

"I'm sorry, I don't remember you telling me that."

"But I did ..." Then he closes his mouth on what he was about to say.

"Let's get out of here, Billy. This place is terrible. I think something bad happened here."

Billy and I step out into the clearing and walk around behind the cabin. Now we can see a small pond shining through a narrow belt of birch saplings. There's an old tumbledown woodpile there too, a chopping block and an axe leaning against it.

I stare at the scene, wondering. There are thousands of ponds in this part of the country, I tell myself.

Billy walks ahead to the edge of the water. He stares down into its depths. Without warning, he drops onto his haunches and removes his shoes and socks. Rolling up his pant legs, he wades into the pond.

"Don't go in there, Billy!" I yell, my voice high-pitched.

He pays me no mind and walks out farther. Suddenly he bends over and reaches in, soaking his sweater to the shoulder. Rising, he lifts up a square of green.

"Computer part," he says, and bends again to look for more.

"Bottles, lots of bottles."

Again he straightens, hands on hips. He is shaking his head, puzzled, as if to say, *Why am I doing this?*

Returning his attention to whatever he is seeing beneath the surface, he takes another step forward and stops.

He reaches into the depths and pulls up something small. Slowly he wades back to shore, pondering intently whatever he holds in his hands. After sloshing it clean with water, he looks at me somberly and holds out the object toward me. It is a child's toy, a tiny yellow racing car.

I choke and double over, coughing. Fear is a lump in my throat, my scalp is stinging, my skin convulses with chills. I cross my arms over my chest and hold my body tightly to keep it from shaking to pieces.

Billy quickly puts his socks and shoes back on and guides me away from the pond, with a firm hand on my arm. We have gone only a few steps when he halts and lets go of me. He is staring at a bundle of shadows beneath a tree.

"It's a body," I cry. "Don't look. Don't touch it."

Ignoring my pleading, he bends and pokes at whatever it is.

"It's men's clothes," he says. "Good clothes. Everything. A ski jacket, shirt, pants, underwear, socks and shoes—very good shoes."

He lifts each item one by one and sets it aside.

"Whoever put them here did it in midwinter," he murmurs, as if to himself. "Why?"

I am shivering uncontrollably now.

Billy checks the pockets of the trousers and the ski jacket. The clothes are wet, beginning to grow mold.

"Nothing," he says. Thinking again, he turns the jacket inside out and unzips an inner pocket. He extracts a man's wallet from it, opens it, and drops the jacket to the ground.

Back in the van, Roberta gets the engine running and the heater blowing.

"We can return to New York now," Billy tells her in a subdued voice.

"Okay, homeward bound it is. Is your friend all right?"

"He will be."

We retrace our route back through Tadd's Ford, up the hill and over the ridge to higher roads leading south. My shivering declines and then stops. The fear is receding.

"Did someone drown in that pond?" I ask Billy.

"No. No one drowned," he says.

He opens the damp wallet and shows me a driver's license. The photograph is my face. Beneath it is a name.

It is not Francisco de Goya.

7

East side, west side

It is close to midnight when Roberta drops us in front of an older five-story apartment building on Twelfth Street, in the East Village neighborhood of lower Manhattan. It is not unlike Billy's building, though better maintained. It is red brick with black trim and wide fire escapes. The front entrance is engraved glass panels in a brass frame. Inside the foyer, Billy bypasses the apartment buzzers. He finds a single key in the wallet's coin purse, and sure enough it opens the door to the lobby, which is brightly lit, floored with maroon carpet. A potted fern adds a dash of green. On the left wall is a bank of mailboxes.

"Do you remember it?" Billy asks.

I shake my head. If I once lived here, all traces are gone.

The building is a walk-up, no elevator, so Billy heads for the wide staircase and begins to climb, his thumping steps softened by runners. I follow with some trepidation, fearing unknown revelations that may soon be made manifest. Lacking a key to the residence of the man on the driver's license, we might learn nothing. I feel certain it would be better to remain ignorant.

Nevertheless, in fairness to Billy's determination, I let him lead me from floor to floor. Arriving at the top, we find ourselves in a corridor with four numbered doors. Billy checks the license again, and then strides to the end of the corridor, halting before 5-D.

He knocks.

I wait nervously a few steps back, ready to make a bolt for the staircase if need be.

He knocks again, then puts his ear to the door.

"Not a sound," he says.

Without knowing why I'm doing it, I step along the corridor to a wall-mounted fire extinguisher. Tucked behind its hose, invisible to the eye, sits a key. I retrieve it and hand it to Billy. He inserts it into the lock and turns it. A click, and the handle revolves. A push, and the door opens.

Ducking his head, Billy enters first. It is dark inside, though city lights are visible through curtainless windows on a far wall. They provide just enough illumination for me to grope along the entranceway to a switch. A single overhead light pops on above me. I close the door. Flicking another switch makes a lamp turn on in the room ahead of us.

"Hello," calls Billy. "Anyone home?"

Proceeding farther into the apartment we enter a living room, and stand there gazing about. Clearly, this is the residence of a moderately well-off person. The floors are shining hardwood, the furniture is avant-garde design but looks comfortable with thick cream-colored cushions. The lamps in the room are oval unglazed clay with golden shades. A single floor lamp is a metal rod with a white shade, embroidered with flower motifs.

The rug looks hand-woven, Scandinavian, warm hues of russet and rose.

To our right is a kitchen with a humming refrigerator and an electric range, its digital clock marking time in small glowing numerals. A teak table and four matching chairs are in the open dining area to the left. A green glass vase in the table's center contains wilted flowers, their black petals scattered about. One chair appears to have been used recently, then pushed back against the wall. A drift of letters, bills, flyers, is spread on the table before it. A ballpoint pen lies on top of an open bill.

The air is stale. Unlike the cabin at Tadd's Ford, there is no smell of decay, though the background odor is that of a place hastily vacated with chores left undone. There are unwashed dishes in the kitchen sink. Among the plates and cutlery are the shattered remnants of a drinking glass. An ice cube tray lies upside down on the floor, with faint water stains around it. A cardboard box beside the refrigerator is full of empty wine and liquor bottles. I open the fridge, releasing the smell of vegetable rot. I close it quickly.

Returning to the living room, I see that Billy has turned on all the lights. The teal-blue walls are hung with a few paintings and photographs, placed here and there, not crowding each other. Billy is standing between the two picture windows, gazing out at the apartments across the street. There is no balcony. He presses a button in the central frame, and wood-louvered shades descend slowly on tracks.

Covering one of the walls is a set of shelves, half of which hold books and the other half a music console, compact discs, freestanding photographs, and an amethyst bowl. In the bowl I find a set of keys.

Watching me, Billy asks, "Do you remember it now?"

"No, nothing," I whisper. "Whoever lives here is a stranger."

"He hasn't been here for some time ... maybe three or four months."

"It's not me, Billy. I don't know this person."

He says nothing, regarding me thoughtfully for a few moments. Looking up at the ceiling, he whistles.

"More than twelve feet high. Higher even than my place."

Two doors lead into rooms we have not yet explored. The first is a bedroom. Rumpled clothing is scattered about; dresser drawers yawn open. The double bed is a tangle of musty sheets, with blankets and pillows tossed to the floor. An empty liquor bottle lies there too. On the bedside table sits another. Jumbled around the bottle are a wristwatch with a metal-link band, an empty plastic pill container, an empty bullet box, and a cell phone. From out of nowhere, I recall how to turn it on. I press a button, and a screen glows, informing me that 138 new voice mail messages are waiting. A larger number of text messages remain unread. I turn off the device and drop it, filled with inexplicable loathing.

Now we enter the last room. It is as spacious as the living room, though not a square. It is a long rectangle with a wide window on the end wall, reaching nearly as high as the ceiling. An artist's easel sits in the center of the room, beside a table heaped with tubes of oil paint. Stretched canvases lean against the wall, unframed. The flooring is paint-spattered tiles. The atmosphere is pungent with evaporated turpentine and a lidless jar of linseed oil.

A canvas sits on the easel. The work is unfinished. It portrays a screeching human face in lurid colors; in the background are two narrow vertical boxes, like apartment buildings. Smoke is pouring from one of them; a small aircraft shape is heading at an angle toward the other. My stomach cramps painfully and I turn away from the image, only to see a large poster taped to a wall. It is a print of one of the frightening paintings we saw in the Metropolitan Museum of Misplaced Memories: a crazed monster with wide-open jaws devouring a naked, decapitated man.

Billy is observing me.

"Come on," he says, taking my arm, "Let's see if we can find out more."

Back in the living room I sit down on the couch and hold my head in my hands. It's too much. Submerged in this tsunami of things that are supposed to have meaning for me, I feel more than ever my dislocation. My life was a current in the continuous flow of time. I drowned in it, and now that I have risen to the surface I still do not know where I have come from or where I am going.

"It's not me, it's not me," I groan.

"Look at this," says Billy, kneeling beside me. He hands me a framed photo of a man seated at the stern of a sailboat. A triangle of white sail is visible in the foreground. In the background the blue horizon tilts at a wild angle. The man's hair is whipped by high winds, his head lifted high, his hand firm on the tiller. He is grinning, proud and in love, his eyes fixed on whoever held the camera.

"Written on the back is *Chesapeake Bay, 1988*," says Billy. "So it's not you, Francisco, but he sure *looks* like you."

I shake my head, at a loss for words.

"We've found out that your name isn't really Francisco, but we could still use it for a while, if you like."

"But I *am* Francisco. I know I'm Francisco."

In his kindliest tone, he lowers his voice and says, "Your real name is Paul Maximilian Davies. That's the name on the driver's license."

"No! It's a mistake."

"You were born in August—same as me—but the year is 1990."

"No, no, no! It's a big mistake!"

He hands me a postcard. It's an art reproduction, the red-suited boy with the jackdaw.

"My self-portrait," I say.

"It was painted by Francisco de Goya, all right," says Billy, "but it's a portrait of somebody else."

My mind swirls.

"Let's look at some other things I've found," he says. He helps me to my feet and takes me over to the bookshelves. There on a shelf stands a photo of a boy wearing a blue hockey sweater emblazoned with a white maple leaf. He is holding a hockey stick.

"This isn't me," I protest.

"No, it isn't, Francisco. Written on the back, it says he's a boy named James Davies. It's dated forty years ago. I'll bet he was your father."

He points to another photo, lying face down on the shelf. I pick it up:

A young man who looks like me is standing beside a very beautiful young woman, their arms around each other, their cheeks pressed together. The Eiffel Tower rises behind them. The woman is not floating sideways in the air. The frame's corner joints are broken; the glass is fractured. I slam it back down on the shelf.

Billy takes me next to the dining room table.

"Most of this mail is addressed to Paul Davies," he says. "Or to P.M. Davies. A couple of envelopes are addressed to 'Max'."

He points to the bill lying open on the table.

"It's a bank statement," says Billy. "Looks like your rent is deducted automatically every month, the utilities too."

I return to the couch and sit down. I hold my head in my hands. I rock my body forward and backward. I hit the sides of my skull with my fists.

"Don't do that," Billy pleads, kneeling and grabbing my wrists. "Stop hurting yourself, buddy. You gotta stop hurting yourself."

Eyes closed, heart racing, I fall back and rest my head on the cushions. He lets go of me. For a time we say nothing.

"I want to go home," I groan.

"This is your home," he replies.

"I want to go *home*," I insist.

Neither of us wears a wristwatch. The stove clock tells us it is nearly two in the morning. Billy goes about the room with a gold shopping bag in hand—*Hugo Boss*—filling it with small items. Still rocking, holding my head, I pay little attention to what he is taking. Finally, he appropriates the keys from the glass bowl and tells me it's time to go.

After locking up the apartment, we head down to the street in search of a taxi. Eventually, we hail one on First Avenue—that is, one that will stop for someone of Billy's stature. The sleepy-eyed cabbie hardly glances at him as he folds and squeezes his body into the backseat. I take the front. The taxi brings us across town to the west side and then north to Hell's Kitchen. The streets are relatively deserted, and we arrive home within half an hour.

It has been twenty hours since we embarked on our journey to Vermont. I crash onto my mattress and fall instantly asleep.

Later—I'm not sure how much later—I awake with a start. The room is still dark, so I must have slept only a few hours. I can hear Billy's breathing nearby. Restless, I get up and pad to the bathroom. Then I drink a glass of water at the kitchen sink. I cannot fall back to sleep, so I go out into the corridor and feel my way in the gloom toward my hidden room of the mind. I open the door and flick on the light switch. The chandelier ignites, blinding me. When I can see again, I notice the gold bag by the doorframe, empty. I throw it out into the hallway and close the door. The horse painting hangs where I last saw it. There are now two yellow racing cars side-by-side in the middle of the floor. Spread around the room, propped against the walls, are photographs, which Billy must have taken from P. M. Davies' apartment.

I turn off the light and sit down with my back against a wall. The window is a pale rectangle of night glow from the city. I close my eyes.

I see golden rings, pulled from fingers in anger, hurled through cold air, descending in an arc, hitting the ice as chariot wheels, rolling, zinging, spinning out of orbit, and wobbling into immobility with one last echoing zing. The rings splinter the ice, collapse the hard surface of the pond, and then pull down the water itself as the weight of a star sinks the invisible graph of time.

Into the great sea are hurled signs that contain unbearable memories. The sea takes them all and returns only a few of them, altered in shape and hue. There are currents and tides and storms in the sea, and because of this, one may find washed up on shores the half-forgotten words of love and hate.

When I was very young, the pond behind Grandma and Grandpa's house was my ocean. Mom and Dad brought me and Puck there for two weeks every summer. When our family of four drove up the lane, we erupted into our annual cheering at the first sight of our old friend, the big painted horse on the wall of the brewery. Then Grandma came out onto the porch, waving, her hands sometimes colored by the dyes she used to stain her weaving wool. Then Grandpa came out of the brewery doors wiping his hands on a cloth, ambling toward us with a grin and a Santa swagger and hands contorted into claws on his huge belly, ho-ho-ho, an old joke between us, bending over to embrace us, his shoulder-length gray hair tickling us, his beard long and scraggly, with two chin braids that he called "fairy twine".

When we could get away with it, Puck and I swam in the reservoir above the waterwheel, chilled and exhilarated by our first plunge, and slid down the old stone race onto the motionless wheel, which was locked against such forbidden mischief. We clambered down its slippery steps like monkeys, dropping into the creek below. Sputtering, shivering, happy, and a little scared, we scaled the mossy creek bank, our skin alabaster white with blue veins, as Grandma came out of the house with warm towels and hot muffins and scolding and nervousness about little boys drowning. Then we danced around in the hot sunlight with the crickets and grasshoppers, got dressed, and went into the brewery to watch Grandpa filling the Benny horse bottles, while Dad stretched out on a deck chair on the porch, reading his reports from the city, and Mom picked wildflowers for the supper table. There were woodpiles to topple too, and the pond, the pond, the great sea to wade across, up to our necks in the middle, feeling the warm muddy leaves on our toes, catching frogs in the shallows, skipping flat shale stones.

Every second year we came for a week at Christmastime. The brewery was shut down then, the hired men gone for the holiday, though the ales and lagers never ceased working on their own. The woods were white, the reservoir frozen over, all sounds hushed in the still air. The parlor was merry with the Christmas tree that Grandpa and Puck and I cut down in the woods and brought in on his ten-foot toboggan.

Grandpa and Dad would drink whiskey, and talk, and tell stories. Dad was different when he was here with Mom's family, more careful with his words. He laughed less, and sometimes stared off into space over the white-powdered mountains toward the south, where our city and our most-of-the-time home was.

"I can tell you about those days," Grandpa once said from his armchair by the woodstove, stroking his long gray beard, snapping his suspenders, patting his belly, while Puck climbed up his legs and draped himself over the huge chest and arms. "The Rolling Stones and the Grateful Dead."

I listened with one ear as I scooted my new racing car, a Christmas gift, around the ornate patterns on the threadbare rug. Mine was yellow; Puck's was blue.

"Not in front of the lads, please," said Dad with a short laugh, and Grandma looked worried.

"I was at Woodstock," Grandpa said, refilling their glasses. "Same beard, another body. Like a young god, I was. Girls going crazy over me, half of us naked, or all of us half-naked, I can't remember which. You should take notes. I'm a walking heritage site."

"It was pandemonium, Ben," said Grandma with a look.

"With an emphasis on demonium," said Mom with a sideways smile.

"You weren't even born, Sarah," Grandpa snapped at her.

"Let's change the subject," said Dad.

"Can't stand conflict, can you," Grandpa snarled.

"If you want conflict, I'll be happy to supply you some."

"Supply and demand, that's you all over."

"Jamie, Dad, take a break, will you," said Mom.

"No, no," said Grandpa. "It's time we had it out."

"Ben, you've had far too much to drink," Grandma interjected.

"In vino veritas," Grandpa shouted.

"In cannabis veritas," said Dad with a snort of disdain.

Puck and I looked back and forth between them.

Grandpa struggled to his feet, and Puck rolled off him onto the rug. My brother and I sat up on our knees, cars in our hands, wide-eyed, intrigued by the argument but somewhat astonished. Before now, we had never seen the grown-ups lose their tempers.

Grandpa hovered over Dad, his face contorted with rage, his finger jabbing:

"You sit there in your tower every day, sneering, looking down on the world. You call yourself a broker, which is a perfect name for what you do, breaking people's lives so others can make piles of money without lifting a finger."

"My company isn't into shark feeding frenzy," Dad answered, unruffled. "We specialize in low-risk investments, and we do everything we can to help middle- and low-income families, and keep them from getting hurt."

"Sure, sure, and you skim off your take."

"My take?" Dad replied without raising his voice. "My take—which I work hard for, by the way—feeds your daughter and your grandsons."

"She shoulda married an honest working man, like me."

"An honest working man like you, Ben? An honest Son of the Revolution like you?"

Grandma hastened out of the room in tears, off to the kitchen where she began moving crockery about, in preparation for an unneeded round of baking. Mom stayed seated on the arm of Dad's chair, looking up at her father with a pained expression.

"Max and Puck, go up to your room," my mother said quietly to my brother and me. "Get ready for bed and I'll tuck you in. You can read until I come."

We scurried up the staircase and into our room, a little alarmed but mostly excited by the drama. In seconds we were into our pajamas and threw ourselves onto the floor, pressing our ears to the circular heat vent above the parlor woodstove. We could see reflections of Christmas tree lights below. We could hear Grandpa's volume increasing, and our father's voice maintaining a steady calm.

"Which revolution was it, Ben?"

"Don't mock my ancestry," Grandpa bellowed.

"If you honored your ancestors half as much as I do, you wouldn't be doing what you do behind the scenes with your—"

"What are you talking about?" Grandpa interrupted.

"I'm talking about an honest merchant like you," my father continued, "with the best darn revolutionary grow-up crop between Manchester and Montpelier."

Silence.

"You call the cops on me and I'll blow your head off," Grandpa shouted.

"Dad!" cried my mother's voice.

We heard boots thumping out of the house, a door slamming.

"Oh, Jamie, you provoked him."

"I do believe, honey, that your father provoked me."

"But you *know* what he's like when he's been drinking."

"And smoking. And selling."

My mother broke into sobs.

"O sweetie, sweetie, I'm sorry," my father murmured, and I knew he was hugging her, because that is what he said whenever he put his arms around her and held her close.

My father's footsteps climbed the stairs. His head peeped into our room; he smiled reassuringly and sat down on the edge of the old four-poster where Puck and I slept together.

"Dad, is Grandpa mad?" I asked.

"It was just an argument, boys. A little tiff. Grownups sometimes have 'em. Nothing to worry about."

He kissed us, and leaned over and turned out the bunny lamp.

"Love you, Max. Love you, Puck."

"Love you, Dad."

Leaving the room, he pushed the old mangy rocking horse, making its runners *squeak-squeak-squeak*. We laughed, because it was our ritual. He left the door open for light.

Later our mother came up. We could tell from her voice that she had been crying.

"I love you so much, boys."

"Love you too, Mom," we recited in unison.

"Night-night, now. Sleep tight."

"Don't let the bedbugs bite," we giggled.

She went out, forgetting to push the rocking horse.

Sometime later, after Puck-boy was sound asleep, I got up to make a final trip to the toilet down the hall. I heard my mother and grandmother conversing in low voices in the parlor. Passing my parents' bedroom, I heard through the open doorway my father talking to someone in the dark.

"He's sleeping it off in his cabin," said my father.

A silence followed.

"No, I don't think he's dangerous," my father said.

Another silence, and I realized he was speaking into his cell phone.

"He's a sad and angry man who hates anything that threatens his addictions and his pride. Not to mention his illegal profits."

A pause ~

"I'm sorry. I didn't mean to sound so harsh. But if I say anything that he interprets even remotely as a slight on his twisted honor, he counterattacks in overkill mode. Sometimes it's a preemptive strike. I don't know how Dorothy puts up with it."

~

"Summers are unbearable, all of us pretending he's gone mushroom picking in the woods when he's really somewhere out there tending his secret garden. I just don't know what to do. Is he selling it to kids? Is he hooking innocent gullible people, or just supplying his cronies? If only I had a flamethrower."

~

"Yes, you're probably right. I don't think he ever really recovered from the war. Too proud to get help."

~

"I'm trying not to be. I'm really trying not to judge him."

~

"I'll surely give her a hug from you and Mom."

Now I realized that my father was talking with his own father, my other grandfather, who lived in Maryland. We called him Granddad, not Grandpa.

"She's doing her best to love them, not so easy with parents like that. It never has been easy, which is why she left home so young. She's a real hero, Dad. She's the best thing that ever happened to me in my life—her and the boys."

~

"Yup. See you at New Year's."

~

"I love you too—very much."

I tiptoed back to bed.

In the morning, everything was fine between the adults.

Puck was called Puck because my mother loved a character in a Shakespeare play and my father loved hockey. My little brother's name, in fact, was Philip. Mine was Paul. We were Puck and Max. We lived in a split-level house in the Bedford-Stuyvesant neighborhood of Brooklyn, so close to New York City that it was virtually part of it. Dad commuted every weekday to an office where he worked, a soaring structure, two structures actually, which we could see from our front porch.

"Those towers are the tallest in the city," I would tell my school friends, stating the obvious, pointing across the East River to the monoliths.

"Probably in the whole world," a friend would say.

"My dad works there," I would brag.

Puck was five years younger than me, a cute little guy with a goofy smile, always begging me to pack him around on my back. Strangely, I never felt—or perhaps never remembered—any sibling rivalry between us. I always loved him. I taught him to climb monkey bars in the park near our home. I once got a bloody nose stopping a bully from hurting him, and felt quite proud of it. I read stories to him. I quieted his fears when he was scared of the dark.

On Sundays in summer our family sometimes rode a bus into Manhattan, and my brother and I sailed our toy boats on a pond in Central Park, the boats Dad helped us make. In winter we learned to skate on a frozen lake near the zoo.

When I was ten years old we spent our last Christmas with my Vermont grandparents. My grandfather had given up his illegal trade, because my grandmother threatened to call the police if he didn't (I overheard my mother tell my father), and moreover he was drinking less. Throughout the visit both he and Dad made valiant efforts to get along, keeping their conversation to less personal topics, such as the masculine currency of local political news, the benefits of certain tools, and ponderings over the financial stability of the brewery. My father, who had little money to spare, offered to help out with a loan. My grandfather adamantly refused and went into a funk of wounded pride. For the sake of the women, we did not depart immediately for the city but determined to tough it out a few more days.

It was my custom each year to borrow a broom from Grandma and sweep snow off the pond ice, making a path carefully toward the center, hoping to see down through the glass to the secret life of the bottom. I loved the thrill of splintering ice, though it never failed to support my weight. However, that winter was warmer than usual, and the ice deceived me. At first it splintered nicely beneath my rubber boots, fractures spreading around me like a spider web, and then without warning it collapsed.

I plunged in up to my neck. Panicking, I was sure I would drown. Panting, yelping, I struggled back toward shore, pushing the floating fragments aside, until I reached the shallows and broke through the remaining ice shelf with every step. Back in the kitchen, after gasping out my story, I was unabashedly stripped and dried and dressed in warm clothes, and set on a chair by the fire. When the last of my terror had been wiped away by the outpouring of adult sympathy and anxious admonishments, not to mention a mug of steaming hot chocolate, I felt that the accident just might have been worth it. The only loss was my beloved yellow racing car. It was now lying at the bottom of the pond.

A few weeks after my eleventh birthday, my father woke my brother and me very early one morning and told us to get dressed, to "hop to it," as he liked to say. Mom was downstairs making breakfast. She and Dad and Puck would take the bus into the city, where they would share the special treat of strawberry milkshakes and doughnuts in his office. Afterward, Mom would take Puck to his monthly appointment with a downtown speech therapist, who was helping him with his stuttering. My own stuttering had all but disappeared, but Puck's was still pronounced.

That day, he was in one of his fussy moods, tromping barefoot around the bedroom, aimless and sullen and complaining that he had no socks.

"You've got plenty of socks in your dresser drawer," I said.

"I d-d-don't want to g-go!" he said.

"You have to go," I told him, plopping him onto the edge of the bed. I fetched his favorite socks, pale green with red stripes. One had a big hole in the heel, but neither of us cared. I pulled them onto his feet just as Mom yelled from downstairs, "We're going to be late!"

"I d-d-don't want to g-go, Max," he said, his lips trembling, eyes filling with tears.

"Don't be silly, Puck. You get Mom and Dad all to yourself, and I have to go to school."

"I'm s-s-scared."

"There's nothing to be scared of. You've been to Dad's office lots of times. Now put on your shoes or you'll get heck for making Mom and Dad late."

After they rushed out the door to catch the bus, I finished eating my cereal, brushed my teeth, read a Spider-Man comic, did the last bits of homework, and stuffed my books into my backpack. That done, I went out and locked up the house behind me. The morning was bright and cool, with a hint of early autumn in the air, a few leaves prematurely turning color. I ran all the way to school, leaping over cracks lest I break my mother's back.

We were minutes into the first class of the day when the school principal opened the door to our room and called the teacher out into the hallway. When she came back in, she went straight to the window and stared out, one hand to her chest and the other to her throat.

"Boys and girls," she said in a tone of deliberate calm, "there has been a terrible accident in New York, a plane crash. The principal has called an assembly, and we are to go to the gymnasium now."

As we took our places on the gym bleachers, my fellow students and I felt excited by the drama of a terrible accident happening so close to home. Giggling, whispering head-to-head, we hoped it would be a bad one, like a thrilling disaster movie.

We all fell silent as the principal stepped onto the court and turned to face us. A jet plane had crashed into an office tower in Manhattan, he said, and it now looked like many lives had been lost. Firefighters and police were rushing to the scene. Our families would want to talk with us and have us close to them as soon as possible. Classes were suspended for the day. Students who lived nearby could walk home, and those who lived farther away could start boarding the school buses. However, any who wanted to stay here were welcome to do so—teachers would remain on duty.

I ran back to my classroom, grabbed my jacket off its hook, and bolted for the hallway, elated by this unprecedented freedom and by the prospects of learning more about the disaster. As I passed the big window of the secretary's office, I saw several staff members crowding around a television set, but I didn't linger. I was out the front door and down the steps in a flash, racing for a better view of Manhattan. I saw smoke rising above the Brooklyn rooftops in the direction of the city, but it was not until I reached our house that I was able to get a better view. From the front steps I saw that the smoke was rising over the lower end of Manhattan.

I unlocked the door and entered our home, worrying a little that the fire was in the general area where my father worked. But I felt sure that disasters never really happened to people like us. Remembering that on the previous weekend Dad had been replacing damaged roof shingles, I went out through the kitchen door into the backyard, where I knew he had left the extension ladder leaning against the porch. I climbed up onto the porch top and crossed it to the roof over the garage, which was three feet higher. A short jump brought me to the next level, and from there I could pull myself onto the highest part of the roof, above the second-story bedrooms.

Sitting down on the tiles near the peak, I gazed across the East River, and my heart began hammering, my mouth dropped open. Not long after, I heard the faint ringing of the telephone in the house below. It rang and rang and would not stop.

I saw the first tower slowly descend into the canyons of the city, and a few seconds later I heard the roar. The other tower continued to discharge massive clouds of smoke, but it was standing. I was sure that my father worked in it. I knew that his office was very high up, somewhere close to the top. Maybe helicopters would come for him. Maybe Mom and Puck were at the therapist's.

The phone rang again and again. It would not stop ringing.

I climbed back down the way I had come and entered the kitchen, my legs vibrating, my hands shaking. I picked up the receiver and put it to my ear.

"Sarah, is that you?" said a woman's voice. "Sarah? Sarah? Talk to me, honey!"

"It's me," I choked out. "It's Max."

"Max, Max, is your mother there?"

It was my Grandma Franklin's voice. She and Grandpa didn't have a phone, so I knew she was calling from the pay phone in the corner store in Graniteville, where they usually went for mail.

"Is your mom home, Max?"

"No," I said and burst into tears. "She went to work with Dad and Puck."

"Honey, try to concentrate. Try to think. What did you say?"

"Mom went to Dad's office with Puck."

I stammered out the rest of what I knew, though it wasn't much, and as I related the details I began to feel a monumental shadow approaching me—a sense that the impossible might have entered my life.

Grandma began to cry, a wretched, broken kind of sobbing. It was a horrible sound. I couldn't stand listening to it. I put the receiver back on its cradle and went into the living room. I'm not sure why I did it, but I took a framed photo off the mantelpiece, the one of Dad when he was a kid in hockey gear. I sat down on the couch and stared at it.

The phone rang and rang. It quit and then rang again. And again.

Finally I responded to one of the calls. It was my Granddad from Maryland. He asked the same questions Grandma from Vermont had asked, and I told him what I knew. His voice was very calm. I heard sobbing in the background, my other grandmother.

"Are you there alone, Max?" Granddad asked.

"Yes."

"Are the neighbors at home? Go next door and ask if you can stay with them. No, wait, forget that! Don't leave the house, so we won't have to look for you. Roger that?"

"R–roger th–that," I stammered. This phrase was the old code we shared, always delivered with the smile of a captain confidently entrusting a mission to a junior officer.

"And don't turn on the television. Promise me?"

"Okay."

"Good," he said, strangely. "We're getting in the car right now, and we should be with you by one P.M. Are you frightened?"

"N–no," I said, drying my eyes on my sleeve. I was indeed frightened, but did not want to admit it.

"We'll see you in three hours, Max. We love you very much. Don't go anywhere."

"I won't."

I sat waiting in the silent room, a space full of absence. I heard a second roaring in the air. It seemed to go on and on before tapering off.

I turned on the television. Mesmerized, I watched jets flying into the towers, fireballs, debris, shattered windows, people falling. Again and again and again. Channel after channel, the people leaping from windows, falling through space. Interviews with crying people, bleeding people, firemen, policemen in shock, business people like Dad covered with dust and describing body parts on the sidewalk. The north tower slowly going down, people on the streets running away from the choking storm clouds of dust.

Voices called from the front entrance hall, and Mr. and Mrs. Beamish walked into the living room. They lived next door. I cut their lawn in the summer and ate a lot of their homemade cookies. Mrs. Beamish was a retired nurse; Mr. Beamish was an administrator for the

Brooklyn city bus line. Like a couple of other families on our street, they were black people. Their grandchildren sometimes came to visit from North Carolina. I liked one them especially, a boy named Jeffer Beamish, because we were the same age and he was witty in the way Granddad Davies was witty. He made me laugh all the time. He was also an incredibly fast runner, and we enjoyed racing each other around the block. I was always the loser, but I didn't much mind because the challenge made me push harder against my limits. Any narrowing of the gap between us was a triumph. We argued sometimes over whether Batman or Spider-Man was the better superhero.

"Where is your mom, Max?" Mrs. Beamish asked, sitting down on the couch beside me.

"I don't know. She went with Dad and Puck to the office."

"Your father's office?"

"Yes."

"O Lord," she whispered. "O Jesus."

Mr. Beamish quickly crossed the room and turned off the television set. He sat down on the other side of me and put an arm around my shoulder.

"Don't worry, now, don't worry," he murmured with little pats. "They're saying on the news that a lot of people got out in time."

Mrs. Beamish went into the kitchen and returned with a glass of milk for me. I took a few sips and left it aside. Later she brought sandwiches on a plate, which none of us felt like eating. Mr. Beamish answered the constantly ringing phone, and explained the situation to callers, telling what he knew.

Shortly after noon my grandfather phoned again, to say that he would be delayed. The tunnels and bridges into New York had been closed. He was going to drive farther north to the bridge at Tappan Zee, cross the river there if he could, and double back to Queens and then enter Brooklyn from the east.

There was a third phone call from him around two in the afternoon.

"No, sir, James and Sarah haven't called," I heard Mr. Beamish say. "There could be any kind of reason for that. Maybe they're just fine, and it's the overloaded lines or they can't get access to a phone."

A silence. I listened to the clock ticking too loudly on the kitchen wall.

"Uh-huh, it was more than an hour and a half between the plane hitting the north tower and when it went down. There was time for plenty of people to get out."

Another silence as he nodded and nodded, listening intently to my grandfather.

"We have to hope," he said at last.

More silence.

"The boy is hurting, but he knows you're coming."

Later, Mr. Beamish got up and crossed the room to the television set, intending to turn it back on. His wife stopped him with a look.

"It's broken," I said, and began to wail.

The towers, the world, my family, my life were broken, and nothing would ever put them back together again.

Mrs. Beamish sat down beside me and drew me to herself, holding me tightly. And we were still in that position when my Maryland grandparents walked into the room hours later.

During the next few days, I slept no more than an hour or two at a time, curled in the fetal position. I wet the bed. The images I had seen on the television played again and again in my mind, and in half sleep I saw my father and mother and little brother plummeting through fire, holding hands as they fell, and smashing on the sidewalk below. I woke up screaming. Later we would learn that they perished inside the tower during its collapse. When it fell they may already have been dead from fire and smoke. They had not jumped. It made no difference to me when I heard the truth, because my mind had conflated the mixture of reality and hallucination into a single memory, imprinting in me an image that would always represent the way they had died.

There was no funeral, because there were no bodies— only ashes, my parents' and brother's ashes mingled with those of thousands of other people. Ashes in my mouth, ashes in my waking mind, ashes in my dreams. There was a memorial Mass in my grandparents' church in Maryland, standing room only. Throughout the ceremony I sat and stood and knelt between the two pillars of my father's parents, conscious that the bottom had dropped away beneath my feet, and yet aware that I was held up by their sure hands. I felt panic at moments, but mostly I was numb, watching it all as if I were seeing through a thick glass. I did not consider what they were feeling, to have lost a son, a beloved daughter-in-law, and a grandson. They were strong; I was demolished. I wanted to hide, but wave after wave of sympathy would not let me.

My Maryland grandparents were now my legal guardians and thus were first in line to take me in. My dad's several brothers and sisters made offers, but they and their families lived in other parts of the country, in the Midwest and the Deep South. I had met my cousins over the years, at family reunions and weddings, but I didn't know them well. In the end, the choice was mine. I decided to live with my grandparents.

On the mantel of their fireplace sat a photograph of a young man in a sailboat. His hair whipped about in a high wind, his hand was firmly on the tiller, his eyes turned to look with a powerful, bursting love at whoever had taken the photograph.

"Your mother took that snapshot out on Chesapeake Bay," my grandmother explained. "Your dad loved her so much, Max, so much," she said, her voice trailing off.

Grandma Dorothy soon came to visit, traveling by Greyhound all the way from Vermont. She was mourning terribly and looked unwell, her skin yellow gray. She brought me a gift, a scarf she had made for the coming winter, hand-carded wool, her own dye, her own knitting.

"Did you know that before you were born, Max, your mom used to write plays for the Little Theater we were involved in then, in Stowe?"

I did know it, because from kindergarten onward my mother had written plays for my school concerts, and the background stories of her life were plentiful. But I shook my head, *No, I didn't know*, because I instinctively understood that Grandma needed to give me something of my missing mother, to make her present somehow.

"Yes, and that's where she met your dad. They were playing the lovebirds in *Our Town*, and it wasn't long before the acting became the real thing."

At night, I could hear her in the guest room, trying to suppress the sound of her crying. She hugged me too often, squeezed me too hard, dropped tears on me, forcing me to tighten my body in self-defense, and once to struggle out of her embrace. She did not stay long.

"How is Grandpa?" I asked during the car ride to the bus station.

"He is feeling very sad, Max," Grandma replied, delicately, precisely, with her habitual compassion.

At the station the three grieving grandparents and the single orphan all hugged each other.

"Come and see us soon," Grandma said as she stepped up into the bus. Though there were plenty of empty seats on the side of the aisle that was closer to us, she found one on the opposite side. It puzzled me that she didn't choose a seat with a window view of the three of us standing on the concrete ready to wave good-bye. As the bus drew away, all we could see was her silhouette, hunched over, enclosed within her loss.

8

The end of the world as I knew it

In early November, two months after the catastrophe, Granddad Davies and I drove up to Vermont in his 1975 ruby-red Ford station wagon, a gas-guzzler in near-mint condition. He had been busy during the previous month, beginning legal work on my behalf, a bureaucratic complexity that he did not discuss with me. He had also closed up the house in Bedford-Stuyvesant and listed it with a real estate agent.

We stopped at my family home on the way north. I dropped in to see the Beamishes and cried in their arms, though I had fully intended not to. I asked them to say hi from me to their grandson Jeffer in North Carolina, and I jotted down on a piece of paper my new address in Maryland.

"He could visit me there," I said.

Granddad and I walked together from room to room in the empty house, saying nothing, both of us afraid of our emotions, both of us focused on memories in our minds. He unlocked the garage, where the furniture was stored until it could be sold, nothing with highly personal meaning other than an armless "nursing rocker" that had belonged to his great-grandmother. This and a few cardboard boxes we loaded into the back of the station wagon.

There were dustings of snow on the hilltops of northern Massachusetts and southern Vermont, heavier falls as the route took us higher into the Appalachians, though the valley bottoms remained green. Wherever deciduous forests dominated the landscape, they were leafless gray washes with touches of the last purple oak and yellow beech. The sky was deep blue.

I did not know what to expect as we drove through Tadd's Ford and along the fork to my grandparents' place. I did not break into cheers at the first sight of the great sorrel horse. It was the first time I had ever come here without my parents. The smoke rising from the chimney of the old white house lifted my spirits, however, and the reunion with Ben and Dorothy was moving, if somewhat awkward. Grandma cried, and Grandpa grew teary, though silent and holding himself back. He initiated a hug, which I appreciated, though it seemed different from the hugs he had given me throughout my childhood. It was brief, tentative, lacking a smile or eye contact. He cast a contemptuous look at the huge station wagon, but made no comment.

My grandfathers had met only once or twice since my parents' wedding. On some primitive level I knew that they were not comfortable with each other and strained to maintain the courtesies. They had made fundamentally different lives for their families, and while both had been military men in their younger years, this bond was fragile. Ben had suffered something hard and bad, which had never been explained to me, and I now recalled my father's words about my mother's father not recovering from a war he had played a part in. Granddad, by contrast, had retired from the U.S.

Navy as a well-loved, much-admired ship's captain. He was unfailingly kind by nature, a listening person with several close friends who were humorous, reflective men like himself, ever concerned with others and never self-preoccupied. Everyone in the older generation called him Robbie, an affectionate diminutive bestowed on him, without loss of respect, by his wife Helen and his peers. For some years during my father's childhood, Granddad had been a visiting lecturer at Canada's Royal Military College. Like my father, he was a hockey man—hence the Toronto Maple Leafs sweater my father had worn in the photo. He had university degrees and read heavy books. He was a patriot of a certain thoughtful kind, loved the sea and sports, and above all, his family. He was strong, my Maryland grandfather, but never mean.

After a supper dominated by amicable clichés, and a somewhat-guarded discussion about the new war on terror, the men went into the parlor for a glass of whiskey. I stayed to wash dishes with my grandmother. She looked worse than ever. After carefully piling her antique plates into the cupboard, I filled the woodbox with a few armloads of birch while she sat down on the chair by the stove and picked up her knitting basket.

"Remember the time I fell through the ice, Grandma?"

"How can I forget!" she said with a smile, then peered intently at her project, counting stitches.

"Are they treating you all right down there, Max?" she asked.

"Yes," I answered truthfully, wondering if she would have preferred me to live with her and Ben.

"I go to a new school," I added by way of detail.

"Is it a good place?"

"Uh-huh."

"Any new friends?"

"Uh-huh," I said, nodding, though it was not true. I still saw airplanes crashing into the towers several times a day, and I didn't want to talk about it to the other kids my age. Somehow I knew that my childhood had ended, while theirs continued onward seamlessly.

"Do they make you go to church?"

"Uh-huh," I said glumly, "they do."

"And how is that working out? Do you mind?"

"I don't mind."

And I didn't, because it was simply what my new family did, though I sat numbly through their services week after week, staring at the alien decorations, the crucifixes, the various sufferings on the walls, while towers fell and fell and fell in my mind.

"How is Grandpa?" I asked her.

"He's not doing very well, Max. He's drinking again, far too much for his health. And the ..."

"And the cannabis crop?" I asked.

She looked up at me sharply.

"There's no crop. He doesn't do that anymore— grow it, I mean. But he spends a lot of time smoking in the cabin by the pond. It makes him sicker and sicker, but he can't stop himself."

Stunned by her candidness, I had no idea how to respond.

"He loses his temper without it," said Grandma with a weighted sigh. "It might be better to give him some elbow room, Max. Stay back a pace or two and stick by your Granddad Davies while you're here."

This did not make any sense to me, but I told her I would.

"He says hard things, you see. Things he doesn't really mean. He's hurting and angry at life. Angry at the way things have gone in *his* life."

I nodded, yearning to change the subject.

"We brought you some of Mom's stuff," I said.

"Oh, that's very nice," she answered distractedly.

I went into the parlor, where I found Granddad bringing the last of the cardboard boxes in from the car. He had set them in a pile by Grandpa's armchair and was explaining what they contained.

"Half of her photos are for you and Dorothy, but I thought Max should have a selection to remember her by.

"And this is her little computer, one of the earlier models. She bought it so she could compose her plays on it. It's a lot easier to edit with one of these machines. There must be three or four dozen plays here. I was also wondering if you'd like to have her old Underwood typewriter. Anyway, I brought it along for you."

"We have a typewriter," said Grandpa, refilling his glass.

"And a box of her letters to Jamie from their summer theater days. I hope it's all right, I kept back a few for Max."

"Fine by me."

And so it went. Before long, my eyes were drooping. I stood and said good night to the men and went upstairs to the bedroom where Puck and I had always slept. I pushed the rocking horse and listened to it squeak. I undressed and crawled under the quilt. Lying in the dark, listening to the drone of my grandfathers' voices in the room below, I tried to remember the best things about Puck. I wanted to cry. But at the moment I was capable of neither and fell right asleep.

Granddad and I spent the next morning visiting with Grandma in the kitchen, drinking tea and nibbling her date squares, listening to her stories about my mother. Grandpa was nowhere to be seen, and my grandmother had no idea where he had gone off to. At one point I wandered into the brewery hoping to find him, and was surprised to see no one working in the building, though the vats were fermenting their beer as they should.

Deciding to have a look at the pond, I went around behind the house and through the saplings into the small field beyond. And there I found Grandpa just coming out of his cabin with a cigarette clenched in his lips. He was hunched over and stumbling, carrying a cardboard box. He did not at first see me.

He took my mother's computer out of the box and placed it on a chopping block beside the woodpile. He lifted an axe in both hands and swung it down hard on the top of the computer, which bounced and cracked. I yelped with surprise, but he did not hear me as he smashed it again and again. Enraged, snarling, gritting his teeth on ugly words, he picked up the pieces and hurled them into the middle of the pond. His chest and belly heaving, he pulled a long black bottle from his trouser pocket, put it to his mouth, and clamped his teeth on the cork, which he popped out and spat onto the ground. Tilting his head back, he gulped down the bottle's contents. When it was empty, he lifted his arm to throw it into the pond.

"Grandpa," I called nervously, "it's almost lunchtime. Would you like to come in and have lunch with us?"

He stared at me, scowling, not replying, his body weaving a little. Staggering over to me, he shoved the beer bottle into my hands.

"Here," he growled, "cash it in for a two-cent refund."

I was frightened by his mood but glad to receive the bottle. On its label was a sorrel horse.

His mouth twisted bitterly, his eyes snapping with hatred.

"You killed them, you little parasite!" he seethed.

Now my fear became terror and I backed away from him.

"Get out!" he bellowed. "Go back to your nice safe life, you little accident!"

I turned and ran to the house.

Bursting into the kitchen, I stammered incoherently.

"Grandpa's m-m-mad," I said, bursting into tears. "He y-y-yelled at me. He t-t-told me to g-g-get out."

Stricken, Grandma got up from her chair and came to me with outstretched arms. Granddad rose to his feet, his lips tightening.

"What happened, Max?" he asked.

"He told me to g-go. He said I k-k-killed Mom and Dad."

"What!" Grandma cried. "Oh, nonsense, nonsense, Max. He didn't mean it."

Without a word, Granddad went outside through the kitchen door, his pace slow and deliberate, his face as quiet as a grave. I had rarely seen this before—once, when he heard a neighbor beating his wife and went over to stop it. And another time when his Irish setter died and he buried it in his backyard. And lastly when he went up to read from scripture during the memorial Mass for my family.

Ten minutes later he was back, just as slow, just as determined.

"You didn't hurt him, Robbie," Grandma pleaded.

"No, I didn't hurt him, Dorothy. I said a few things he'll have to ponder, maybe have to live with the rest of his life. But I didn't lay a hand on him. He went off into the woods when I was finished." Granddad turned to me. "Okay, Max, let's get our gear together and push off. Homeward bound, lad. Hop to it."

Out in the yard, we made a messy disjointed farewell with Grandma. Granddad hugged her a long time and she clung to him. He kissed her forehead. We drove down the lane waving good-bye, my head out the window, watching her wave back until we rounded a corner of the fork and were gone from her eyes. It was the last time I ever saw her.

Grandma Franklin died of cancer the following spring. Ben died the year after that. By then, the brewery had closed down, neglected and finally bankrupt. I never learned what caused my grandfather's death, or perhaps Granddad Davies chose not to tell me. In any event, he died as a long-term guest in a commune of young people trying to live close to nature, a category that included the cannabis plant. Hard drugs were looked down upon by these sensitive, creative people, who on the whole meant well and had some good ideas about gardening and self-sufficiency (I was later to learn), but their attachment to certain altered states of consciousness induced by their chosen natural ingredients tended to cripple their dreams. What most of them were really looking for was a stable family and community, a human birthright that was natural enough but declining in our world.

Ben was buried somewhere out in the hills, after a spiritual rite performed over his body by the community. In my late teens I visited these people, wanting to find his grave and reach some kind of closure, but the ones still living there had forgotten where they'd buried him. They were hospitable to me, and remembered a few details of his life, most significantly that he had once owned a brewery and had given it all away in order to embrace their "lifestyle". He was remembered as something of a sage, and one person went so far as to declare that Ben was Gandalf reincarnated. I left soon after hearing this and spent some time at Dorothy's gravestone in a Montpelier cemetery. There I remembered her countless acts of kindness to me and my brother, her inexplicable patience, her goodness that had so often lacked focus or direction.

During my high school years I tried to imitate my absent father. Granddad taught me how to sail a little racing skiff, which we rented on weekends during warmer months. I toyed with the idea of joining the navy, but never did. With the small allowance I received from the trust fund my grandfather set up for me from my parents' estate, I tried my hand at being an amateur broker, operating through a real broker. The investments earned a little money and lost a good deal more, and I gave it up.

Track and field consumed my extracurricular activities, and running became my drug of choice. I ran in the Boston Marathon three times, finishing among the hundred frontrunners. Jeffer Beamish and I were reunited at one. He had finished far in front of me, and I was proud of him for it. Afterward, we shared a coffee together and caught up on our personal histories. He was an honors student and was planning to attend college, majoring in biology. I was lagging in my final year of high school with no plans for the future, and not much else to say for myself. We had become strangers to each other.

When I was eighteen I took an art class, and then as the thing took hold of me I signed up for summer classes offered by local artists. It was landscapes at first, and I discovered I had a flair for it. Little by little the natural talent grew. I won a prize for a watercolor that was a blatant imitation of Winslow Homer (subconscious on my part, understood in hindsight), though no one seemed to notice, or perhaps did not want to discourage me.

Now and then I would take the bus to Washington, D.C., and spend a day in the National Gallery. More often I went to New York City, mainly to spend a few days in the Metropolitan Museum. I was charmed by the Chagalls and passionately loved the Goya collection. I revered Homer's seascapes and those of the darker, brooding Albert P. Ryder. And I developed a nostalgic attachment to early American folk art, for the pure pleasure of it, which may have been my sole cultural inheritance from the Franklins. I never revisited Bedford-Stuyvesant, and managed to avoid lower Manhattan altogether.

In all my activities I preferred to be alone. Though I had friends, I did not speak to them about my loss, nor did I develop any degree of intimacy founded on trust. I did love Robbie and Helen, actually very much, though with an undercurrent of fear that I would lose them too someday. I chewed endlessly on what Grandpa had meant when he called me an accident, and why he said I had killed my own parents. It took a couple of years before I could bridge the topic with Granddad, determined to face the painful truth, whatever it might be. But my grandfather was as perplexed as me, and conjectured that Ben had blurted the most devastating thing that had popped into his distorted mind, and that it had no basis in truth. It was "catharsis of the most irrational kind," Granddad reassured me.

He became skilled at engaging me in thoughtful discussions about life and destiny, fate and providence, vocation and suffering, human struggle and religious faith, and so forth. He never lectured. Rather, he probed and pondered and evoked my own thoughts on various matters.

Once, when I captured him in his study for the purpose of making a pen-and-ink portrait of him, he put on his reading glasses and wrote quietly on a tablet while I drew his likeness. When I showed him the finished drawing and gave it to him to keep, he beamed.

"It's great, Max ... it's masterful."

He handed me the sheet of paper he had been writing upon.

"Not quite a fair exchange," he said with a smile. "Just some of my jottings, but maybe you could tuck it away for a rainy day."

He had written:

Men are accustomed to making objective assessments of devastating situations, as long as they are not immersed in them. Rare is he who maintains objectivity in the midst of personal affliction.

*

In a season of high emotions, declarations and avowals tend to become adamant. By such, many a man seeks to reassure himself that a path opens before him through the forest of adversity. He asserts his inner need against a battering of confusions. He becomes resistant to all questioning. Yet in his declarations of certainty he reveals his uncertainty.

For some, this takes shape in the mind as dreams of ambition fulfilled, earthly securities seized at all costs and held at all costs. For the best of men, it is a yearning forward to a better self. In most, if not all, there reign the soundless alarums of fear. By love do we cast out fear. By love do we become who we are.

I thanked my grandfather for what he wrote. Though I did not understand it, I felt no inclination to try to grasp its meaning. But I wondered over the odd use of tenses, which was quite unlike him: *Become* who we already *are*?

Grandma Helen was less philosophic and less articulate about life, but she had a lot of wisdom. Hers was primarily the way of the heart, as was my Grandma Franklin's, though the Davies women were stronger and less anxious. She and Granddad prayed a lot for my conversion, I suspect, but I did not feel ready for any kind of commitment, least of all to an omnipotent God.

I was not blind to the factors in my emerging personality. I sensed that the damage done by the end of my world would have long-term effects, but I felt that I could live with them—with myself. Of course, there were moments of happiness, and yet these were most often the fruit of solitary achievements. I had no human loves, though I felt strong attraction to a few young women in my school and at the local parish, which I continued to attend dutifully until the end of my high school years.

On my twenty-first birthday, Granddad sat me down in his study and informed me that I had "come of age" and that my inheritance from my parents was entirely at my disposal. It was not a grand sum, he explained, but enough to fund a college education. Since my graduation from high school, I had wandered in a state of indecision through courses at a community college, studying art history, psychology, and conversational French and Spanish. I had also taken a few studio classes under professional artists.

"Have you given any more thought to what you would like to do in life?" he now asked.

I had indeed.

Thus it was that I awoke one morning in a third-floor flat in the rue de Babylone in the Saint-Germain-des-Prés district of Paris. I was not enrolled in any college or institute, but as the privileged recipient of a freedom that very few people on the planet enjoyed, I was determined to develop my art independently, without burdensome debt or anxiety. If I wanted to, I could live the rest of my life, so to speak, in the temple of the Louvre. Where New York's cultural life had been nearly inexhaustible, the queen of cities was meta-inexhaustible. For four months I soaked it up to the point of saturation, and then I began to paint.

My flat was a two-room affair under the eaves of an ancient stone tenement. One of the rooms contained my cot, hot plate, and sink, and the other was a bare space that I used as a studio. I purchased a tall easel and a stack of canvases, and an arsenal of brushes and oils, and threw myself into *becoming* what I *am*, as my grandfather would have put it. Predictably, I tried to be everything at once, the classic American in Paris. I was, of course, infatuated with the pre-Cubism masters of the nineteenth century. I was not above borrowing from the Symbolists and the ' Fauves, but for the most part I settled into a style that was a mix of my beloved, brooding Ryder and the melancholic end of the Impressionist spectrum. I was, during that period, constantly happy.

My neighbors in the building were heard but mostly unseen. From time to time, we crossed each other's paths on the staircase or at the communal *toilette* down the hall, shared by the other tenants on my floor, most of whom were students at the Université de Paris. On weekends the air in the hallways was nauseating with the aroma of marijuana. It was not unlike the culture of the Vermont commune, though more intellectual and artistically sophisticated. As a cliché specimen from abroad, young and artistic, I was invited to their parties and encouraged to share a variety of beds, though I managed to decline most of the former and all of the latter. Their jaded romanticism was ostensibly anti-romantic, endlessly playing with revolutionary roles ranging from Marxist to Existentialist to Islamic terrorist to Nouveau Absurdist, though everyone understood that these were personas that people tried on and discarded—a process essential to "finding oneself." Their exaggerated individualism became tiresome, and I soon learned to excuse myself from their rites of spring. They were not offended. It was understood that artists are a breed apart, to be forgiven everything, even dissent from revolutionary conformities—or worse, isolationism. I bought myself a set of earplugs to reduce the noise of my environment, I kept up a vigorous jogging routine, and I slept deeply every night.

On a morning in the spring of my first year in Paris, I happened to be painting outdoors in the Jardin du Luxembourg. The tulip beds were in a riot of bloom, children and nannies strolled the pathways, the weather was mild and the din of traffic bearable. I was taking a break from visual brooding and enjoying the rendition of a flowering horse chestnut tree, with a nod to van Gogh at the asylum of Saint-Rémy. I had set up my mobile easel near the Medici fountain.

Whenever I painted, I seemed to lose all consciousness of time, and, to a degree, awareness of anything outside my subject matter. However, on this loveliest of mornings my concentration was broken by a nagging sense that someone was standing a little too close behind me.

"*C'est très belle*," said a feminine voice, which I tried to ignore.

"Even geniuses must eat," the woman continued in English. "Are you not hungry?"

It was a young voice, and in a moment of weakness I turned around to look at the one who had spoken.

Before me stood the most extraordinary person I had ever met in my life. She was shockingly beautiful and very much my age, and yet so guileless that I did not suspect her of flirtation. Her blond hair was wind-blown, cut stylishly short *à la parisienne*; her clothing was comfortable but *chic*, a cream-colored jacket and skirt, high black boots. Without any loss of élan, she carried a frumpish leather valise, which appeared to be bulging with whatever it contained.

This is not real, I told myself. *This is an apparition.*

I suppose I was standing completely still, staring at her with my brush suspended in midair, my mouth hanging open.

She smiled at me, and I was lost forever.

"*Bonjour, Monsieur l'Américain*," she said with a little laugh, a mixture of amusement and affection.

"*Bonjour*," I said in a throttled voice.

"Would you like me to sing for you 'La Marseillaise'?"

"*Pardon, mademoiselle?*"

Again she laughed and I lowered my brush, still unable to take my eyes off her.

"How do you know I'm an American?" I asked.

"It is extremely obvious," she said, in English.

"Extremely?"

"*Oui*. Extremely. Would you care to join me for a simple repast? My *maman* packed far too much for me."

She turned and proceeded to an empty park bench a few steps away. I followed her meekly. We sat down side by side.

Is this really happening? I asked myself.

She opened her valise, a battered thing as wide as a suitcase. Inside were notepads, books and binders, and a laptop computer. A woven wicker box filled the rest of the space. She pulled it out and busied herself untying its clasps. Imprinted on its lid was the logo of a champagne company, *Pommery et Greno, Maison fondée en 1836 ~ Reims*. It contained four neatly packed sandwiches, a glass container of vegetables, a single wine glass wrapped in a cloth napkin, and a quarter-liter bottle of red wine, rolled in a thicker table mat.

"The sandwiches are Normandy Camembert and Brie," she said. "That is, two are one kind and two are the other. If your tastes are not discriminating, may I make a selection for you?"

"Please," I murmured.

"*Tiens, le camembert* is yours, *monsieur*, for it is stronger and more flavorful."

She handed me a package, which I unwrapped. Inside were inch-thick slices of white bread, heavily buttered, with a half-inch-thick slab of soft yellow cheese in its characteristic white rind. The woman was now setting the mat on the stone bench between us, opening more packages, popping the cork from the wine bottle, clinking the little glass against it.

"The wine is for you, *Monsieur l'Américain*. You may proceed."

I remained somewhat immobilized, dealing with confused emotions. I took a large bite from the sandwich without taking my eyes off her. She poured the wine and offered me the glass. I took a sip.

"*Merci, mademoiselle.*"

"You are silent, after the manner of the authentic artist," she mused. "There are numerous ones in this city who are not so genuine. They speak much theory and create little art."

She took a bite of her sandwich, not taking her eyes from me. Oddly, her manner or approach, or whatever it was, did not seem predatory. If anything, I sensed, she was an unusually open person engaged in a moment's curiosity or kindness. I fully expected her to pack up the remains of the lunch, after it was completed, and to disappear forever. At this point she stood and walked to my easel. Carefully she carried it over and set it up beside the bench. She sat down again and examined my partly completed painting.

"You understand light," she said. "But you understand it as a mariner would—yes, I am certain this is an ocean light you have used. Even so, *monsieur*, you have been faithful to the *being* of the tree. The *esse*—*l'être*. Do you know what I mean?"

"Are you an artist?" I asked her.

"No, I am a student at la Sorbonne. Do you know it?"

She pointed to the roof of a large old building, its upper stories just visible above the treetops.

"What do you study?" I asked.

"Psychology. Also philosophy."

It struck me that there was nothing for me to lose.

"It seems I cannot stop looking at you," I said. "I am sorry if I seem rude."

"You are not rude, not the way your eyes are. I can see you are not a selfish person."

"I hope that is true. You are extremely beautiful."

She blushed and dropped her eyes. Looking up at me she said:

"To contemplate beauty is natural and good. It is what we were made for."

"Some ways of looking are not so good."

As if startled, she gazed at me without blinking. Then she said, "Yes, this is true."

"It is admiration on my part, I hope you know. It is not ... it is not anything base that would dishonor you."

"You do not need to explain yourself or apologize. What century have you come from, young man?"

Young man?

"This one. And you?"

"The same."

I stood and brushed crumbs off my lap.

"I cannot finish the wine," I said. "It is very nice, but I am not much of a drinker."

"That is a pity. I will drink it for you, then."

"You are exceedingly kind, *mademoiselle*. I will remember our meeting all my life."

"I will remember it too."

"If life were different ...," I said, my voice trembling. "If life were different, I would propose that we choose a path on which we might frequently remind each other of this encounter."

"But why should we not!" she exclaimed with a smile.

Because life does not give us paradise, I thought. *Never does it give us paradise.*

"Because life is not so simple," I said.

"We make life too complicated," she replied.

I stood looking down at her upturned face. To venture is to risk loss, I told myself; and to seek a treasure that is beyond valuation is to risk monumental, devastating loss.

"W-would you c-care to see more of my work?" I asked. "My p-paintings?"

"I would be very happy to. May I ask what is your name, *monsieur*?"

"It is Maximilian."

"I am Françoise."

Françoise, Françoise, Françoise.

She stood and glanced at her wristwatch.

"Oh, I will be late for a lecture," she said. "I must go."

I have lost her, I thought. *I have lost her forever.*

"Can we meet later?" I asked.

"*Oui, c'est possible.* Where may I meet you?"

"Anywhere!"

"Do you know the little café by l'Odéon Théâtre?"

"I will find it."

"It is in the rue de Vaugirard, just behind the Palais. I will meet you there at five o'clock, if this suits you."

It suits me.

"I will be there."

"*C'est d'accord.* Agreed. *A bientôt*, Maximilian."

I watched her walk away in the direction of boulevard Saint-Michel and her Sorbonne. And when I could no longer see her, I felt again that I had lost her. At five o'clock I waited by the café entrance, dreading that she might not come. A few minutes later my pulse quickened when I saw her moving energetically toward me along the sidewalk, her face radiant.

We shook hands. I did not want to let go of her hand.

"Now, *Monsieur l'Américain*, I would like to remind you of our meeting earlier today. Do you remember it?"

"I remember it. I will remember it always."

"You see how the path did not end in the garden? We have decided to walk together and remind each other of beautiful moments that are too easily forgotten."

I nodded mutely, and we went inside.

Our meal was a simple feast of Italian pasta and sauces. I ordered a bottle of wine.

"You are an impoverished artist, Maximilian. You should not."

"I am not so impoverished, Françoise, that I can fail to celebrate the most beautiful moment of my life."

"Is it truly so with you, in your heart?"

"Yes. It is."

We ate our meal in silence, every so often looking up at each other, breaking into smiles.

"Who could have predicted this day," she said.

"Where will the path lead us?" I asked.

"We do not yet know."

"We cannot see all ends."

"Yet for now, here we are."

"Here we are."

After our second glasses of wine, I told her a little about myself, that my home was a small town in Maryland, near Washington, D.C. I had come to Paris in the hope of developing my skills as a painter, to see the original works of masters and to live in the lands they had walked and loved.

"Do you sell your work here?" she asked.

"I have sold only a few of my paintings, one to my grandmother, who refused to accept it as a gift and insisted on paying for it. Two others went to elderly ladies in a painting class on Chesapeake Bay. You see, I am not very talented."

"Do you know, Maximilian, one of my uncles, who lives in Bordeaux, is a famous painter. He is quite rich. He is very talented and knows it too well. I do not like his paintings. I do not think they are real art, though they are clever. He exhibits at a gallery here in Paris. But I do believe your tree in the Luxembourg is better than anything he has made. It is beautiful and pure and it reverences the *being* of your subject."

"*L'être.*"

"Yes, *l'être.* That is what true art gives us."

"Françoise, why did you speak with me today in the park?"

"Because I saw that you respected the tree in a way that was unfamiliar to me. I do not mean like the silly ecospiritual people and their obsessions. I do not mean that at all. I mean, I saw a man with love in his heart and reverence for his subject matter. It seemed to me, as well, that you had given away many things to arrive at this point of seeing. You had sacrificed much. Or you had lost much."

I did not respond to her searching look. I sipped my wine and felt my heart beginning to race.

"I am sorry, Maximilian," she said with a rueful look. "I am being the intellectual. Forgive me; it is the curse of the academic life."

"Do not apologize, Françoise. I am thinking about what you said. I believe it is true what you said."

"Oh, and I should point out, in all honesty, that I also spoke to you because you are an extremely beautiful-looking man."

I burst out laughing, sputtering wine onto the tablecloth.

"Extremely?" I asked when I could speak.

She began to laugh with me.

"*Oui, oui*, I admit it is a favorite word of mine. Extreme people use the word too often—we cannot help ourselves."

"It is you who are beautiful," I said.

She looked down at her empty glass. I refilled it and ordered another bottle.

"Ooh, you should not. Poor starving one, I saw the way you gobbled my sandwiches."

"Will such a night ever come our way again, Françoise? This is an occasion for wine."

"Excuse me, but that is not a very good wine. It is extremely young."

"I am also extremely young and feeling very happy."

"And so am I."

I walked her back to her residence, a flat she shared with three other women in an ancient building, deeper in the Latin Quarter, not far from her university. On her front doorstep, we shook hands again. We did not kiss, but we did not let go of each other's hands.

"Your paintings!" she said with a flutter of confusion. "I did not see them."

"I could show them to you another time. Not all of them are like the tree."

"Another time, then. When will I see you again?"

"May I call on you tomorrow?"

"I will give you my cell number," she said, rummaging in her purse.

"I do not have a cell phone, no phone at all for that matter. Tomorrow is Saturday. Would you care to visit the Louvre with me? There are certain paintings I would like to show you."

"The ones you love most?"

"Yes."

"Then we will go there."

We spent the day together in the Louvre, the first of many such days. Additional riches were offered by the Orangerie and the Jeu de Paume in the Jardin des Tuileries. Then back we went to the Louvre, again and again. We did not want it to end, and indeed there was no end.

Her studies came to a close, and now we were free to spend all our time together.

"Are there no other young men interested in you?" I asked at one point.

"Yes, several. I am a master of the courteous decline."

"Why do you decline?"

"Because of you."

By now we were walking everywhere in the city, holding hands. We kissed each other's cheeks each night as we said good-bye. I was maddened with love—and paradoxically felt myself growing saner because of this love, the kind of love we were creating together. Was there desire in it? Of course, absolutely, passionately—extremely. But we did not express it physically for fear of losing *l'être*, the deep thing, the indestructible thing.

"We could live inside this," she said, musing in front of one of Chagall's magical floating couples. "We can pretend we are museum janitors, and all the while we will be the true and secret guardians."

"Together?"

"Of course. This is now extremely certain."

I showed her my favorite Goyas. She gazed thoughtfully at them, loved them, though in a different way than I did.

"There is suffering in every eye," she observed. "There is no relief from it. The only relief is blindness."

"I see joy there too," I said.

"Can you point it out to me, please, Max?"

I couldn't for the moment find evidence in the paintings.

"In any event, I see Goya's immense heart, his compassion," I said.

"Yes, his is a very great heart, a great compassion—with, perhaps, a little too much grieving."

On the anniversary of our meeting—that is, the first-month anniversary—we went out to dinner at the Café du Palais. As we drank our *apéritif*, Françoise gave me a gift. It was a book of Goya's paintings.

We plunged into it immediately, and as we waited for our meals to be brought to the table, we tried to decide which images were our favorites. Mine were the dark paintings, *Destiny* and *Snowfall*, the *Colossus* and *Fight with Cudgels*, as well as the horrific *Saturn Devouring One of His Children*. Her preference was for the lighter end of the existential spectrum, pastoral scenes like *The Village Wedding* and *Blind Man's Bluff*.

Françoise suddenly laughed, pointing to a painting of four young women engaged in a blanket toss at a party or a country fair. Smiling with delight, they heaved into the air what appeared at first glance to be a man. He hung suspended in space, his limbs dangling at angles, his head akimbo, his face turned to the sky. The chalk-white face with its rouged cheeks was nearly clown-like, though its surreal expression, despite the superficial levity of the scene, was oddly tragic. The eyes stared upward, as if in resignation.

Its title was *The Straw Manikin*.

"What fun they are having," exclaimed Françoise, as if she were one of the girls.

"The manikin does not seem to be enjoying it," I said.

"Ah yes, the poor nincompoop does not know how to defend himself from women."

She laughed again.

I said, "Is Goya commenting on the unprotesting grief of puppets, I wonder?"

"The secret sorrows of clowns and marionettes?" she mused. "Dear Max, it is merely a literal scene."

"A literal scene can have layers of meaning."

"True. But why should we not interpret on the bright side?"

"I see a victim's abandonment to cruel fate, and to human blindness."

"I see a party game."

At that point our meals arrived, and we turned our thoughts to each other, to the splendid gift of our growing relationship.

There came a day when it was time to show her my work.

I had done most of the paintings before meeting her, mainly images expressing the struggles of the human condition. My brooding Ryderesques, my neo-Goyas. Among them were a number of symbolic works depicting the horrors of September 11.

She came in the evening, blew in through my open door with her hair disarrayed and her cheeks reddened by a rainstorm. I took her coat and hung it on a nail. She was excited, eager to see my soul made manifest.

In preparation for her visit I had leaned about two dozen canvases against the walls. I began by showing her the happy landscapes, which had been painted after our first meeting.

"*L'être*," she said. "The light of the sea."

"Which do you like best?" I asked.

"This one," she said, pointing to a small painting of a man striding between the towering walls of a canyon, a Turner sun spinning down through the royal-blue shadows, illuminating him. A flock of pigeons spiraled above his head.

"It's for you," I said.

She went down on her knees before it, touching the rim tentatively.

"It's dry," I told her.

She picked up the painting and kissed the little man in it. She pressed it to her chest, her eyes closed.

"It is your self-portrait," she said.

I made tea for us. We sat down on the floor and sipped from our cups. She did not seem interested in conversation, and her eyes kept turning to the canvases distributed along the walls.

Then I showed her the rest.

She said nothing as we moved from image to image. She paused over the burning towers, shuddered when her eyes picked out the three falling human figures.

"Two adults and a child," she said, shaking her head. "Did children die in those towers, the ones the terrorists destroyed?"

"Yes," I said.

I d-d-don't want to g-go, Max. Puck's lips trembling, his eyes filling with tears.

Don't be silly, Puck. There's nothing to be scared of.

When she had gone around the room a second time, she took a deep breath.

"It is fine and interesting work," she said, frowning analytically. "You paint the darkness at the heart of the American dream."

Surprised by this, I said, "Is that what you think these paintings are about?"

"Did you intend something else?"

"I try to paint a protest against the forces of annihilation, against hatred, irrationality, violence."

"And you Americans see yourselves as victims?"

"Yes, we do ... at least in the disaster of September 11."

"It is very difficult to see ourselves as we are."

"I would agree with that. Yet it is a sword that cuts both ways."

She pursed her lips, considering.

"You French think there's a darkness at the heart of the American dream," I continued. "Are you saying freedom is darkness?"

"*Non, non, non,* I mean there is a secret heart of darkness *beneath* the heroic myth you have about yourselves. The myth is true, in part, but it is not the whole truth."

"Our myth, you call it. How can you say this, here at ground zero of the French Revolution!"

She frowned. "Of course we have our own myth about ourselves—and our own heart of darkness. Every nation has one."

"So what is the reality behind the myths?"

"I do not know, but I want to find out. That is why I study *there!*" She pointed to the window, more or less in the direction of the Sorbonne.

"Why there? Can you not search for it anywhere?"

"In the Sorbonne you will find wise men, and the self-deceived, and many kinds of mythmakers."

"Why do you entrust your mind to such professors?"

"Why do you entrust yourself to solitude? Is not solitude another sort of risk?"

"A less complicated one."

"But it's dangerous too. You live inside yourself, and no one can get in. You go off by yourself and stop caring about how other people feel."

I thought, *Oh, our love is going to be a long, long marathon. She is a catastrophic phenomenon of beauty and I am on fire. I will become dust and ashes.*

"Ooh, Max, I really like you," she said with a sudden change of tone, her face lighting up, dropping all gravity.

"You don't even know me," I said.

"I know that you like *le camembert* very much. I am wondering if you also like good wine."

I will willingly die in the heart of whatever she is.

"I do like good wine," I said, "though my exposure to it has been limited until now."

"I will teach you."

And she did.

9

A medieval exegesis of love

In midsummer, Françoise helped me move the last of my things from my old flat. As we walked hand in hand along the rue de Babylone, she carried a backpack full of my brushes and paints, while I held an imitation Calder mobile high in my left hand, keeping my right free for her intoxicating touch. We talked all the way to the rue d'Assas and turned onto it, seeing nothing along the way, aware only of ourselves. A few blocks farther on we entered the walkways of the Jardin du Luxembourg.

My new flat was situated in the boulevard Saint-Michel, facing the Luxembourg on the border of the Latin Quarter. It had the advantage, unstated, deliberately chosen, of being only a few blocks from the Sorbonne and from Françoise's residence. I had rented it at an insane price but figured my savings would still last another year—enough time, I felt sure, to win her forever, *éternellement*, as she would say—another of her favorite words. For though she was the type of girl one could too easily summarize as naïve or shallow, prone to frivolity and ready laughter, there was depth there too. She was, after all, a *philosophe*, and the daughter of *philosophes*.

My one supper at her parents' apartment had been an exercise in measured circling and assessment, unspoken but oppressive. I did not like the people. They were solicitous, and attempted to lighten me up with ironic French humor to which I hesitantly responded, after interpretation. There was even some *bonhomie* on their parts, though it was strained. Over dinner, they crabbed at each other intellectually, with a caustic undertone. On the whole, I could not get away from them fast enough.

"I was glad to meet your parents," I said to Françoise as we paused by the Medici fountain. "They are intelligent people."

"They are, Max, and I love them, but I am not quite so blind as you suppose."

"I don't think you are blind."

"Papa is a *rationaliste* à la Sartre. For him, everything is *l'être et le néant*, being and nothingness—oh, and of course *la politique et le vin*."

"Politics, wine, and nothingness—an unusual mix. Perhaps a volatile one."

"*Exactement*," she laughed. "He loves his wine and existential angst, usually combined, and thus we sometimes have combustions, he and I."

"And your mother?"

"*Maman* loves *Papa* and her children with equal portions of devotion. It is she who holds everything together. I do not think I could ever live with such splits, such contradictions."

"And you, Françoise? What do you love?"

"Are you not asking, my dear, transparent Paul Maximilian, *whom* do I love?"

"I hardly dare ask."

"Then let the question age like good wine." She faced me squarely and took my coat lapels in her hands, shaking me a little, smiling into my eyes. "*Si grave, si sérieux, mon pauvre* Max."

"*Ma belle* Françoise."

"I too can be *very* grave and *very* serious," she said in a tone of mock melancholia.

"I have suspected it, but have not yet seen any evidence."

"That is because I try to let my heart live. *Oui*, I just live. Do you know the silly American song 'April in Paris', and the other songs like it? Did you know that for Parisians such songs are very boring! For us, to live in Paris is to *live* in Paris!"

"What exactly do you mean, Françoise?"

"I mean *this*!" she sang, spinning off from me, twirling on the sidewalk, dancing several steps beyond my reach with a backward look calculated to devastate, to deliciously melt all resistance.

"Oh, like *that*!" I cried in a high theatrical shout, and made imitation Fred Astaire steps in her direction.

She burst out laughing, doubling over with hilarity.

I threw my arms wide; the mobile went flying. Still dancing, I sang in my loudest baritone:

> "Boys and girls together,
> me and Françoise *la fille*,
> tripped the Light Fantastic
> on the sidewalks of Paree."

"*C'est fantastique!*" she exclaimed, running to me, throwing her arms around me. Kissing me on the lips. "*Mon doux, beau* Max."

She often asked about my family. I had told her my parents were deceased. But who were they? she insisted.

Were they not too young to die—for both of them to die? The euphemisms for their deaths did not satisfy her. There came a day when I told her everything. She cried; she grew silent. She did not vocally analyze the experience, nor do I think she analyzed me at that moment. I think she was simply feeling it—feeling it *with* me.

"I am grateful you have told me about this," she said at last.

"Grateful, Françoise? I wonder if it will ruin our friendship."

"That is entirely and absolutely not possible, Maximilian."

She had moods. At one moment she would be delicately sensitive to the feelings of others. At another she would be deliriously happy, a girl dancing in the wind. Then, without warning, a serene summer day would be riven by a flash of lightning. I gradually came to understand that the latter episodes always had something to do with her ferocious devotion to truth, as she saw it.

One day, she stood by my large easel in the new studio, examining a work in progress. With folded arms and frowning brow, she spent some minutes with it as I waited beside her, trying to see it with her eyes: a large male face with wide-open mouth, an upside-down torso with arms and hands reaching upward, a man falling through flames.

"Its title is *The Scream*," I said.

"Max, I worry about this," she replied, staring at the canvas. "Why do you repeat Edvard Munch?"

"It's only a superficial similarity—the title. Real screams cross all ethnic and national boundaries."

"*D'accord*. Okay. The title is Munch, but the contents are Goya. Why are you trying to be like him? You are not Francisco de Goya!"

"I know I'm not Francisco de Goya. I simply admire him."

"And emulate him. But why *him*, why this macabre sadness, this bitterness and irony over *la condition humaine*?"

"Because we are birds in a cage, Françoise, and he shows us the cage."

"Like Sartre's *Huis clos*, *No Exit*? Hell is other people?"

"No, not like Sartre. Goya shows us something more human and sad and beautiful, revealing to us our folly, asking us to live a better way."

"Beautiful and sad." She clicked her tongue, shaking her head. "Sad, sad, sad, always the sad."

"You once told me how you yearn for me to speak my heart without hesitation. But when I try to speak that way through my paintings, you are repelled. Do you think this encourages transparency on my part?"

"You simply do not understand me. I am saying that in this life you are not condemned to slavery. You are not the creation of the things that happen to you."

"Really? You must have had a very sheltered life."

"Perhaps. But does this take away all my credibility? To have hope, to have joy—does this make me a spoiled *naïf*?"

"I'm not saying that. I just mean you don't see the whole picture."

"And I am saying, it is you who fail to see the whole picture."

"I paint as a voice for the voiceless."

"Yet this painting is intensely personal. You have been badly hurt by your sufferings, I know, but why do you let them define you?"

"*C'est facile*, Françoise."

"Chagall's early life was painful, *très difficile*. He chose to turn his memories into joy."

"Chagall's family was not burned to ashes in an instant."

"How many of them, I wonder, were burned to ashes in Auschwitz."

"Oh, Auschwitz. How can one argue with Auschwitz? It demolishes every debate."

"Is this a debate?"

"If it is, I didn't start it."

She tightened her crossed arms, frowning. I leaned over to kiss her, for kisses, too, cross all ethnic and national barriers. She jerked her head away.

"Do you love your tragedy?" she asked. "Do you love it more than you love me?"

Speechless, with an ache in my throat, I threw up my trembling hands.

"I love you," I pleaded. "I love you with my whole heart."

"I know you love me," she said, her face crumpling, tears springing to her eyes. "But you cannot yet say, with complete honesty, that it is your whole heart."

"It's the only heart I have."

She wiped her eyes with her fingertips, and said, "I'm sorry. I made this conversation go wrong. But I have to leave, Max. I have a paper to submit in the morning and it is not yet half-written." She smiled sadly. "It is on the medieval exegesis of love."

I walked her back to her residence, and at the doorstep we briefly kissed good-bye.

"Across the barriers," she whispered, and turned away.

Returning to my studio I told myself that she was right—she was almost always right about the important things. But this only made it worse, because, in the end, I was incapable of changing myself.

I threw myself down on the cot in my studio, scrutinizing the screaming face. I suddenly wanted to burn it. I wanted to get up and carry it down to the Luxembourg and set fire to it. To destroy the image of destruction, to silence the cry of protest.

I turned off the lamp beside me and lay back with an arm across my eyes. I fell into a troubled sleep, and during the night I dreamed of a woman reaching out for me. I could not see her face, only a young feminine hand with a gold ring on its wedding finger, offering me a piece of paper. I took it and looked closely. On it was a photo of the New York City skyline and two jets angling downward for collision with the towers. At the base of the image a monumental human figure strode between the buildings with his arms raised to hold off the attack.

Beneath his feet were numbers:

09—11—20—01

As more and more memory returned, it separated into fragments:

Her voice: "You would benefit greatly from catharsis, Max."

My voice: "I do not believe in catharsis."

Her voice: "That is because you have never tried it."

My voice: "It offers only temporary relief. And often makes more damage."

Hers: "How would you know that?"

Mine: "I once was on the receiving end of it."

Hers: "Oh well, perhaps it does not work for everyone immediately."

Mine: "Huh?"

I wrinkled my brow. What was she saying? That victims of catharsis should be considerate enough to give the perpetrators time to get it right? I hated to contradict her, to risk weakening our bond, so I let it slide. I told myself that no one's opinions were perfect, after all, nor were they fully formed at her age. Besides, she was so perfect in every other way.

"My unhappy sisters, for example," she continued. "One of them blames my parents for everything that went wrong in her life. Her counselor tells her so. Her psychiatrist instructs her to vent her rage against them. My other sister punishes them with silence. I'm not sure which sister hates them more." She gave a Gallic shrug. "There have been several separations, you see, then reconciliations, followed by more conflict. These leave their mark on children."

"And you, what do you feel?" I asked.

"I used to storm and scream at *Maman* and *Papa*. It really made me feel better. Now that it is out of my system, I choose not to fall into the gravitational pull of their miseries. I see their flaws but I do not blame them for their humanity."

"So why haven't your sisters come to the same conclusion?"

"Neither of them have yet pushed their catharsis to the extreme."

"Extreme, again. You girls must make your parents' lives rather painful."

"*Oui*," she laughed mischievously. "We give them no relief."

Somewhat appalled, I said, "Really, Françoise, isn't it better to be patient and kind?"

"Why? Repression is not healthy."

"Um ... maybe not in some things. But why not talk it out with them in a calm, reasonable way?"

"They would not listen. They would rationalize everything into molecules."

"Whew," I said, shaking my head, glad that her family wasn't mine. "Sounds like misery without relief."

She squeezed my arm and skipped along like the charming *gamine* she was. "But we, Max, you and me, we have relief."

"Can one build a life together on a feeling of relief?" I asked, still uneasy.

She frowned. "We have more than that."

"Yes, we do," I said, wondering over the frown.

Spring again:

We were standing together at a wine-and-cheese reception in a commercial art gallery of moderate but not insignificant repute. Our arms were around each other's waists. She held me tightly, smiling, smiling. I swelled with pride, exalted by new hope. The paintings were selling.

"You see, my wicked uncle is not so wicked after all."

"Nepotism," I said.

"No, not nepotism. He recognizes your quality. He has friends. Should you have turned your back on this? Your first show and it is in Paris!"

Autumn:

We stood arm in arm on the Champ de Mars, the Eiffel Tower rising above and behind us. A small lady, a dwarf, came up to us and asked if we would like a photograph of ourselves. Françoise handed the woman her camera, and we posed. We talked with her about gardening and painting. She loved irises, above all the dark-purple "flags", though she did not so much like the golden iris. Monet was her favorite painter. His water lilies. And of course Renoir's children. She herself could not have children—a great pity. She hoped *le bon Dieu* would bless us with many. She was very fond of Degas as well, though not everything he had painted. Did we know that absinthe would drive one mad? Yes, it was true, the wormwood in it created insanity. We assured her we would avoid it. Well, it is now illegal, she demurred. Françoise and the woman exchanged addresses and embraced—two strangers, no longer strangers.

That evening we went out to dinner at our favorite café near the Palais du Luxembourg. Over wine, I took a gold ring from my pocket and offered it to her in my open palm.

"It is a promise ring, a fidelity ring," I said. "It means I am yours forever."

You do not have to accept it, lady of sweet fire, but my part is to offer it.

"You must put it onto my finger," she whispered.

I slipped the ring onto her finger.

"I put my whole self into your hands, Françoise."

In answer, she opened her purse and removed a white cloth, tightly folded and bound by red ribbon. Unwrapping it, she brought forth a gold ring and held it out toward me.

"It is a ring of promise, Max, my promise to you. It means I am yours *éternellement*."

The mutual exchange of rings was unplanned, uncanny, and doubly wonderful because of it.

"This is like something in a story," I said. "These things don't happen."

"But they just did!" she laughed with shining eyes.

Another memory:

We were walking the *quais* around the Ile de la Cité, the wind blustery, the sky overcast.

"Do you trust me?" I asked.

"Of course I trust you!" she said. "Do you trust me?"

"Of course. Still . . ."

"Why are we asking this? If we have to ask—"

"Nothing in life is absolutely certain . . . other than death and loss."

"Do not worry, Max, I will fix that."

"You cannot fix human beings," I said. "We are not machines."

"True, we are not machines. But I know my *chevalier du roi* will be healed of his great sorrow one day."

"You wish your knight to become a perfect prince, like in a fairy tale. That is not reality, Françoise."

"I do not wish my prince to be perfect. I want him to be happy."

"I am happy."

"These sweet days, they are not long, Max."

"You are in a dire mood today."

She squeezed my hand and pressed closer as we continued to walk.

"I would give everything, Max. Would you?"

"Yes, absolutely."

"I mean ... *can* you?"

Startled by what she had just communicated, I halted and faced her.

"You don't trust me," I said in a quiet voice. "You don't have confidence in me."

"I ... I have confidence that you are *un bonhomme*, Max, and that you love me."

"But you're afraid I'll turn out to be like your father."

"No, not like him. But I have seen too many of my friends fall in love with men who made them happy for an hour, a day, even a year, and then ruined their lives. Some women cannot resist losing themselves entirely in the love of a criminal or a wild drinker or a tough guy who beats them. They believe his violence is masculine strength. They fool themselves that their love will tame him, make him nice but keep the strength." She dropped her eyes and stared at the sidewalk. "Among my friends there have been suicides."

"I will not ruin your life, Françoise."

"I do not mean *you* would ruin my life. It is just that we must be sure before giving our lives to each other."

"I thought we already had."

We walked on, silently ruminating on the confusion between us. It had been a moment's lapse in our communion, and both of us hastened to shake it off.

Another fragment:

"Why do we not sleep together, Max? Why do you not push for it?"

"I respect you."

"Are you afraid of sex?"

I laughed outright. "*Au contraire*, Françoise."

"Then what? What is the problem?"

"I am afraid of losing you."

"This makes no sense at all."

"*L'être*," I said.

Uncomprehending, her eyes puzzled over me. "*Pardon*?"

"I want you to know—I want you to know deep in your soul—that I love you totally for who you *are*. I would rather die than use you."

"That never stopped the other young men who have loved me totally, who also believed they did not want to use me."

"Are you saying they *tried* to use you, or are you saying they *did* use you?"

She shrugged off the question as unworthy of an answer.

"Do you think men are mainly animals?" I asked.

"You sound so surprised. Look around you, Max. Look at the world."

"The world wasn't always this way. Men were once protectors, not predators."

Again she fixed me with a look of uncertainty.

"So, let me try to understand this, Françoise. You don't trust men who are too moral, have I got that right?"

"Not exactly. I am merely asking, where does this morality of yours come from and why do you need it?"

It was a fair question. I wasn't sure of the answer. I hadn't really thought about it before. Some of my morality may have been instinctive, a sense infused in me from birth that any man worthy of the name respected women. The thought of Granddad Robbie flashed into my mind. And my father. Neither of them had been self-righteous types, but they had loved their wives—passionately and morally.

"There are all kinds of men," I said, "and you'll find that the ones who love best are the ones who aren't slaves to impulse. If I'm your first, well, I think you need to be informed that there are plenty of us out there."

"Do not ruin your chances, Max. I might start looking out there."

I shook my head, still trying to understand. "So, you believe in sexual catharsis as well as emotional catharsis?"

"I believe in love."

"Me too. Do you trust men who can't control their sexual appetites? They may look and feel more romantic, but please explain how this is different from the women who fall for criminals and tough guys."

"*Non, non, non*, it is not the same."

"How is it different? Is it because the users you've known have been sweeter about it? Chocolates and roses and into the blanket toss as fast as we can?"

She gave me a cold look. And now another possibility struck me—and it struck hard. Did some women prefer sexually driven, immoral men because they were predictable and controllable, like the manikin in Goya's painting?

Suddenly she grinned with sly amusement.

"You are a virgin, aren't you? Admit it, Max, you are a virgin!"

"Yes," I said. "I am."

"You need not be so defensive about it," she tittered.

"I don't feel defensive about it."

"But of course you do. All young men are desperate to lose their virginity. And those who have not lost it usually lie about it. They are afraid to admit they have not had sex."

"Françoise, I haven't had sex."

"And it is also complicated by their fear of inadequacy."

"You've taken too many psychology courses."

"Now you are feeling hostile."

"No. I'm feeling irritated."

"Poor boys, until you really know a woman, you do not know what you are missing."

"The poor boys who throw away their virginity don't know what *they're* missing."

"*That* is absolutely a non sequitur."

"They lose their chance for the joys of expectation, and for the ecstasy that comes when longing and self-restraint are finally fulfilled with the one you will love forever."

"Why not have it now?"

"Imagine a prize racehorse. When the gate opens, all that magnificent discipline and pent-up energy are released. Would you rather ride *him* or some pretty pony dribbling around a barnyard thinking he's a wild stallion?"

"This is absurd," she murmured, pained. "We are having our first argument. And about sex, of all things!"

"It seems like a reasonable discussion to me."

"Max, enough! Let's go to a film. After, we will drink wine and you will kiss me with mad passion."

"Yes to all three propositions. But you will have to be strong for the both of us. Otherwise, the animal in me will take control."

She laughed. We both laughed, and the moment of tension was over.

How much later was it? Three months? Six months, perhaps. There came an offer from a gallery in America, a dealer who had visited Paris at the time of my first show and had stopped into the gallery quite by chance. I had to fly to New York for negotiations, to see the exhibition space, to know if I could trust these people. They offered temporary lodgings in an apartment in the East Village of Manhattan, where I could stay rent free.

Françoise drove me to the airport. In the departure lounge I said, "I will see you in a week or two."

"If you must stay longer, I will understand. However, if it is longer than a month, I will fly over secretly and kill you. Do we have an agreement?"

"We have an agreement. And thanks for the warning."

At the gate, she said:

"I love you very much. I will always love you. I will love you forever."

Beyond this, there were missing pieces. I strained to resurrect them. Specters crossed the screen of my imagination. Disconnected evocations of a life in progress, a chronology of narrative amputations.

There was a weekend in Maryland with my grandparents. My temporary lodgings in New York became my permanent abode. I painted with intense focus, time ceased altogether, the surrounding noises and motion faded away to the periphery of consciousness.

I wrote letters to Françoise daily and sent them off by airmail. Hers arrived weekly—in perfumed envelopes, containing her finely penned script, purple spidery ink on mauve vellum paper. I kissed the letters, inhaled her fragrance, smiled over her loving insults:

"My beloved troglodyte, *mon doux beau* anomaly, when will you abandon your antipathy to electronic communications? There is not a single person on this planet who has no e-mail, no cell-phone. Do you love me? If you love me, you will buy yourself a laptop and cease torturing me with these endless delays."

I replied: "I love you so much that I cannot bear to metamorphose the words of our union into cold font on a screen. How much better it is to hold your handwritten letters close to my heart, imagining it's you I embrace. When they arrive by sailing ship or as a scroll in a bottle, crossing the great sea of *l'être*, they are a thousand times more treasured than insta-bites. *L'attente est la langue principale de l'amour, l'attente en presence fidèle à l'autre.* (Forgive my fractured French.) I wish to say, *ma douce belle*, that waiting is the primary language of love—waiting in faithful presence to the other."

In her next letter, she retorted:

"Sweet idiot, you are a pathetic Romantic!"

I begged her to join me here in America, my home-land. She could analyze the myths firsthand, I suggested. But she delayed and delayed: writing her thesis, defending her thesis, tending her mother, who was in the throes of a nervous breakdown.

"Why do you not return to France?" she asked in every letter.

Why? Because the impossible future had become possible. Because I was on the verge of becoming an established artist—a *real* artist. Because I had to work and there was no time to lose.

I had a successful show, the gallery thronged with visitors because of a review in the *New York Times* and an article in the *New Yorker* magazine.

Françoise had been adamant that she would fly over for the opening, but in the end she begged off, pleading unnamed duties to her family. My grandparents came, beaming with pride, Helen watery eyed throughout, Robbie nodding his approval over the paintings, and watching the glittering, beautiful, and bizarre people in attendance with an expression I recognized as his subtlest—amused and ironic. He also eavesdropped on the exquisitely nuanced commentary all around him, and at one point he burst out laughing, offending some-one in a metal-link dress. The dress was not worn by a woman. Another lady, an actual lady, in her sixties or seventies, walked about in a leopard-skin leotard, lead-ing her pet piglet on a diamond-studded leash. Robbie was fascinated by it all; Helen grew increasingly uncom-fortable. They embraced me warmly, and left early.

The *Village Voice* and other papers wanted interviews, but I said no, which made the gallery owner furious with me. He pleaded and tried to bully, but I wouldn't budge and I wouldn't explain. I told him only that, on principle, I felt people had no right to access the personal memories of others.

"We're a generation of entitlement," I said, "and I'm not going to play by its rules."

Though I believed this, I also knew that their questions could split open a healed abscess, hemorrhaging old pain. Thus, without my aid, the journals published their psychoanalytical nonsense, social commentary, adulation, and antipathy. I was by turns a "prophetic articulator of the national trauma" and an "opportunist capitalizing on the sufferings of thousands". Paintings sold well. Another exhibit was scheduled for the following year.

Somewhere in all of this, I gave in and purchased a cell phone so that I could talk with Françoise every day. With instruments pressed to our ears, we communicated amply yet strained with desperation for the sense of communion we had had in Paris, and nearly taken for granted. We talked and cried, and I revolved the ring on my finger whenever we were connected. As I listened to her voice I stared through walls and crossed an ocean, yearning for her. I begged her to consider moving to my city.

In August she phoned me on my birthday. During our conversation she asked me if I had visited the site of my family's deaths. Stricken by the question, I said no, I had not, I couldn't bear to go there. I told her I was afraid of what I would feel, what would happen to me.

"You do not have to go alone, Max. I would go with you."

"Please come, Françoise. Come as soon as you can. But it's impossible for me to go to that place."

"How can you complete your grieving if you do not?"

"I have completed it. They died twelve years ago."

There was silence on the other end of the line.

On September 9 she phoned to say she would be flying to New York the following day. I was ecstatic.

When I asked for her flight number and arrival time, she refused to tell me.

"Do not meet me at the airport," she said. "I will take a taxi. I do not want us to meet in a romantic place, my Max. I want us to meet in the very place where you suffer—this place you call Ground Zero. Let me be with you there."

"Françoise, you have to stop treating me like an invalid. You make me feel like an emotional and mental cripple."

"My prince has been wounded in mortal combat. The dragon has—"

"There is no dragon! It was politics and jihad. It was a declaration of war. And it's in the past."

"It dominates your present ... and our future. Let me be with you there," she said again.

"If you love me, you will not ask this of me," I said, shocked and hurt by her insistence.

"If you love me, you will overcome this thing that is killing you," she said.

"Is this a test?"

"It is not a test. Let our love conquer it forever."

"It doesn't work that way, Françoise."

"It works exactly that way, Paul Maximilian."

Angry now, I raised my voice: "You are so *stubborn*!"

"Do not worry. When we are married, I will not be like this."

"I doubt it very much."

The following morning she called me again. I had prepared a new strategy: I did not know if she had relented of her mad schemes to heal me, but I thought that if she still insisted on me not meeting her at the airport, she might be argued into taking a taxi straight to my apartment. I would promise to consider her proposal, and once she was here with me I would reject it.

But she had already read my mind.

"The flight is boarding now. Tomorrow, Max. Tomorrow at the ground zero of your pain. I will be there at nine o'clock in the morning."

"I won't be there, Françoise."

"But *I* will be there."

"Stop! What's your flight number?"

"*Adieu, mon cœur.*"

On the anniversary of the catastrophe, I awoke from a fitful sleep, afflicted with a feeling of dread. It dissipated only gradually as I showered and shaved and made my breakfast.

I knew that I would have to go. I could not risk letting her be alone, a stranger in a strange land, in that worst of places. If I did not meet her there, she might or might not admit defeat, and pace around the great gaping hole in the city that even now was being reconstructed into something more elaborate and magnificent. Would she become angry? Would she lose heart? When she finally accepted that I could not join her there, would she hire a taxi to bring her to my apartment? Once we were reunited, our long-restrained love for each other might sweep everything aside and restore us to the enchantment of our beginnings. Or she might chastise me. Or, seeing the extent of my fears, she might be overcome by pity, expressing her understanding and compassion. Or, being a person of strong will and varying moods, she might do something else.

I admonished myself severely: This was not about *me*! What about *her* feelings? If I succumbed to mine, would it not be a supreme form of selfishness on my part? Surely I could fulfill such a simple request.

On the other hand, I wondered if this was an ultimate test, despite her protestation to the contrary. Was she testing my courage, my capacity for sacrifice? And, more onerous, was it a test of how compliant I would be throughout the rest of our lives? In other words, was she manipulating me? Was this ultimatum really about who was in control of our future? And if that was the case, what kind of marriage would we have? After the intoxications of passion subsided, would we be left with power struggles and habitual bitterness?

Even if that was the case—and it was by no means certain—I knew that if I did not join her there, I was being unfair to her. I had to prove to her my love. Mine was a love stronger than death, I told myself. I was not a coward. I was a man who kept his word, a knight faithful and true—and, perhaps, the prince she desired me to be.

Shortly after eight in the morning, I left the apartment and headed west on East Twelfth Street, beginning the three-mile walk that would take me to the financial district at the southern tip of Manhattan. My route zigged and zagged out of the East Village and into Little Italy, then onto Broadway, where I turned south. I jogged some of the way, trying to burn up the adrenaline flooding through my system. My heart banged in my chest, and my throat ached.

Once or twice I looked up at the office towers around me, and cringed as I saw jet planes crashing into them, fireballs blowing through their walls, bodies dropping from the heights. I heard screams that began as police and ambulance sirens and ended in wails of despair. I had just passed Canal Street, I think, when I began to see bodies heaped along the sidewalk, and only with an effort of the will was I able to turn them back into garbage bags. My mind told me these were trauma hallucinations, but the knowledge did not stop the bodies from multiplying, block after block. By now I was choking with terror, growing dizzy with insufficient oxygen. I slowed my pace and ground to a halt.

Horns beeped angrily, drivers yelled at me out of their windows, for I had stopped in the middle of an intersection. I hobbled forward toward the Twin Towers, seeing a cloud of ash descend in front of my eyes, bodies hitting the pavement, the pulverized flesh of my mother, my father, my little brother.

I leaned against a brick wall, bent over double, trying to catch my breath. Sobbing, I could go no farther. My hair standing on end, I ran all the way back to the apartment.

When my panic had subsided I called her on her cell phone. It went immediately to her voice mail, so I left a message explaining what had happened. Throughout the morning the phone did not ring. There was no knock on the door. I left numerous voice messages begging her to call me. She would understand; I knew she would understand. But why was she not answering? Had she accidentally left her cell phone in Paris; was it ringing and recording in her residence near the Sorbonne?

Why did she not call me?

I waited and waited. I telephoned the international terminal and gave her name to airport information, requesting that a public announcement be made, calling her to their desk. Nothing came of it. I asked if any flights from Paris had been canceled yesterday or today. None had. Could they tell me if a certain passenger had arrived or not? But they were bound by regulations not to divulge such information.

And so I waited. And waited. Three days passed, and she neither came to the door nor phoned me back. I slept little, if at all. I took sleeping tablets but they didn't help. I went out to a liquor store and bought alcohol. Drinking a bottle pushed me down into a drugged stupor, but it seemed to make my mind more confused than ever.

Finally I called her parents' number in Paris. Her father answered. When I told him who I was, there was silence on the other end of the line.

"What do you want?" he asked at length.

I stammered a garbled explanation, but he would not hear it.

"You have hurt her terribly," he said. "It is better for you to leave her alone."

"This is insane," I cried. "I can explain."

"Insane," he said in a cold voice. "Yes, insane." And hung up.

I phoned him again an hour later.

"She is not here," he said. "She has gone away."

"Away? Where?" I cried.

"That is none of your business. Do not call again."

I could not understand it. It was so completely out of her character simply to terminate all communication. Not a word, not even a sorrowful final conversation ending our relationship. Nothing.

Memories strained to coalesce, to piece together the chronology:

Autumn leaves fell. Snow fell.

I saw myself unable to paint. I saw the empty bottles of wine accumulating, waiting to be taken down to the trash. I saw myself in the mirror with a heavy growth of beard, red eyed, growing thinner. The mirror of my mirrored self, the bathroom cabinet's triple panes receding me into infinity.

I called her cell phone two or three times a day, until finally a French-speaking operator informed me that the number was no longer in service. My letters were returned to me unopened, stamped *No longer at this address*.

After anxiety came frustration, then anger, and then depression.

I showed up at the gallery drunk one evening, and was preemptively driven home to my apartment by an employee.

I could not bear to face my grandparents in my present condition and begged off their invitation to spend Christmas with them. I lied shamelessly. "I'm fine," I said, steadying my voice. "I'm just on a creative roll." Their questions followed.

"Don't worry, I won't be alone for Christmas. Friends want me to join them. I'll miss you a lot. I'll be thinking about you. Love you."

It was true that people had asked me to join them, though they were not, in fact, friends. They were denizens of the cultural circle of the gallery owner, and collectors intrigued by me or sexually attracted to me, or both. I declined the constant invitations to parties and beds.

"A mistake, Max," said the gallery owner. "They're rich and they're in love with you. You're a fatal attraction, you see—they want a piece of history, and more important to them, you're the tragic genius they long to cuddle and heal."

"To heal?" I shouted.

"Uh, in a manner of speaking. Relax, relax. I wasn't saying that *I* think you're unbalanced. I'm just suggesting you go along for the ride."

"I am not a commodity! Cancel my next show!"

"No, I am not canceling the show. You signed the contract, Max, and I have your paintings in secure storage."

"Then I'm not painting anything more for you—ever."

"That's your choice, but the show goes on."

I walked out on him, and from then on I answered none of his calls.

That was a month devoted to liquor bottles, my contribution to the recycling industry, two big boxes of empties a week, which I carried down the five staircases to the save-your-planet bins at the curb, carrying replacements in bags and boxes back up to my apartment. Harder liquor bestowed absinthine dreams, less romantic than wine, less consoling, but vastly more medicinal due to its numbing effect.

My world became infested with the sounds of phonograph records, scratchy, nostalgic, faint through every apartment door in the warren's hallways. Christmas bells in the city. White Christmas. Have a holly jolly Christmas. I entertained murderous feelings toward Bing Crosby. On my CD player I played Mozart's unfinished *Requiem* at full volume, constantly, in honor of my unfinished life. I should have been finished off with my family. I killed them, though I was not yet certain how I had done it. I killed them and I survived. It was the survival that provided the incontrovertible evidence.

Whenever I left the apartment, I was forced to enter the realm of merriment—the amplified colors, the soaring tree-of-lights in Central Park, children skating to the piped music of Strauss the Waltz King, the jingling bells of charity Santas and con-artist Santas, and the plastic Santas staring with manic-depressive glee. I staggered through midtown and uptown and never again wandered beyond the guarded frontier into lowertown, the city of death.

When I was not drinking I was sleeping or checking the in-box of my cell phone for voice and text messages. How did they find me, all these people? How did they track my code? Who told them my secrets? Why so many, when the only person I wanted to hear from would not call?

My bank account was full of money, the last of the old inheritance replenished by the new deposits from the gallery. I was semi-rich. If you sell your soul to the highest bidder, you can become rich, which proves that you are a social parasite, which proves that you are a mistake—a mistake become a fraud, because that is where it all ends, really, that is where you end when you don't know the truth about yourself. Ben Franklin saw the truth. Françoise saw it.

The day after New Year's I received in the mail a small padded envelope, with no return address. It was postmarked Lyon, France. Inside I found a greeting card, a fine art reproduction of a painting—a boy in a red suit, tethering a jackdaw on a string, beside three cats and a cage full of little brown birds: *Boy in Red, Portrait of Manuel Osorio Manrique de Zuñiga*, 1788, by Francisco de Goya.

Penned inside the card:

> *I am not the one you need.*
> *I must cut the string.*
> *F.*

Taped beneath these words was the gold ring I had given to her in Paris.

She had not used my name. She had not written, *You are not the one I need*—though this was the real message. She had not signed it with her full name. It was as concise as a surgeon's incision, as final as an execution-er's slice across a vital vein.

I purchased a handgun and a box of bullets. With these and the ring in my jacket pocket, I rented a car from a city agency and drove north. At Montpelier I dropped the car at the company's local agency. Then I found the closest bar where pickup trucks were parked outside. I went in and negotiated with a young man, long-haired and down-at-the-heels, who agreed, for a price, to take me up into the mountains.

First we loaded his pickup with groceries and boxes of alcohol. Along the way, he asked a few questions. No, I told him, I wasn't planning a party. No, I wasn't heading to a commune. I had an old family place up there, I explained, lots of memories. A retreat, I said; I had some thinking to do.

"Looks like a dandy retreat you got planned," he said with a smirk. "Can I come too?"

"Sorry, I need some time alone."

Did I want a toke, he asked—or did I have a joint or two of my own to share? I shook my head to both requests. He lit up, and I rolled down my window, rid-ing the rest of the way with my head freezing, sucking up the pure winter oxygen. He said no more throughout the winding fifteen-mile journey, and dropped me at the end of the lane leading into the Franklin homestead.

When he had disappeared back down the road, I trudged through deep snow, carrying my gear as far as the house. It took three trips back and forth to bring everything that far. I had hoped to camp out in the house, but its windows had been smashed, and snow had blown into the rooms. It was empty of furniture, the woodstove plundered and inoperable. The mill and brewery were likewise falling apart, roofless, gutted, and vandalized.

But the cabin by the pond was intact. The door was unlocked, the windowpane undamaged. On the collapsing porch sat a row of stacked cordwood, covered by a decaying tarp. Inside, a kerosene lantern hung from the rafters, with oil in its reservoir. The stove was still in one piece and connected to its chimney, with a half-empty woodbox offering enough birch to start a fire. Nothing belonging to my grandfather had been left behind, with the exception of dirty sheets, a pillow, and a blanket on the army cot, as well as a cardboard box under the bed, containing old clothes and a pair of plastic beach sandals. Tacked to the logs beside the cot was a magazine photo of the Twin Towers burning. Someone had used a felt-tip pen to make a black circle around the upper floors of one of the buildings.

I lit a fire in the stove, unpacked my things, drank a half bottle of cheap wine, and settled in to face my past, whatever it might be. I knew that I must do it this way or I would die. I might choose to die anyway, depending on the truth. My own personal ground zero. I loaded the gun and slipped it under the pillow.

Beyond these images there were only fragments of a life splintering and collapsing. I remember emptying bottles down my throat, cooking things, burning the food by neglect, staggering around the cabin, yelling at everything—my grandfather with his disgusting narcissistic fairy braids; my parents for leaving me alone; the woman with the scalpel who severed arteries in my heart, watching me bleed from a distance, detached and philosophical, cultured and sensitive to her final artistic *bon mot.* I also roared at the terrorists and the vast society of malice that had spawned them. And yet, strangely, I could hardly muster any hatred for them personally. This I reserved for the end-of-the-line Ben Franklin, the man whose pain meant more to him than his grandson's.

Through the delirium of rage, I considered what he had told me the last time I saw him. I mulled over numerous interpretations, some of them plausible, most of them contradictory. I still could not understand why he had chosen to hurt a child. Was it because he believed his beloved daughter had been dragged from the life he wanted for her? Had he taken personal insult from her rejection of the safe and natural environment he had provided? She had married a man whose work he despised, had stayed in the city he loathed, choosing to raise her children with more advantages, and as a result had died too young, leaving him afflicted in a life already overloaded with unresolved grief. Again and again the various explanations came down to this: My grandfather had been locked into the gravitational pull of his negative emotions. It was always about him, his miseries, his pride, his happiness, his needs, his sorrows. In his mind, his sufferings were always caused by others, and lest he take an honest look at himself, he must sustain the habit of blaming at all costs, even to the point of absurdity. In my semirational moments, I believed this was the truth of the matter.

Increasingly, however, his hateful words returned with greater force, and under the influence of little food and constant drink, my depression deepened. The words gained credibility, and then assumed an authority that could not be denied.

I watched another sun rising through the stripped birches. I threw two frozen hamburger patties into a skillet and put it on the stove to fry. As I sat and waited for my breakfast to cook, I choked down the day's first shot of whiskey. Followed by another. And another.

I picked up my gun and put the barrel into my mouth, to see what it would be like. I pulled it out and waved it about, and almost without knowing it I squeezed the trigger. The bullet whizzed past my head and struck a pan hanging on the wall. I vomited onto the bed and threw the gun down.

"Nothing makes sense!" I shouted. "Life, death, accident, murder—nothing!"

The pond will tell me, I thought when I calmed down. The pond was my childhood. It was the great sea; all secrets were drowned within its depths. I have to look down through the ice, because the past is buried there, my lost childhood. If I can see it, I may understand it. If I understand it, I may be able to begin again. The little racing car is down there too. I will dive in and find it when the ice melts in spring.

I drank more whiskey, upending the bottle like a true scion of Ben Franklin. I threw on my jacket and staggered out of the cabin, trudging through deep snow to the edge of the pond. The wind had swept parts of it clean, leaving a broad patch of bare ice out near the center. I twisted the gold ring off my finger, and pulled the other ring from my pocket. I tried to crush them in my fist, and then hurled them over the pond. They descended in an arc, hitting the ice, *ding-ding-ding*, rolling, zinging, spinning out of orbit and wobbling into immobility. Their massive weight rested on the ice for a few seconds, bending the surface downward as a star's gravity sinks the invisible graph of time. I ran out after them, intending to smash with the heel of my shoe the garbled trajectory of my manhood. The ice buckled under me and I fell through.

Down through frozen fire, down through the dual rings of death, I am falling from the tower heights. I am screaming, screaming as I go down to shatter on the sidewalk below. On impact, my face touches mud, glass, plastic, matted leaves, memories, and secrets. Then my body revolves and my feet plant themselves in the liquid earth, I bend my knees and push for the surface. My heart skips a beat, and another beat, and even as I strain for the light above, I know I am dying. My heart fails, my lungs fail, and now I am dead.

I break the surface, hacking water from my lungs. Gasping, panicking, pushing the floes aside, I gain the shallows, smashing the ice shelf with my every step. Reaching the shore, I fall onto the snowbank. Rising on all fours, then standing, I strip off all my clothing, which is beginning to burn me, freezing solid against my skin. Then I am running barefoot through the trees, my flesh burning, shaking uncontrollably. Back in the cabin, I crouch by the stove until my body ceases its convulsions, then dress myself in old clothes I find beneath a bed. I pull a dirty blanket over my shoulders.

I look about, wondering what has happened.

Where am I? I do not know this place.

I walk along a country road. An old man in a pickup truck stops and offers a lift. I get into the cab beside him, still shivering.

"Did ya have an accident?" he asks. "I didn't see no car off the road."

"F-f-fire, ice, water," I stammer.

"Okay, hang in there, boy. I'll take you down to the hospital in Montpelier."

Next I am stepping out of his truck, then walking out of the hospital parking lot, the old man calling after me, shaking his head.

After that, I stop beside the cabin of a sixteen-wheeler idling at a gas station.

The driver rolls down his window.

"Where you goin' dressed like that?" he asks.

"I d-d-don't know."

"Well, I'm goin' to New York City."

"I-I-I'll go there too."

"Okay. It looks like this is your lucky day. I ain't got no partner on this run."

I remember nothing about the journey.

I am standing on a sidewalk in a city, the truck roaring away, leaving a trail of exhaust. I need to get out of the wind; it's burning me. I climb cement steps, push a splintered door that is barred by yellow tape. The latch gives a little, then breaks. I go inside and climb the staircase. On an upper floor, I enter a bare room, littered with broken glass, mouse droppings, a frozen bat, a metal bed without a mattress. I lie down on the rusty springs, wrapping the blanket around my shoulders.

I will rest awhile. If I can sleep, I may dream, and when I awake from the dream I may remember where I should go.

The shivering returns, waking me from a dream, but the images dissolve and I cannot recapture them. I gaze through the window at the world, at the layers of phenomena. Many of these are visible, though flattened into a single plane. The invisible layers of secrets and lost memories are present but incomprehensible. They may be seen in brief flashes, though they are beyond counting. They are in relationship, yet how it works, and why it does, remains indecipherable. I exist as an element of the whole and may observe parts of it—myself a part, of course. Yet to see and understand the whole, I must wait patiently.

10

The grammar of memory

I raise my head and see that I am again in my room of hidden memories. Yes, here are the photos spread around the walls, the two little racing cars, the old painting of the horse. Beside me the giant is seated with his back to the wall, his knees up, chin on his chest, breathing lightly.

"Billy," I say, shaking his arm.

"Huh?" he says, startled. "Oh!"

He yawns. "I'm awake, Francisco."

"You can call me Max," I say. "That's what people mostly called me."

Openmouthed, he stares at me. His face lights up.

"Yes, Billy, it's coming back. I'm remembering things. Not everything, but pieces are coming together."

"That's wonderful!" exclaims the giant, clapping his hands like a child. "Oh, that is wonderful!"

"Some of it's hard, Billy. I know now why I lost my way. It took a couple of hours to go through it, just the bits and pieces, like a trail through a dark woods."

"Longer than a couple of hours, Francisco. When we got home from Vermont, you slept through the whole day and into late last night. I heard you get up around midnight."

"What time is it now?"

"Nearly morning."

"I'm sorry. You should go back to bed."

"No, I can't. I'm too happy. Can you talk about what happened to you?"

"I'll tell you more soon. But it's enough to say that I had an accident. I fell through the ice and nearly drowned."

"Francisco, I'm so glad you survived."

"I wouldn't have, without you."

He tilts his head reflectively.

"You know, I've often thought that we look at a pond and think it's an ocean. Other times, we look at an ocean and think it's just a pond."

"You mean we don't really understand what's important?"

"Something like that. We get large and small confused sometimes."

"Billy, can you tell me about the time you lost your memory? When we first met, you said you once were crazy but now you aren't. Were you really crazy?"

"I don't know for sure, Francisco."

"Max."

"I don't know for sure, Max. My thoughts weren't working right for a while—a few months, if I remember correctly. Most of the time was spent in a hospital bed. Then another thing happened. And maybe I was truly crazy for the second part. But it's in the past now. Twelve years ago, and it hasn't happened again."

"Billy," I say, choking up, "all the time I've lived here, I've been thinking mostly about myself. You've been looking after me, and I hardly gave it a thought."

"If you break your leg, Max, your leg demands all your attention for a time. If your mind gets hurt, it tries to possess your attention too."

"I know. I understand. But I can see now that you worked hard to keep me alive, and it must have taken a lot out of you."

"Nope, Max, not much. And you gave a lot in return."

"You're good."

Billy smiles.

"No," he says. "I just remember what it was like when it happened to me."

"When you lost your memory, you mean?"

"When I lost everything."

"You've been a true friend, Billy. And it's time I started being a real friend to you. I really would like to know what happened to you."

He ponders this a few moments, gazing far away, his childlike face growing older as he considers my request. Coming to a decision, he looks down at me and slowly gives a nod of affirmation.

"All right, Max," he murmurs. "If you wish."

I listen without interruption as he tells his story:

The car accident was in early April 2001. I remember nothing more than a deafening bang and then the car buckling and tumbling, my body and head lashing around, and blood flying everywhere. My seat belt was a World War II parachute harness, and it didn't break, but it wasn't tight either. My head and shoulders were inside the hopper, which Dad had padded with styro insulation because we have cold winters in Iowa. I guess that's what saved me.

The next thing I remember is waking up in a hospital bed, wondering where I was, hurting all over, an oxygen mask on my face. I tried to tear it off, but my arms wouldn't move. Nothing would move. I was encased in plaster, and whatever part of my body wasn't in a cast was bandaged.

The light in the room was too bright. Whenever I opened my eyes I saw people moving back and forth around me. I heard constant *beep-beep-beep*ing, and a voice on an intercom. Now and then, faces bent over me. I felt the sting of needles. My body was turned and cleaned. I felt sick when I saw the tube trailing out from between my legs, dripping yellow fluid. Other tubes went into my arms and belly through open ports in the plaster.

I couldn't think at all, but I was aware enough to wish I could slip away and die.

There were voices—doctors, nurses, medical students:

"He's hanging by a thread, but the thread is getting thicker day by day."

"Heart of a lion."

"Head like an oak."

"An oak hit by lightning. No one can survive this."

"Do your best."

"I've never seen anyone this tall in my whole life."

"He was a basketball player."

"The MRI and X-rays show no tumor on the pituitary gland and no osteogenic malformations, so this has to be genetic."

"The parents are dead."

"Next of kin?"

"None."

With eyes closed I listened to it all, trying to patch it together.

"William," a voice called. "Come on, big boy, wake up."

"Can you wiggle your toes, William?"

They called me William and Willy and Will and Billy—also the names of famous giants whenever they thought I couldn't hear.

Needles pricked my exposed toes.

"The automatic reflex is working fine, indicating no permanent nerve damage, as far as I can see. Any regaining of consciousness, Nurse?"

"He opens his eyes for a few seconds, Doctor. Just a few flutters a couple of times a day."

"Is he conscious enough to feel pain?"

"He groans whenever he comes out of it. The pattern is consistent—consciousness equals pain."

"The morphine drip should be keeping it under control."

The morphine drip kept it barely under control, though never quite enough. Whenever they turned my body, I opened my mouth to scream, but only croaks came out.

More and more I remained awake, listening, waiting, hoping that someone would let me die. I tried to recall beautiful things, happy memories to distract me from the pain. But nothing would come. There was nothing there. I had overheard someone say my parents were dead. I felt perplexed. Who were my parents? No images arose in my mind.

Sounds drifted in from time to time: a cow mooing, the roar of a crowd in a stadium, the pounding of a basketball on a wooden court.

Then the visitors came:

"Yo, Billy, it's Coach. I brought the guys to see you. Can you hear me?"

"I'm sorry, sir," said the nurse's voice. "He can't hear anything."

I tried to call out to them, *I can hear, I can hear!* But my mouth issued only its groans and croaks.

"I think he hears me," said the coach. "We love you, buddy. Keeping fighting now. Keep fighting."

"We love you, buddy, we love you!" came a chorus of voices, and I opened my eyes on a forest of tall trees surrounding the bed, white and black and yellow trees bending close, with faces worried or encouraging or sad. I saw a hand spinning a basketball on a fingertip.

"He sees it, he sees it. I saw him smile."

"That ain't no smile."

"Sure it was. You know the way his eyes go when he's happy."

Then I dropped down into the arms of my mother morphine.

In the middle of the night I was stabbed by new pains, my skull cracking open, but my hand could not reach the call button. Suddenly there was someone with me, standing beside the bed. I tried to turn my head to see who it was, but a blinding headache would not allow me to. I smelled a beautiful fragrance so subtle and unknown to me that I was bewildered by it. The woman put her hand on my bare forehead and held it there gently. She did not speak. The headache receded and I fell asleep.

When I awoke it was morning. My first awareness was a feeling of amazement over the goodness there was in the world, the presence of so many kind people in the world. Then came the conviction that I did not want to die.

Another day, another night, more voices in empty rooms:

"It's me, Billy. It's Carl Friesen."

A hand grasped my hand.

I opened my eyes on a stranger, a middle-aged man.

"Thank God you're going to make it, boy. Marian sends her love. Everyone back home is pulling for you."

"Who are you?" I groaned.

The man looked away, sighed, squeezed my hand.

"I'm a distant cousin of your mom's, Billy. I guess you're too unwell to remember me right now. I'm the executor of your parents' estate. You mustn't worry about anything. Just concentrate on getting stronger."

"Okay," I croaked.

"This is the first time he's spoken," said a nurse to my visitor, as if I wasn't there.

I remember the day they cut the casts off my body. My exposed skin looked yellow and was covered in a million red spots. It was tormentingly itchy, and the first thing I did was to scratch and scratch and scratch. I felt incredibly free, though I was shocked at the thinness of my arms and thighs.

There were physical therapy sessions, followed by the first attempts at walking, supervised by doctors and nurses. Because of my size, two hefty orderlies helped me to shuffle back and forth across my room. But I couldn't support my body at first.

"You've lost a lot of muscle mass," one of the doctors explained. "Don't worry, you'll rebuild it."

I sat up in bed most of the time, staring out the window at nearby buildings, or watching TV. I couldn't bear the programs for long, the noise and franticness, and I always switched it off. Neither could I focus on reading anything people brought me. Mostly I slept. Four times a day the staff made me walk up and down the ward, pushing a rolling walker that was specially made for a person my size. My greatest pleasure in life was to go to the bathroom on my own—the hateful catheter had been removed. Next favorite was the simple act of feeding myself, which was a return not only to liberty but to adult responsibility.

Pieces of memory:

Three of my teammates dropped in to my room by surprise one day, bringing me a gift. It was a New York Knicks tank-top shirt, signed with felt-tip pen by some of the major players. I could talk now, no longer rasping and croaking. I thanked them, but I didn't know what else to say. I didn't know who they were, really—not as individuals.

"I can't remember your names," I said.

One of them, a big black guy, started crying. One of the other guys punched him hard on the shoulder and said, "Stop that!"

"Sorry," he said. "Sorry, Billy."

He later joined the army, the young man who cried. He won medals and was killed in Iraq.

Another memory:

A box full of get-well cards had been saved for me, hundreds of them. It took a whole day to go through them, squinting my eyes at the messages, straining to recognize the senders' names. I could identify none of them.

There were a series of tests and interviews with doctors.

"That's why we suggest you stay with us a while longer, William. Unless we put you on the rehabilitation program immediately, you're going to have problems with arthritis when you get older. We want to start you on a combination of general and sports-injury therapies. Of course, it's your choice. You can go home whenever you wish, and you could take the outpatient route."

"I don't know where my home is," I said.

A much longer course of testing followed, including interviews with psychiatrists and other physicians.

"William, your body has recovered remarkably well. The physical therapy department tells me that you're gaining muscle and mobility. I think they'll soon be letting you get around without the walker."

"I practice walking without it whenever no one's looking," I told him.

"Any dizziness or falls?"

"None."

"Excellent, but you're not quite out of the woods yet. Your medical team would like you to be admitted to a psychiatric facility here in Manhattan, the Wilder Penfield Institute. Would you agree to that?"

"Am I crazy, Doctor?" I asked with a sinking heart.

"No, not in the sense of mental derangement or dementia. You're quite sane, William, but you *are* suffering from amnesia."

"I know I can't remember a lot of things. But I feel sure it'll all come back to me."

"That's very much what we're hoping for. There are various kinds of amnesia, you see, and with most of them there's partial or total regain of memory. I think your prospects are very good."

"What kind of amnesia do I have, Doctor?"

"You have what's called Retrograde Amnesia, which means an inability to recall memories from before the onset of the condition. In other words, from before your accident." He paused. "Do you remember the accident, William?"

"A little bit, maybe a second or two. A loud bang, rolling upside down, blood. But I don't know what happened."

The doctor then proceeded to tell me more details. When he described my parents' deaths, I wanted to feel something but couldn't.

"Those poor people," I said.

"Do you remember your parents' faces from the time before it happened?" he asked.

I shook my head.

"Do you remember seeing them during or immediately after the accident?"

Again I shook my head.

"We don't believe you're suffering from Dissociative Amnesia, which has purely psychological causes, the repression of memory due to severe emotional trauma when seeing something horrifying; for example, a child who witnesses a fire that destroys all his family, or a person who sees the violent dismemberment of a loved one. But we haven't entirely ruled out dissociation as a partial influence in your present condition. Clearly, you've suffered severe trauma to your body, including skull fractures and internal bleeding in the brain, specifically in the medial temporal lobe. The tests show good physical recovery in that regard, but for the time being, the aftereffects of the head injury remain."

"Will I always be like this?"

"Most people retrieve what they've lost, though it takes time and some professional help. In summation, William, you have a fairly common form of amnesia. The good news is that it's usually temporary. You'll probably find that most or all of your general knowledge is still available to you, though occasionally weak on specific information. Also, the hospital staff informs me that you've been learning new things and remembering them. This means you're not suffering from associated Anterograde Amnesia. Can you remember all this? Can you say it back to me?"

"I have head-trauma retrograde amnesia. I probably don't have dissociative amnesia, but you haven't ruled it out."

"Excellent."

"But why can I access some things and not others?"

"Because different parts of the brain do different jobs, and the zone regulating your pre-trauma memories has suffered quite a blow. You might say it's in deep storage. It's all still there, and the odds are in your favor that everything will eventually reconnect."

"Thank you, Doctor."

The middle-aged man from Iowa returned during my third month of recovery. By then I was living at the Penfield Mind-Brain Institute.

"Hello, Carl Friesen," I said when he walked into the room, which made him grin and shoot two thumbs into the air.

I still couldn't remember anything from pre-trauma times, but Carl told me a great deal about my past. It seemed abstract to me, like hearing the details of another person's life. He had also been given Power of Attorney, he told me, and had opened a bank account in my name, here in New York City. I had to sign documents for the selling of the farm, and other documents directing the funds into my new account. There were insurance settlements as well.

He came to see me three more times that week. During the final visit he asked if I would like to return to live in the Des Moines valley.

"You could stay with me and Marian until you get settled," he offered. "Make a fresh start. You could continue your therapy at the local hospital."

I considered it, but felt that it wasn't a place I really knew. I thanked him sincerely, explaining that doctors here at the psychiatric institute were working with amnesia patients in a special way. I might move back west someday. Or I might return to school in the fall, if I had improved enough by then. And there was basketball too. I needed more time to think about the future.

Carl was an honorable man, and he did everything he promised. He left me with a box of photographs, offering to send me my high school trophies and other personal effects as soon as I decided where I would live. I wrote to him in July, asking him to wait on sending me any objects from my past. The photographs were enough for now. I spent long hours gazing at the faces in them, especially my mother's and father's. A trickle of emotion began to flow, along with a few flashes from my childhood and youth, no more than quickly passing scenes.

Daily I swam in the institute's ground-floor indoor pool and lifted weights in the gym. I hiked up and down the staircases, to and from my tenth-floor ward, avoiding elevators, doing everything possible to increase my strength. Each day I spent two hours with a speech-language therapist, seeking reconnections by working on word association, language skills, general knowledge, and dialogues. My room was a private one, modern and sterile, warmed a little by a soothing art print of a landscape and a pot of plastic flowers. Eventually I replaced them with the photos from my past, taping many to the walls. I felt depressed at times, seeing little progress with the amnesia, and sometimes I awoke at night in a state of panic—feeling that I was completely alone in the world, without a family.

I made an effort to spend more time in the common room. There were a lot of suffering people in the institute, all of them afflicted with mental troubles, most of them on medications that kept them tranquil. It seemed that by engaging them I lifted their hearts a little. I frightened some of them at first, because they believed I was a hallucination. As we got to know each other, however, things settled down and I learned that I had a gift for making people smile.

One old man in a wheelchair caught my special attention. He looked very angry and never spoke with other people. I sat down across from him in the recreation room one evening and asked him if he would be interested in playing a game of checkers. He glared at me suspiciously, grunted, and then said in a conspiratorial tone of voice:

"Are you the count of Monte Cristo or the prisoner of Zenda?"

"Mmm, neither," I answered.

"Me, I'm the man in the iron mask."

"I'm Billy Revere," I told him, offering my hand for a shake.

"Watch out how you use that thing," he grumbled, indicating my hand. Nevertheless, he took it and gave it a single pump.

"Okay, I can see you're one of us prisoners, so I'll trust you. My name's Giacomo Loncari. My children put me in here because they're after my money. Non compos mentis, if you know what that means."

"I don't, sir."

"Psycho, nuts, buggy, schizo."

"Would you like the black markers or the red?" I asked him.

"Black. I prefer to be in the black, not in the red. So, what's your opinion? Am I crazy?"

"I have no way of telling at this point, sir. I myself am not in the best of condition."

He laughed. "Seems like you're not only industrial size, you're also an honest guy."

"I hope I am, sir. However, I have no way of knowing if I was honest before I lost my memory."

"Oh, you were honest, all right. It's written all over your face. You're so honest it's sickening."

"Your move, sir."

"Stop calling me sir. And here's my card. Call me when they set you free. My lawyers are busy trying to get me out of this hellhole even as we speak, so I should be home soon."

"Thank you, Giacomo. I will call you."

On the first day of August, I went to bed in a state of anxiety, realizing that at the present rate of progress, my full mental recovery could take years, if it happened at all. I hadn't slept during the previous two days and nights, and now exhaustion overrode my fears.

During the night I awoke, groggy and somewhat disoriented, my heart banging hard from a nightmare. I had dreamed of two skyscrapers burning, people jumping and falling out of them, and then the towers collapsing. I felt a hand placed gently on my forehead. Only half-awake, I thought it was part of the dream, until I smelled an enchanting fragrance—the same scent associated with the warm feminine hand that had come to me during a painful stage of my time in the hospital.

The door of my room was open partway, and the night-light from the ward hallway filtered in. I tried to sit up, to see who was touching me, but the hand and the scent faded away.

I reached over and turned on the bedside lamp. I was alone in the room. Restless, I padded barefoot in my pajamas down to the nursing station. The nurse on duty told me there had been no visitors; no one had entered or left my room.

I wandered into the darkened games room and over to the large picture window—made of very thick glass, to prevent anyone from breaking it and committing suicide.

I stood for a while looking out at the city lights, a million stars blazing from hundreds of office towers. The winking lights of a jetliner passed from east to west. I gazed at it all until my heart grew quiet again. And then it skipped a beat and began racing, because I noticed that the two highest towers were the ones in my dream. I had seen them many times before, but had taken no particular interest in them.

The next morning, August 2, 2001, I asked for a day pass, explaining to my psychologist that I needed to have some fresh air and to see the outside world. He wrote out the permission slip and gave it to me along with a card, on which was written my name and the clinic address, and a message requesting that any person or persons reading it would return me to the institute if I should lose my way.

When I set out on my walk, I thought the towers were almost next-door. But block after block seemed to bring them no closer. The nearer they came, the higher and higher they rose in the sky. So enormous were they that when I arrived at the plaza half an hour later, I put a crick in my neck looking up at the top. Entering one of the towers, I crossed a lobby as big as a cathedral, and at an information desk I asked a uniformed man if the building had water sprinklers in case of fire. He told me that it did.

"Why are you asking?" he said with a look.

"I had a dream that it was on fire," I answered. "The other building too. They both burned from the top and then they collapsed."

He smiled. "Well, pal, the chance of a fire in one of these is just about nil. As for both of them catching fire at the same time, that's impossible. And nothing is going to bring them down, not even the worst kind of earthquake. They're built to last forever."

"That's very reassuring," I said. "Thank you for your time, sir."

"No problem. Hey, how tall are you anyway?"

I left the building and crossed the plaza to the other tower. There I asked the same questions of a man at the lobby desk. He gave the same answers.

Greatly relieved, I went back outside, and sat down on one of the low benches around the golden-globe fountain. I guessed the globe was supposed to represent the world, but I thought it was a poor design, the way they'd made it out of broken pieces.

I chided myself for taking a dream too seriously. People dream all the time, I thought. Dreams are produced by the imagination. You had a hard blow, losing your family and your past. Your world fell apart. So you had a nightmare about a disaster striking the city. Your subconscious turned your tragedy into someone else's tragedy, so you could look at it from the outside, symbolically.

I was glad to realize I knew words like *symbolically* and *subconscious*.

It was a warm summer day, and I was tuckered out from my long walk. I lay back on the bench, with my knees sticking off the end and my feet on the pavement stones. With my arms behind my head I stared up at the sky. Without warning, an airplane shot like an arrow across my field of vision, hitting the tower on my left. A huge fireball blew out through the side of the building, close to the top. Instantaneously, a second plane hit the other tower, with more fire and smoke. Tiny human shapes began to fall like rain.

I jumped to my feet, throwing up my arms to catch the people and to stop the buildings from collapsing. Then I blinked and everything was normal again.

I went back into the lobbies of both buildings and spoke to the guards on duty.

"Airplanes are going to hit these buildings," I told them. "I don't know when but it'll be soon. You've got to warn people, you've got to get them out of here."

The guards' reactions were mixed: some were amused, some were suspicious, a few questioned me about "inside knowledge". When I told them I had seen it in a dream and a vision, I was escorted out of the buildings.

"That's the third one this week," I heard a guard say.

Back at the institute I realized my foolishness. I had tried to warn them with no evidence whatsoever. How were they to know I wasn't a crazy person? How could they tell whether or not it was all in my mind? Then I thought maybe it *was* all in my mind. What kind of medication were the psychiatrists giving me? Could there be side effects like this?

I described to my psychologist what had happened. He informed me that I wasn't on any medications, because there was no pharmaceutical treatment for amnesia, and otherwise my mental condition was stable. They were, however, giving me a heavy dose of vitamins with every meal, including a concentrated dose of the Bs. He attributed my dream and vision to anxiety.

"The human mind projects," he explained. "We exteriorize a shapeless inner sense of dread by giving it visual form. No matter how fanciful a phantasm may seem, it functions as a focal point for the rational mind to process the irrational irruption. It's basically chemistry, Billy. If you like, I could ask a physician to prescribe medication to help you with it."

I thanked him and said I would go for a swim instead. Swimming always made me feel better. So I swam forty lengths, and I tromped up and down the ten staircases, and felt better for it. I napped in the afternoon, but woke abruptly from another nightmare. It was the same as the first, with the addition of two jets and falling bodies. Moreover, as I came fully awake I heard a voice say, *Forty days more and the towers will fall.*

On August 3 I returned to the World Trade Center plaza. I entered the south tower and tried to arrange an appointment with the building's manager or security department. Again I was escorted from the premises. A guard at the entrance to the north tower wouldn't even let me in, and told me he would call the police if I returned. Discouraged, I sat down on a bench by the fountain, wondering what to do. I must have remained there without moving for hours, watching hundreds, then thousands, of people entering and leaving the towers. How many of them would die?

Every day that week I returned, sitting and watching. At times I strode around the entire complex, looking for exits, safety measures, anything that might be of help when the blow fell. If only I could enter the buildings and reconnoiter the elevators and emergency staircases. I knew what it was like to climb ten floors, but I had no idea if I could climb a hundred and more. And what about these people, most of whom were less fit than I was? Of course, they would be trying to come *down* the stairs, but it was still a long way to descend with a fire raging above your head. And what about smoke?

During the following week, I tried to engage people entering and leaving the buildings. No one would listen. A few thought I was a carnival act. Others were sure I was a mentally ill street person. Guards began watching from the doorways. Two city policemen stopped and questioned me, read my card, and told me to go back to the institute. They were friendly but firm. Day after day, I kept trying, but now many of the people who worked in the buildings swerved to avoid me as they arrived in the morning or left for the night. I could still engage visitors, but I knew they might not even be here on the day of calamity.

On August 15, the staff and patients at the institute surprised me with a birthday party. It was my twentieth. There was a cake with candles, party hats and balloons, and everyone sang "Happy Birthday" to me. Giacomo was scheduled to be discharged the next day and was in good humor because of it. He handed me an envelope containing a stack of ten-dollar bills—two hundred dollars' worth—and told me to "get a life when you get sprung." He also exacted a promise that I would call him as soon as I was a free man. I gave him my word. He had a proposition to make, he said. He needed a caretaker for a building he owned on West Forty-Fifth Street. He lived on the ground floor and needed someone with "muscle" to keep things in line; the other tenants were "fly-by-nights and yahoos". I could live there rent free if I checked the boiler, took out the garbage, and kept "druggies and squatters" from moving in.

"Do we gotta deal?" he asked.

"It sounds like a very good deal, sir."

"Stop calling me sir!"

The next morning I rode the elevator with him down to the ground floor, where he was met by a chauffeur and limousine, which drove him away, cigar in mouth and waving a hearty good-bye. Immediately I set forth with his gift in my hip pocket. Along the route I purchased a large backpack, and then stopped in at a photocopy store. I handed an employee a sheet of paper on which I had written:

> If you are employed here, please arrange
> to be absent from work
> from September 10th through the 12th!
> YOUR LIFE MAY DEPEND ON IT!
> Please feel free to make copies of this warning
> and pass them on to as many people as possible.
> THIS IS NOT A HOAX!

I ordered five thousand copies and waited while they were printed. When the job was done, I loaded the stacks of paper into my backpack and hurried onward to the plaza. There I began to distribute the warning.

"Twenty-six more days and these towers will fall!" I declared to anyone who would accept one.

From time to time, people asked if they could have their photo taken with me. I always agreed. It was my size that interested them, I suppose, though the warning probably added a little flavor to the stories they would tell about the characters you meet on the streets of New York City. I wasn't the only odd person in the plaza and surrounding area. There were people with political causes to promote, others who were advertising theatrical performances or products for sale, and even a few with personal grievances, such as the lady whose husband owned a corporation headquartered in one of the towers. She was handing out sheets of paper describing how her husband was reneging on his alimony payments. I asked her what alimony was, and she explained. She asked me what I meant by the towers falling. She didn't look convinced by my account of what had happened to me, the dream and the vision and the voice, but she did keep one of my papers and promised to make her own copies to distribute. She told me her name, and I told her mine.

"I can assure you, Billy," she said, "there's one tower here that's definitely going to fall!"

Throngs of Japanese tourists came every day, following their guides, who spoke through mobile microphones and led their flocks under red umbrellas. Invariably, they swarmed me for group photos, and not one declined to take my warning paper as a souvenir.

As I said, I wasn't the only odd person in the plaza, but I was surely the most visible. Which meant that, from time to time, I would be stopped by a policeman and questioned, and told to leave the plaza. I would then circle the streets surrounding the World Trade Center complex, handing out my warning to any who would take one. I was saddened by some of the rude things people said, but occasionally moved by individuals who would stop and carefully read what I wrote. A child gave me a candy in a cellophane wrapper. A beggar offered me half of his sandwich. A lovely young woman who worked as a secretary in one of the towers surprised me by buying me my first espresso, giving it with a smile and an apology that it might be too strong for my liking. One old lady embraced me and cried. An old man kissed my cheeks and cried. For the most part, people swerved to avoid me.

And sometimes, if the truth be told, I sat down on the benches by the fountain and cried too. I'm not sure why exactly. Maybe it was because I felt such awful sorrow over what was going to happen. Or maybe it was because it struck me that nothing whatsoever would happen and that I was, in fact, a genuinely crazy person. Of the two possibilities, I felt that the latter was preferable by far. Still, to be crazy—to be deranged and delusional, to spread false alarm and strike unnecessary fear into hearts—that was a sad ending to the hope-filled journey that had begun in Iowa only two years before.

On September 5 I was arrested in the plaza as I was handing out papers to people leaving work for the day. The police held me overnight in a cell. In the morning, my psychologist arrived and had me released. He brought me by taxi back to the institute, and there I was given a new room on the ninth floor in a locked ward. Later in the day, staff brought me my photographs and I spent an hour or two taping them to the walls. During the next few days, the seventh to the tenth of the month, I grew increasingly frantic, for I knew that with every passing hour opportunities to warn people were lost.

My psychiatrist prescribed a medication that would make me tranquil, but I hid the pills under my tongue and spit them into the toilet when no one was looking.

The night of the tenth was the worst. I did not sleep at all. I was allowed to sit in the patients' common room, which, like the one in the open ward, faced south toward the towers. I stood and gazed at its lights for hours, agitated and weeping.

As dawn crept over the city, I dressed myself and waited in my room for an opportunity to escape the ward. Shortly before 8 A.M., the night staff prepared to depart as the day shift began to arrive. A cleaning man made a last swab of the floor in front of the emergency exit, and unlocked the door to the stairwell. He pushed his rolling bucket through and propped the door open for a few seconds while he made a final squeeze of his mop in the janitor's closet beside it. In an instant I was out and galloping down the back staircase three steps at a time. I was two floors below when I heard the sound of his carefree whistling while he methodically mopped the ninth-floor landing and the steps behind me. Within a minute or so I was at the bottom, pushing my way out the exit door and into an alleyway. A bell started ringing as I jogged onto the street. I turned south and began to run.

The clock on the wall of a passing bank told me it was now 8:15. I did not know when the catastrophe would happen, but my every instinct told me it was near. I arrived in the plaza completely winded, and stopped to catch my breath beside the golden globe. A minute later the passenger jet hit the north tower, and debris began to fall. A chunk of building material landed on the globe, denting its top. Flames and smoke poured out of the tower. Gasping, I ran toward its ground-floor entrance, without a thought in my mind, driven by the certainty that I must do whatever I could to help. But the way into the building was blocked as people began streaming out of it. Many of them looked stunned, or irritated, or simply confused. Everyone was asking questions, looking up at the tower above them because at this point few if any of them knew what had happened.

I stood in their path, yelling, "Run! Run! Get as far away from here as you can!"

More and more people stumbled out of the tower. I heard the distant sirens of fire trucks, ambulances, and police cars.

"The elevators aren't working!" someone screamed.

"There's fire inside!"

"Explosions!"

"Run!" I yelled above the tumult of voices, but no one listened, no one seemed to see me, though they continued to pass around me as a river divides around an island.

Then the second jet hit the south tower.

Women screamed and sobbed, men cried out and swore, stumbling backward, staring upward, walking, running, or frozen immobile in horror. People shouted into cell phones, wept into cell phones, tapped numbers on their cell phones. Others held each other tightly and simply watched. Glass rained down, and bits of burning flesh, and bound documents and electronic instruments and briefcases and wristwatches. Myriads of small objects floated about in the air, black and white ash, foam coffee cups and fluttering credit cards, while a hail of heavier wallets and shoes continued to thump onto the ground.

Now an army of firefighters and police had arrived, hoses snaking toward the buildings. I tried to go with them, but they pushed me away.

Back on the plaza, I resumed my yelling, but nothing could be heard in the din of sirens and cries. Human shapes were dropping out of the upper stories, sometimes alone, or holding hands.

"Run!" I yelled again. "The towers are going to come down!" And I was still yelling when rescue workers herded me and everyone else out of the plaza. I was a block away, still trying to find a way in but held back by a barrier, when the south tower boomed and slowly collapsed downward onto its very roots in the earth. A storm cloud of ash and smoke rolled our way, and now everyone ran from it. Old and young tripped and fell. I picked them up and hurried them on, carried some of them to the safety of alleys and recessed storefronts. When the cloud hit us, we all fell down and ash covered us. Something hit my head.

I lost consciousness, maybe for no more than a few minutes. I was struggling to my feet when the second tower went down and another wave hit us. A single sock blew past my eyes—light green with a red stripe and a hole in the heel—a child's sock. Confused and dizzy, I picked it up, pushed it into my pocket, thinking that I would try to find the child and return it to him.

When I could stand again, blood was streaking me from a wound on my forehead, and all around me other survivors were bleeding too, trying to rise, red on gray and white, all of us ghosts in a city of ghosts, hacking and spewing ash from our throats and lungs. Together we staggered toward a hint of light in the distance, for it was like night under the cloud.

People helped each other. I remember that. Yes, people helped each other.

I know there were selfish individuals among the survivors. I saw things they did. But they were few in number. Many turned their hearts to the needs of others. The strong helped the weak.

On that day we were revealed to ourselves. We had thought we were indifferent, and we learned it was not so—most of us, I should say. Most of us remembered who we were. We saw that we had forgotten important things, that we had lived as if great things were small and small things were great. We had been asleep, or forgetful of the state of man and his vulnerability. We awoke for a moment, an hour, a day, and knew ourselves as better than we thought we were, knew for a brief burning instant that we might yet become what we truly are.

But why did we fall back into unremembering, Max? Why did we resume our older ways? I do not know. And now I wonder if I will ever know.

Billy opens his eyes and raises his head to look at the window in my room of hidden memories. Morning light shines through the translucent glass.

"I have to go feed the girls," he says.

"I'll collect the eggs," I say.

Up on the roof we stand side by side, straining our eyes southward to the tip of Manhattan, where the sun is glinting on the new tower, nearly completed.

"We could go down there together," he says. "We could go down there and remember."

"Yes," I answer. I am afraid, but, strangely, no longer very afraid.

He is making coffee and frying an omelet for our breakfast.

"You did your best," I tell him. "You gave everything."

"It wasn't enough, Max."

"I know. It's never enough. And even if we could give more than everything, even then it wouldn't be enough."

He nods in agreement, focusing his eyes on his cooking.

"There's no explanation," I say. "No explanation for why some people die and some are rescued."

"None that would fit into our little minds, Max. But we can choose to do what we can."

"And we can choose to remember them."

"Which is a way of loving them. So that nothing is lost, nothing is wasted, and the goodness they left behind is still alive in the hearts of others."

"We can't know them all, Billy. We can't know their stories, why some were there that day and some were not."

"We can know them in another way. There are hints scattered about the earth, I think. Little things, very little, but pointing to a bigger story."

"Like the things in your hidden room of the mind, Billy?"

"Uh-huh," he says with a nod, and flips the omelet, still absorbed. "Fingerprints, unspoken words, traces left everywhere, seen and unseen. They're waiting to tell their story, if we stop awhile and listen."

I tell him about Puck on the morning of September 11, how my little brother had been so afraid that day, without reason, and how I had reassured him that there was nothing to fear, that all would be well.

Wordlessly, Billy goes into his hidden room of the mind and retrieves the sock he had saved. He gives it to me.

The following day we go to the site of the World Trade Center. There is a museum now, and other memorials. Colossal new buildings. Many tourists. Busloads full of school children for whom this place is ancient history. For me, for Billy, it was yesterday.

We stand silently side by side, trying to absorb the reality: Yes, this was the place. For me, the site of my parents' and brother's deaths. I feel disturbed, with a confusion of emotions, but I am unable to cry.

When we leave and head back uptown, I am different. I cannot say for certain how I am changed, but I am.

I return to live in my apartment—the apartment of Max Davies—and spend a week cleaning it and reacquainting myself with myself. I put my photos from the room of my hidden memories back on the shelves and walls. The two little yellow racing cars have a prominent place.

I visit Billy's apartment most evenings. He is often out on his night errands around the city. I now understand that this is his role—the rescuer.

We share a supper together once during that week, doted upon by our Chinese friends. We share an afternoon coffee at Dina's.

I notice that her elephant tattoo is entirely gone.

"I see you've had the Greek-Indian elephant tattoo removed from your arm," I say, having a momentary relapse.

"Whaaat!" she loudly exclaims. "You lose your marbles, Frankie? I ain't got no tattoo. Never did have one." She shrugs. "'Course, my dad was Greek and my mum was from Bangalore. That's in India. But there wasn't no elephant in the mix."

"How old are you?" I ask her.

"Thirty-seven, kiddo. Hey, don't you ever learn your lessons?"

"Sorry. I would have placed you in your mid- to late twenties."

"Yeah, right. So, you guys want the special or your usual?"

"The special," we say in unison.

"Comin' right up, boys."

Alone, I visit the Metropolitan Museum to see *Boy in Red, Portrait of Manuel Osorio Manrique de Zuñiga* by Francisco de Goya. The jackdaw is still pecking the piece of paper, but the image on it is something indecipherable. It is not the skyline of New York City. The scratchings beneath it are not numbers, not even remotely 09-11-2001.

Each day brings small leaves of memory floating to the surface. I am coming to see how complex my former life was.

"I've been away," I tell the curator-owner of the gallery where I exhibited.

"I'm not canceling your next show, Max. So go ahead and sue me."

"I'm not going to sue you," I say. "And I'll show up for the opening, if you still want me. Sober too."

"Uh, sure. Yes, I'd like that. What's come over you?"

"I've been ill. I'm doing better now."

"That's good to hear. Now tell me why you ignored all my calls and the media requests."

"I was totally out of contact. Just got home, and I'm trying to plow through the backlog."

"Sounds like you had a good vacation."

"Yes," I say sincerely, nodding. "It was very good."

"Any new paintings?"

"A few unfinished. I'll try to have them completed by the opening. They'll probably be somewhat different from what I've done before."

He looks suddenly worried. I'm his moneymaker, his cash cow.

"Okay. Bring them in and we can have a look."

There are phone calls to return, a few dozen urgents out of the hundreds of loud superficials. Not a word from France. A flood of messages from Maryland. I call my grandparents and arrange to visit them soon—a long visit. There are also bills to pay, and banking to do, the landlord to placate, the very last empty bottles to be taken down to the bins at the curb. There are plenty of things in the apartment I want to sell—the expensive ornaments and jewelry and clothing with which I used to console myself. A week or two passes and they are all gone. I donate the proceeds to the churches where Billy tends his breadlines and soup kitchens. I feel poorer and more buoyant, and in the process have learned that deprivation can be good for the soul—the nouveau-riche boy returning to his essential form. With some reluctance, though with a feeling of the rightness of the move, I consign the broken photograph of Françoise and me to a burial at sea—via the Liberty Park ferry. Images of other people are sacred, in a sense, but if we cling to them like talismans we run the risk of obsession with unreality.

I go down to the site of the catastrophe one more time, alone. There I weep openly, sobbing loudly and grieving completely at last. I walk all the way home to the East Village suspended in a feeling of peace.

Returning from Maryland, I take up painting again. The flow of creative intuition is more difficult, perhaps from lack of use, but more likely because the themes of my 9/11 paintings have altered in meaning. On one level they are the same. On another, I see them with new eyes—see my own experience with greater understanding. A trauma can keep you stalled at the age it happened to you. You can bury the memory and think it's dealt with, done and gone. It is never gone, but it must be transformed into something that gives us life. To overcome death, you must create life. But we have to choose to undertake this hard labor, if we would grow older and wiser, and—as Billy said, as Granddad Robbie said—become who we are. Part of me, until now, has remained eleven years old. Now I can begin the long process of growing up.

Billy arrives at my apartment late one afternoon. I had left a note at his place, inviting him for supper. After some bone-rattling back thumps, we eat the meal he has brought in shopping bags—Chinese, of course. There's also a gift of three dozen eggs, small and large. We don't say much. It's just good to be together again.

"Billy," I venture as we sip our tea (his in a soup bowl, mine in a mug), "Billy, this is a pretty big place I live in. I've been wondering if you'd consider a change of scene. I'd be honored if you'd come live with me here."

He screws up his face in indecision, smiles, laughs. "The ceilings are right," he says.

"Yeah, and we could try to find an extra-long Lincoln bed for you, or maybe build one ourselves."

"Ah, Max, you know I prefer the floor. It's better for my back."

"And if you're worrying about where to put all the memories from your hidden room of the mind, there's a loft for rent just down the corridor. I'd be happy to cover the cost."

"Mmm, Max, that's very generous, but you have your future ahead of you."

"Well, think about it, would you?"

"I will."

Two days later I am hard at work painting in my studio. It's something new, a kind of landscape with symbolic implications, not quite coalesced into specific form. It's full of lavish color. I'm not entirely sure what it's going to be, what my heart is saying through it, but I can already tell it will be beautiful.

There comes a moment when my concentration is broken by a sense that there is someone else in the room. Startled, I look around to see Billy standing in the doorway, smiling paternally over me.

"How long have you been there?" I ask with a laugh.

"A while," he says.

"I'm getting a little obsessed with this," I tell him, turning back to the painting, and laying on a brush stroke.

"It's very fine, Max," he says. "It's a new kind of work, isn't it?"

"Uh-huh," I say with a nod, and continue painting, loath to lose the inspiration of the moment. "Gimme a second, Billy, and I'll be right with you."

"I love you, buddy," I hear him say. "Keeping fighting now. Keep fighting."

"Love you too, buddy," I murmur distractedly.

Minutes later, when I turn around to ask him to put a kettle on the stove, he is no longer there. I search through the apartment, but he is gone.

Light fantastic

It is a measure of how absorbed I was in my art that a week passed before I ventured over to the west side to see my friend. I was perplexed when I found the front entrance of our old building boarded and padlocked.

I returned to my apartment, thinking that Billy would soon show up with an explanation. Another week passed, and still he did not appear. By then, my autumn show was looming, and I was busy with the gallery people choosing frames and deliberating over my new work. Of course, they had an assured winner in the older pieces dealing with death and destruction, and thus they looked dubiously upon my neosymbolist landscapes, with their not-quite-visible influence of the happier kind of Chagall and the relatively unmelancholic end of the Goya spectrum. A few of these paintings were added to the show, to test the waters.

The opening went very well, with more than half the work sold that night, the disasters going first, the new work following close behind. Reviews were mixed.

By then it was a month since I had last seen Billy. Now I made a concerted effort to find him. Our Chinese friends had not seen him since our last meal there.

Our favorite waitress at Dina's reported the same. The people at the soup kitchens and breadlines where he had regularly volunteered were as concerned as I was. No one had seen him. I dropped into Giacomo Loncari's apartment building on Lexington, only to learn that the man was recently deceased. Neither the doorman nor the manager had seen Billy since the funeral, though they knew him well. I wondered if he was ill, perhaps a patient in one of the city's many hospitals. I telephoned every one, as well as the psychiatric institute where he had lived for some months around the time of September 11. He had not been admitted to any of them.

By now I was feeling a little hurt, and more than a little worried. Remembering that he jogged daily in Central Park, I sat for three days on a bench among pigeons and falling leaves, reading books and waiting for the vibrations in the earth that presaged the sound of pounding feet. He did not come. The local police precinct informed me that not a single body of a giant had turned up in the city morgues. I left a note inserted into the door crack of our old apartment building on West Forty-Fifth. Returning a few days later, I found that it hadn't been touched. Again and again I returned, sometimes at night, hoping to see a light in an upper floor window. Nothing.

In the end I decided I had to get on with my life. It was what Billy would have wanted me to do. *Keep fighting now*, he had said the last time we saw each other. *Keep fighting*. They were the last words he had spoken to me.

In early March I returned to the building for a final visit. A crew of workmen were carrying lumber and sheets of drywall up the front steps. The sound of circular saws and hammering came from within. The foreman told me that the building had been sold and that the new owner was turning it into luxury apartments. I explained that I had lived here until only recently and would be grateful for a last look around. He gave me ten minutes. The fourth floor was a maze of open wall studs. An electrician high on a ladder was removing old wiring from the ceiling. Two broken chandeliers had been heaped in refuse bins by the staircase. The room of Billy's hidden memories was still exactly where it had been, though it was now empty of all furnishings. Only the paler squares and rectangles on the walls testified to paintings and photos that had once hung there. My own room of hidden memories was likewise bare.

In April 2014, I purchased a used minivan. It was an ugly, rusty old thing, but it had a motor and transmission built to last forever, and the gas mileage was moderately good. Though I had plenty of money, there was no guarantee that it would last as long as the vehicle. Besides, I had resolved to live more simply. Along these lines, I had also decided that I would soon try to find a cheaper apartment, maybe something farther out toward the edges of the galaxy—that is, a suburb of New York.

A year had passed since the return of my memory. Recalling the day Billy and I had driven north to Vermont in search of clues, I thought I might make the same journey, a kind of final step of closure.

The morning was sunny, the hills washed with mint-green new leaf and the occasional bursts of white and pink apple and cherry trees enduring in the midst of old farms encroached upon by young woods. I stopped at every place we had stopped, trying to regain a sense of what I had felt that day, how limited my consciousness had been, how damaged my emotions. By the Connecticut River and later a branch of the White, I paused and stepped out of the vehicle to breathe the clean air and listen to the soft flow of the waters. I drank coffee from my thermos and ate my chopped-egg sandwiches in the village that had a bronze memorial to the fallen Civil War soldiers of the region. I read the names of young men not much different from me, more than sixty of them, the loved and bereaved of another century, boys who had turned the fields with plow and oxen, and hunted the forests in search of game, dreaming of love and fruitfulness and plenty, not knowing they would be felled in their prime.

As I took the road that went over the mountains and down into the valley of Tadd's Ford, I felt a vague apprehension. There was no fear in it, however, and along with the most recent, most unhappy memory of the old homestead, there were numerous beautiful memories that rose to greet me: me and Puck and our mischievous adventures, the thrilling dangers of the reservoir and waterwheel, the molting rocking horse, the endless affection of our grandmother Dorothy, and even the less frequent kindness of Ben. I was not entirely sure if I was ready to have a look at the dark cabin, or at the pond, which for me was a well at the world's end, containing, I knew, both evil memories and the mementos of permanent loss.

Entering the village, I coasted slowly between its few buildings and rolled to a stop in front of Myrt's Café. The memory of the tang of lemon pie leaped to my tongue, and my fate was sealed.

The doorbells jingled as I went inside, but Myrtle was nowhere in sight. The place was deserted, save for the old man who had been sitting at the same table a year ago, and perhaps had never vacated it. He looked up from his newspaper, took a sip from his coffee cup, and went back to reading. Looking around, I saw that nothing had changed. The glass dome covering the pie racks was still there, along with the crossed snowshoes and the bobcat pelt. A few colorful quilts hung from the rafters, with price tags pinned to their borders.

I sat down at a table by the front window and waited. Presently a young woman came out through the kitchen doors, wiping her hands on an overly large apron. She swung around the end of the counter and approached me with a somewhat amazed, pleased look, as if the arrival of a new customer did not happen very often.

"Hi," she said in a cheery voice. "I'm afraid the lunchtime menu is closed for the day, but I can offer you coffee and pie, if you'd like to try a slice."

She was about my age, pretty and eager, dressed in a blue denim skirt and white blouse, and lacking any hint of either the sultry or desultory. She wore no makeup, and wisps of dark-brown hair escaping from bobby pins fell over her clear brow. A local girl, I supposed, hanging on to the last scraps of wholesomeness in the midst of a jaded era.

"I would love a piece of your lemon pie," I said. "It's famous."

"Famous within a five-mile radius," she said with a smile, without a hint of sarcasm. The joke made her face shine, and I laughed without any effort at all.

She went off to cut me a piece, and returned shortly bearing a plate with an extra-large helping and a cup of coffee I hadn't ordered. She placed it before me just as Myrtle had done a year ago.

"How do you know about our pie?" she asked, hovering.

"I stopped by last April," I explained. "That's why I've driven hundreds of miles for a second piece."

"My goodness, that far! Hmm, your accent isn't Boston, which stands out a mile. My guess is somewhere in southern New Hampshire."

"I was born in Brooklyn and spent my childhood there. I live in New York City now."

"But you don't sound like New York at all."

"I guess my accent has changed, kind of a mix of everything, Maryland mostly. Maybe even a drop or two of Vermont. My mother's family used to live around here."

"Really?" she said, looking closely at my face, and sitting down across from me. "What was their name?"

"Franklin," I said with a note of apology, for I wasn't sure of their reputation.

"*Dorothy* Franklin?" she asked.

"That was my grandmother."

"Oh, I remember her so well. A very nice lady. She taught me to knit and weave when I was younger. She ran a craft club for girls around here. We used to have it in the village hall before the roof collapsed in the bad winter of—mmm, I forget what year. Not many of us, three or four girls, but that didn't stop her. I still love weaving."

"I'm Max Davies," I said, offering her my hand. She shook it firmly, and then leaned forward, crossing her arms on the table, silently examining my face.

"You don't look like a Franklin, not that I knew any other than her."

"I resemble my father," I said. "And your name, miss?"

Before she could answer, the old man at the other table piped up:

"I'll have one of them lemon custards, Katie."

"Coming right up, Cory." She went back to the counter, unhurriedly going about her business, and when the old man was served she returned to my table and sat down again.

"Do you live here in Tadd's Ford?" I asked.

"Just returned," she said with a whimsical look. "I went off to see the world for a time. Got myself an arts degree and a graduate certificate in education, but decided enough is enough."

"So you're a teacher," I said disingenuously.

"Nope. Pie maker. Too much ego and ambition in all that education racket, too much 'quiet desperation', as Thoreau called it. People forget what life is about."

I indulged in a swift glance at her fingers. No rings.

"They never learn about the art of the pie," I said between bites.

"That and weaving and splitting kindling. The smell of wood smoke on a winter's eve. Stars you can see at night." She smiled. "And the world's chock-full of great books. By the way, Max, I hope I haven't offended you. Are you educated?"

"Informally."

"More pie?"

"I'd love a piece of Myrtle's pumpkin. By the way, where is she today?"

Her face saddened. "Grandma had a stroke last fall. She's in a nursing home in Montpelier. I make the pies now. I try to follow her recipe, but people tell me it's not quite up to her standards."

"It's still good pie," the old man interjected. "Though you go too heavy on the nutmeg."

"Thanks, Cory, I'll do some experimenting. You can be my taste tester."

"Glad to."

Katie and I shared a conspiratorial look.

"So," she said, turning back to me, "are you heading up to the old place?"

"Yes," I said, nodding. "I spent most of my summers there when I was a boy."

"It must have a lot of memories for you. It's really a pity what happened to it after your grandparents died. First the neglect and then the vandals. A fire took the roof off the mill and the brewery a few years back, though no one was ever caught. Such a fine old place with plenty of history."

"You've been there, then?"

"I used to pick berries on the property after it was abandoned—blackberries and raspberries running wild, and also the blueberries on the higher ground, among the junipers. There's that sweet pond out in the back. Migrating ducks land on it in the fall."

"Your grandmother told me that a bank took the property."

"Uh-huh, I think so," she said, with a sigh. "But no one has ever wanted to buy it. It's not good-enough soil for farming, and the timber is poor. I expect the bank would let it go for a song."

I glanced across the room in search of a clock, because I wanted to visit the homestead before the afternoon sun began sinking. I planned a short visit—my last, forever—and a return trip that would bring me back to the city by midnight. And then I spotted a framed painting of a horse hanging on the wall above the cash register. I stood up and crossed the room to look more closely. It was a painting very much like the one I had seen in the room of hidden memories.

Benny's Vermont Dark Ale.

For a moment I wondered if it was merely a copy of the one Billy had owned. But the crack across its middle was the same.

"Where did you get this?" I exhaled in wonder.

"Grandma told me a man gave it to her."

"A giant?"

"A giant, I don't know. She said he was a 'Paul Bunyan sort of gentleman'—her exact words."

"Did she tell you anything else? When was he here?"

"Late last fall, I think, because the painting wasn't there at Thanksgiving, when I came for a visit, and she had her stroke in early December. I moved home for good after that, you see."

"Katie, do you think your grandmother's well enough to receive a visitor?"

"Oh, she'd dearly love to have a visitor. She doesn't get many. She can't walk anymore and part of her face isn't working right, but her mind's as clear as ever."

"I would like to visit her, if I may."

"You surely may," Katie replied. Her eyes grew moist as she suddenly made herself busy wiping off the counter with a rag.

"So you're not going back to the city just yet?" she asked in a quiet voice.

Not yet, I thought. *I'll sleep in the van.*

"No, I think I'll stay awhile."

"Well, that's fine," she said. "That's just fine."

In June I moved the last of my belongings up from New York, and began the herculean task of sorting order out of the Franklin place—now my place. Local roofers repaired the tin shingles on the white house, and carpenters raised the fallen porch roof to install new posts. They also buttressed the staircase leading to the upper floor. A major project was a roof for the brewery. Over sturdy new trusses went barn-red metal sheets that did no disservice to the style and history of the venerable old structure. Its stones were still intact and needed only a scrubbing with lye and water. Katie helped me with that, as did three of her five brothers, hearty lads who looked as if they were descendants of the boys who had once lived in these hills, hunting squirrels and deer, their lives pondered by only a few after too long a passage of time, their courage and sacrifice memorialized by bronze sculptures in the declining villages of New England.

Summer brought an increase of tourists through the valley, not as many as one would meet in other places, but enough to keep Myrt's Café in operation. Busy with her pies and serving, Katie bicycled up to my place once or twice a week to give a day of free labor.

"This is what neighbors do," she scolded me, a little affronted by my attempt to pay her. "So put your money back in your pocket, buster." It was the last time I made that mistake.

She preferred the tasks I least wanted to put my hand to: painting the rooms in the house, cleaning cupboards, caulking the new window glass, and ridding the place of an army of mice. *My trapline*, she called it.

I liked her for her generosity, her perkiness, and her resolve, which was never intense, just focused. Despite what she had said about the "education racket" and "quiet desperation", she told me she still wanted to be a teacher. She was devoted to the ideas of Montessori and Cavalletti, which she explained at length as we scrubbed the vandal soot from old stones. If people started having children again, she mused, and if a schoolhouse could be reopened in Tadd's Ford, she would put all her energies into helping rebuild what she called a "rooted life connected to the land and human-scale community". She believed it was still possible. Clearly, Katie was capable of serious thought, reflective and insightful but never intellectualized. She also joked a lot. She was, for a time, the little sister I never had.

We twice drove down to Montpelier that summer and spent a few hours with Myrtle. She had heard much about me, I could tell, which she communicated by oblique questions and probing looks, cautious but ultimately approving of my presence in her ancestral valley. Occasionally she allowed herself a quiet, knowing smile that verged on the philosophical and timeless—perhaps the perspective that can be reached only by patient creation of quilts and families.

With her damaged mouth she asked me about Billy.

"Your friend, now," she said. "I liked that boy. You should tell him to come back here."

"I haven't seen him in a long time, Myrtle," I explained, "and I miss him a lot. But if I ever track him down, I'll bring him to see you."

"Well, that's just fine. You tell him I'll make him a right good lemon pie. Or this granddaughter of mine will. He likes lemon custard, doesn't he?"

"I think it was pumpkin."

"Now, that ain't exactly right, Max. He liked lemon *and* pumpkin. I'll make him both. And Katie here can order in some espresso coffee for him. You tell him, will you?"

"I will tell him."

"That is a first-rate man," she added. "A *legend* man. And I don't mean how tall he is."

I nodded. "I know what you mean."

"Good to know they still make that kind."

I nodded again, but I thought to myself that Billy was who he was not only because of his nature and upbringing but also by his personal sufferings—rather, by what he had done with them.

Sometimes Katie would bring a picnic lunch to my place and we would walk up the hills beyond the pond, onto the higher, drier ground where the blueberries were ripening. We would sit side by side, leaning against boulders and surveying the receding lines of ridges, dark green to purple to blue to gray dissolving into the sky in the north. Neither of us felt compelled to say much whenever we hiked there. It went without saying that I was beginning to wonder if she wondered if I wondered if she wondered what we two might become together. The subject was never discussed, nor was it broached by any liberalities of touch. For both of us, I think, the question was merely savored as a possible future. Would we be friends and neighbors, or would we become something more? Little by little I wanted us to become something more.

For the most part, I was too busy for any preoccupation with love. And she was absent most of the time. Yet there were hot nights in August when I lay alone and sleepless on the old brass bed I had purchased at an auction, wondering if she would ever share it with me. I wondered as well over the generations who had been conceived and born and had grown to maturity and old age and natural death upon it. The window of the bedroom I had once shared with Puck was full of stars, and the violins of crickets and flute notes of peeping night frogs evoked profound feelings that I think were more about longing for a constant love than about passion.

Deciding to delay the restoration of the mill—which might be possible next year, finances permitting—I partitioned the ground floor of the brewery with new and well-insulated walls and ceiling, leaving one section for an art studio, three of its walls unaltered stone, one with a wide window exposed to northern light. I also installed a chimney and an airtight wood heater, which would ensure a snug place to paint during the swift-approaching cold months.

"We have two seasons in this neighborhood," Katie quipped. "Winter and preparing-for-winter."

Early on, I had purchased a chain saw, and throughout the warm months I cut down the dead trees close to the house, and buzzed them up into firewood for the coming winter. Dry, seasoned by age and weather, they made excellent fuel for the stoves I had installed in the studio and the kitchen. By the time summer drew to a close, I had stacked about twenty cords for each—forty cords in all. My muscles felt perpetually sore, and despite my youth I came to the end of each day overwhelmed with fatigue and ready for deep sleep. Yet it was a good tired, a satisfied tired, and not once during those months did I wake in the mornings with more than a moment's remembrance of a dream. The dreams, without exception, were good.

Behind the house and along the pathway to the cabin, wildflowers bloomed, withered, formed seeds, giving way to other species in turn, the foxglove, red columbine, and blue lupine nodding, entangled with roses, the remains of Grandma Dorothy's old garden run amok. The raspberries and blackberry canes spread rampantly throughout July and August, heavy with fruit. Katie came more and more often to reap the harvest, leaving me homemade pies by way of exchange, or generosity, or—I hoped—undeclared love.

The cabin out back was scoured and repaired—slowly healed, to a degree, of its darksome memories. I had not yet tackled the condition of the pond, which to the naked eye appeared to be thoroughly natural and *sweet*, as Katie had described it. Beneath the surface, however, were layers of murk containing the detritus of rage and despair, and who knew what else. For a week in September—sunny, warm, Indian summer days—I hired Katie's younger brothers to help me dredge the pond. In our swimming trunks, and shod with work boots in case of broken glass, we waded in with burlap sacks, wooden hay rakes, and hoes, pulling up a surprising amount of man-made objects. Three heaps grew on the banks. The first was a mound of brown beer bottles of recent design (Ben's, I presumed), the second a motley collection of genuine junk, including smashed computer components (my mother's), rusty tin cans, broken glass objects, and such. These I transported in my van to the local municipal dump.

The third was the smallest, where we deposited anything antique or verging thereon. Numerous medicine bottles surfaced, many from past centuries, smoky with age and filled with dirt, their embossed letters testifying to the popularity of what we might call snake oil remedies. To these were added clay and ceramic pots of quaint design, usually with only a crack or a chip to hint at why they had been discarded. I wondered at first over the country habit of depositing trash in a water source, for there seemed too many objects here to explain them as accidental losses. Had the pond once been a family dump? Had it once been a dry hollow? I reminded myself that in the days before garbage collection and public dumping grounds, each family dealt with its own refuse in whatever manner they thought best.

Not content with these finds, the enterprising brothers decided to dig deeper into the muck. They took turns walking back and forth endlessly, up to their necks at times, exploring the entire bottom with finer rakes and sieves. Though the pond was a stone's throw across and half again longer than its width, it amounted to a good deal of square footage and demanded an investment of time and patience. The treasures brought up from the depths proved to be well worth it. There were horseshoes and square hand-hammered spikes; parts of farm implements of ingenious, mysterious design; three blades of strap-on ice skates; several brass spigots; the long blade of an ice-cutting saw; and a ring of old-fashioned keys. There were also a few heavier items, such as stove trivets and boat-shaped weights for ironing cotton clothes. Finally, and most significantly, the boys found dozens of silver coins blackened by tarnish, with dates and features still readable. Most were from the nineteenth century, though three large ones were from the late seventeen hundreds. It was an astonishing find, and though the boys offered them to me as the rightful owner, I insisted that the treasure was theirs.

As I pored over the antique items, cleaning them by the water's edge, I happened to glance into an enameled kettle. Sitting in its muddy bottom were two gold rings. Later I mailed them to the people who manned one of Billy's soup kitchens, requesting that the rings be sold and the money used to feed his street friends.

The autumn turned glorious, the hills changing at a leisurely pace with successive waves of red and gold and yellow and purple. Light itself was transformed, alternately crystal clear and hazed with wood smoke. I sometimes wandered in the woods with my portable easel under my arm, and sat for hours making painted sketches on small pieces of hardboard, planning to work them up into larger pictures during the coming winter.

One whole afternoon I sat on a massive, lichen-covered rock at the height of land, working on a painting of a sugar maple flaring crimson against its background of tinted hills and azure sky. At one point I heard a little cough behind me, and fearing it was a black bear, I jumped up and prepared to bolt. But it was Katie, sitting in the grass about ten paces away with a berry pail at her feet.

"Oh, I didn't want to interrupt you," she said with an apologetic dip of her head.

"You're not interrupting me," I said, overjoyed to see her.

"May I look?" she asked.

She knelt down on the rock beside me and closely examined the painting. I expected she would give it a quick glance and then offer a standard compliment such as, "It's pretty." Instead, she kept on looking, and then sat down and looked some more. I began to wonder if she didn't like it, or thought it was nothing more than calendar art.

At last she turned her eyes to me.

"You love this tree, don't you?" she asked.

"Uh, yes, I guess I do," I said.

"It shows. What you feel for it is all here." She paused. "And you understand light."

She returned to the painting while I absorbed this.

"People look at things and never really see them," she went on in a reflective tone. "No flower, no sky, no tree is entirely like another. Each marvel in the world has its own place and character, its own beauty. And you respect it as something unique and glorious."

"Do I do that?" I asked with a smile, at first amused by her seriousness. Then struck dumb by it.

"Yes," she said. "You do."

I didn't see Katie for a couple of weeks as she harvested pumpkins in her family garden, and boiled them, spiced them (hopefully with not too much nutmeg), and canned them for next year's pies. In early October she and I took a daylong hike up the mountain behind my house, for the first time following the creek to its source in a convergence of springs near the top. There we picnicked and said little, gazing out over the ranges, content to rest in each other's company. At one point I reached for her hand, and she let me take it. Suffice it to say that our hands stayed united until we took leave of each other, hours later, at the end of my lane, where she hopped onto her bike and cycled for home, looking back at me with a smile. I was still waving good-bye when she rounded a curve and was gone from my eyes. Immediately I began yearning for her next visit.

I was invited to share Thanksgiving dinner with Katie's family. They lived on the outskirts of Tadd's Ford in a three-story clapboard house firmly planted on its fieldstone foundation, with its back to their hundred acres of pasture, garden, and woodlot. Considering they were a family with six children, among whom were five hearty boys with enormous appetites, I could not begin to guess how they made enough money to survive. I presumed there was income from the fiddles Katie's father carved and lacquered in his shed, and from the hand-planed refectory tables and Shaker chairs he built. Her mother made quilts and sold them at the café in the summer, and drove a small yellow bus for the remnant of local children who commuted to a school in a town ten miles away. The family must also have received a stipend for managing the little post office in the café, and doubtless Myrt's itself showed some modest profit. In any event, they were prosperous in a personal way, though not in the line of possessions.

I liked her parents very much. They were uncomplicated people who could surprise you with an insight or a carefully considered word. Their humor was gentle, their conversation was of the taciturn Vermont variety, kindly but not inclined to arrive at hasty conclusions. Their eye, so to speak, was turned to the lessons of the earth and the seasons and the endless marvels of fate and grace and nature—the intermingling of phenomena, the surprises to be found in the ordinary.

That weekend the house and table were full of the vital uproar of youth. An older brother and his wife were present with their three children. Another older brother, studying at a nearby college, had brought his girlfriend and two foreign students. Katie's siblings all played musical instruments, mainly fiddle, accordion, and an out-of-tune upright piano. Katie played a dulcimer that her father had made for her when she was a little girl. The singing and camaraderie went on into the wee hours of the night, long after the old folks had gone upstairs to bed. By the time I left to drive home, the sky was paling in the east and guests were spreading sleeping bags on couches and the rug in front of the fireplace. The foreigners, an African and a South American, both of them aficionados of beer, begged me to show them my "brewery", which I did the next day.

The snow began falling after Thanksgiving, and I tucked myself in for a long winter. Painting in the studio each day filled my hours, though I should say that this expression is not precise. The hours were neither endured nor measured nor filled. They had become my friends, time itself a boon and blessing. There was always something new: the last of the Canada geese winging southward, high up and honking; the cries of blue jays arriving to squabble in the woods; the visit of cedar waxwings passing through, gorging for three days on the wizened crab apples in the neglected orchard.

I was dazzled by the ever-creative displays of color that appeared in the sky before sunrise and sunset. The full moon rose, casting blue shadows of branches through the night woods. I came to love the cycling of the moon and the constellations revolving around the dependable polestar of the north.

All sounds were cleaner, sharper than the background cacophony of the city. The crunching snow beneath my boots. The snapping of morning fire in the cookstove. The sighing in the trees. Owls hooting in the woods. Strong wind or deep freezes made the house creak and groan, as old houses should, as habitations long loved will do.

At one point I swept the edge of the pond clean, and stepped out onto the ice. It crackled deliciously, fractures spreading around me in a concentric web, and I smiled. Good memories from of old merged with this newly forged memory of victory over terror, creating a new thing.

On the morning of Christmas Eve, I found a small blue spruce higher up on the mountain, cut it down, and brought it home for the parlor. I made popcorn strings and colored paper stars for its decoration. It wasn't exactly a work of art, but it was lovely and it was mine. In the afternoon I dug the van out of a snowdrift at the end of the lane, and drove down the other side of the mountain to Graniteville. From a pay phone there I called Robbie and Helen to wish them Merry Christmas. They would be driving up here for New Year's, I knew, but I wanted to tell them how much they meant to me, and how I wished we were together now.

"I love you more than you will ever know," I said.

"We know," they answered, each in turn. "We know."

In the evening I drove over to Tadd's Ford and shared a frugal Advent meal with Katie and her family. Later we all went to the little country church where they regularly worshipped. Katie stood and knelt and sat beside me throughout, dignified and recollected in her forest-green duffel coat, with her shining brown hair plaited down her back. She turned the pages of the hymnal, leaning into my arm so I could read the lyrics with her. Her voice was melodious, with shimmering depths of womanhood in the lower notes. Now and then she glanced at me with a reassuring smile. *Don't be a stranger here*, her eyes seemed to say. *Don't feel left out. We're with you.*

I was not a believing person, and yet I did not feel out of place. It was as if I had always known this small island of light in the surrounding darkness, these people, the embraces and the sincere greetings, the sounds of children singing, the ringing of bells, and the flickering red lamp behind the altar. As if this, *here*, was the humble center of the universe, and I had reached it at last. No one, not even a person like me, was excluded. Though I did not yet fully know it, I was home.

Afterward, back at their homestead, the feasting and gift giving began. For each of the pond boys, I had brought a bag of foil-covered chocolate coins. For Katie's mother, a set of quilted oven mitts. For her father, an antique wood planer. They gave me the painting of the sorrel horse that had once belonged to the Uffingtons, then to the Franklins, then to Billy, and now, coming full circle, to me.

After numerous toasts with apple cider and elderberry wine, and too many mincemeat tarts, I reluctantly prepared to go. They all saw me to the door, exacting my promise to return for the morrow's great feast. Katie threw on her coat to walk me to the van. Outside we paused under the porch lamp.

I had saved a gift for this private moment, a gift I had made for her. We stood shivering under the stars as she unwrapped it. It was a little painting of the mountaintop where we had first held hands. She knew the place immediately.

"The light is fantastic!" she breathed, and looked up at me.

"Light fantastic," I said, smiling.

"But I have nothing like it to give you, dear Max," she said. "The horse was from all of us, and my canned preserves, but ..."

"You are the gift, Katie," I said. "You."

She embraced me and then she gently broke away. As she turned to go back into the house, she told me everything with a look. And I knew by her look that there would be time enough for kisses, and that we would have a lifetime's worth of kisses.

On Christmas morning, I awoke with a feeling of peace, brilliant sunlight pouring through the bedroom window. The glass was covered in frost, a garden of ornate swirling luxuriance. I hopped around the freezing floor in my long johns, pulling on clothes and hunting for socks. Downstairs in the kitchen I got the fire going and the coffee started. I heard blue jays whistling outside in the yard.

Yawning, peering out the window, I noted that fresh snow had fallen during the night, though the day was going to be clear and bright. Opening the front door, I stepped out onto the porch to gather a few sticks of birch, and nearly trod on a cardboard box tied up with red ribbons. Opening it, I was at first puzzled, then speechless. Inside was a crested merganser duck, preserved by a taxidermist, lovingly repaired by two sets of hands. Leading toward and away from the porch, large footprints had been impressed in the snow.

I wanted to call out, to make my voice ring through the woods, to leap off the porch and run after the prints, until I realized they had been half filled by new snow. The giver had departed hours ago.

I stood without moving for a time, with the merganser cradled in my arms. As the sun climbed higher, a golden light spread slowly across the yard. I gazed long at the south, over the mountains, toward a city where a giant roves by day and by night in search of the lost. And I knew that its best son, its uncrowned prince, is ever vigilant, ever awake.